B. J. Rockliff was b................
childhood in the N...... ...gland. Illness and a
lengthy convalescence meant that most mornings
were spent reading or listening to the wireless and
inventing stories to tell her favourite toys. She trained
as a secretary and worked in the oil industry before
getting married and helping to raise three stepsons.
She began writing when she was forty and her first
thriller, *Paydirt*, was published by Headline in 1988.
She lives with her husband just outside Lymington in
Hampshire.

Praise for *Paydirt*:

'A spirited and fascinating heroine . . . a minefield of
deadly perils . . . fast-moving, intelligent and topical.'
Look Now

'A fast-moving novel of high-living, ambition,
skulduggery and greed.' *Publishing News*

Praise for *Crackerjack*:

'Tough and tender is our heroine, Meryl, and I'd put
my money on her any day.' *Woman's World*

Also by B. J. Rockliff

Paydirt

Crackerjack

B. J. Rockliff

HEADLINE

First published in 1988
by HEADLINE BOOK PUBLISHING PLC

First published in paperback in 1989
by HEADLINE BOOK PUBLISHING PLC

ISBN 0 7472 3174 5

Printed and bound in Great Britain by
Collins, Glasgow

HEADLINE BOOK PUBLISHING PLC
Headline House
79 Great Titchfield Street
London W1P 7FN

For my faithful friend, Mr Brown

Acknowledgements

Many thanks to B.P. plc for supplying data on oil shale and tar sands exploration.

PROLOGUE

The notice summoning members of the Amalgamated Union of Petroleum Workers to a meeting to be held in the recreational centre at six o'clock sharp had been hastily written in bold capitals. Few of the crackerjacks even bothered to look at the bulletin board as they filed into the canteen.

Jim Stanton caught up with two tail-enders and clapped a hand on each of their shoulders. 'Seen the notice, guys?'

'What notice?' One of them glanced over his shoulder at Jim.

'Come on!' Jim gave a heavy and audible sigh. 'See that board on the wall over there. That's called a bulletin board. And on that same bulletin board there is a large piece of white paper with red lettering on it. That is called a notice.'

'O.K. O.K. O.K.'

'Come on, guys; this is an important meeting. It's our futures that are at stake. Brian Whittaker has had a further meeting with Barclay about the Discus Petroleum bid. He described it as a full and frank exchange of views.' Jim slapped the two men on the shoulder again. 'I think you should all hear what Brian Whittaker has got to say.'

'The guy's an asshole.' The man who spoke picked up a tray and slapped it down on the rail in front of the self-service counter. 'He just says what Barclay tells him to say.'

A flicker of annoyance crossed Jim's face. 'I am going to pretend I didn't hear you say that. O.K.?'

The man shrugged.

'Look, be there. It's in your own interests. If Discus Petroleum succeed in taking us over, we'll need a voice. Old

Beaumont isn't going to live for ever, you know, and we have to be ready to meet the changes as they come, and they surely will.'

'Sure.' The man pushed his tray further along the rail, leaned forward slightly and called out to the girl serving hot dishes. 'Hey, sweetheart, what's your special today?'

Jim puffed his cheeks out. He picked up a tray from the stack at the side of the counter. What do you have to do, Stanton, to motivate these guys?

Brian Whittaker stood up and spread the thumb and forefinger of each hand along the edge of the table in front of him. 'I am in a position to inform the meeting that this morning I had a meeting with David Barclay, which I have no hesitation in describing as a full and frank exchange of views.' He paused and glanced around the room allowing a few moments for the enormity of his first statement to sink in. Jim Stanton quietly stretched his legs out in front of him and leaned back in his chair. The guys were right. Whittaker was an asshole.

Two men sitting at the back of the room exchanged swift glances, but remained silent.

Brian glanced down at the table and cleared his throat. 'As I say, we had a useful exchange of views, in which I expressed the AUPW's concern that the rights of its members should be fully represented in any dialogue brought about by the threat of Tundra Corp being taken over by Discus Petroleum.' He cleared his throat again. 'I have been assured by Barclay that it is Tundra's intention to vigorously defend itself and to remain a strong and independent organisation. Tundra and its workforce can have every right to feel confident that the proposed takeover is a threat, and nothing more than a threat. It is not the first time that Tundra and Discus have clashed.' Brian paused again and gave a thin smile. 'Old adversaries would be an appropriate description.' He glanced quickly around the room. His attempt at meaningful menace had not impressed his silent audience.

Jim Stanton allowed his mind to wander as Brian's voice droned on relentlessly. Old adversaries. He picked at the side of his thumbnail. 'Old' was the operative word. Beaumont was in his late seventies and in failing health. The fire had gone out of his belly. Jim bit his splitting thumbnail. And Barclay, the whizz-kid from Ottawa, was just marking time. Jim glanced up at the sudden shuffling of feet and the scraping of chairs. Brian had already begun fussily pressing papers back into a zip-topped document wallet. Jim rubbed a hand across his eyes. He couldn't for the life of him recall what Brian had just said. He stood up and pushed his chair up to the table. He turned to Brian and rocked his hand back and forth in front of his mouth in a drinking gesture. Brian nodded.

The bar was crowded and emitting its usual nightly noise level. The two men pushed their way to a table at the back and sat down. Jim took a long pull of beer then wiped his mouth with the back of his hand. 'What's really going on, Brian?'

'What do you mean?'

Jim gave a faint shake of his head. 'Don't play games. Not with me.'

'Who's playing games? Tundra's going to win this one. Don't worry. We're going to win.' Brian nodded to himself, as if reinforcing his own belief in the idea.

Jim set his glass down on the table. 'Bullshit. Who did Tundra lose out to in the Beaufort Sea concessions? Who did Tundra lose a piece of the action to in the NWT Pipelines sell-off?' He picked up his glass again. 'Discus, that's who.' He took a quick mouthful of beer. 'And Mallory, the guy who runs Discus, he's a corporate raider, an asset stripper. And you're trying to tell me that Tundra is going to win this one? Like I said. Bullshit.'

Brian turned to look Jim full in the face. 'If I read you correctly, you're not going to be around for much longer?'

Jim gave a short laugh. 'I don't much care for deathbed vigils. Tundra's or anyone else's.'

Brian stared down into his glass of beer.

Jim checked his watch. 'I've got to go.' He pushed his chair back and stood up.

Brian looked up at him. 'I think you're overstating the case. Even if Discus did take us over, there wouldn't be any asset stripping. Investment Canada wouldn't allow the deal to go through.'

'Investment who?'

'Used to be called the Foreign Investment Review Agency.'

Jim gave a small laugh of undisguised cynicism. 'See you, Brian.' He slung his raincoat over one shoulder and pushed his way out towards the door.

PART 1

Traffic approaching the Marunouchi district, the financial and banking centre of Tokyo, consolidated into its early morning snarl-up, giving the occupants of the cars time to gaze upon the outer gardens of the Imperial Palace, if they so wished. Teriyaki Iwano had more important matters on his mind. His hand reached for the in-car telephone almost as soon as it warbled. He listened intently for a few moments and nodded silently to himself, then replaced the handset and carefully lit up a cigarette. The information was interesting – extremely interesting. He picked up the handset again and punched in a local telephone number. The line was engaged. He pressed the recall button and drew on his cigarette.

It wasn't until he had reached his office that the line he had called was clear and he could pass on the information he had received. He twirled the gold fountain pen in his hand base over apex; the only sign of his growing irritation. 'Discretion in this matter is crucial, I agree, but I believe that it is time that we act. The unexpected rise in the share price of Tundra Corporation on the London Stock Exchange is of great significance. No one in London is prepared to speculate as to why the share price has risen. That can only mean one of two things. Either Charles Beaumont is dying: his health has been in question for some time; or Discus Petroleum of America has been forced to increase its bid for Tundra Corp. It is time to act. To delay now could mean the consortium losing an opportunity vital to its future expansion.' Teriyaki placed the pen down on the desk. 'That is my carefully considered opinion as the consortium's consultant.'

'I do not doubt your opinion for one moment, but . . .' The voice on the other end of the telephone sounded hesitant.

Teriyaki picked up the pen again and rolled it between his fingers.

'But,' the voice repeated, 'perhaps it would be wise to see what developments there are, if any, when the Toronto Stock Exchange opens. If what has happened in London is reflected in Toronto, then I agree it is time to make our move.'

Teriyaki nodded as if speaking face to face to the man on the other end of the line. 'If that is your wish.'

'I think my fellow members of the consortium would consider it wise.'

'Of course.' Teriyaki stood up and pushed his chair back from his desk. 'I will be in touch as soon as there are further developments.' He put the telephone down and tapped his fingers on the handset. What the consortium continually failed to realise was that Western business did not operate on consensus of agreement. It was not unusual for decision making, if need be, to rest solely in the hands of one man. He glanced at his watch. Several hours would pass before the Canadian Stock Exchanges opened for business and much could happen in the meantime. Much.

The nightclub in the expensive Ginza district was reputed to have the most beautiful and congenial of hostesses. Teriyaki declined to have his whisky glass refilled by the young girl kneeling by the side of the velvet covered sofa. He would have liked another drink, but he still had a little unfinished business to attend to before he could truly relax for the night. The business of Charles Beaumont. A man with a paranoid hatred of the Japanese and a not much smaller hatred for Christopher Mallory, the chief executive of Discus Petroleum, and instigator of the takeover bid for Tundra Corp.

A figure appeared out of the semi-gloom and plugged in a

telephone by the sofa. Teriyaki picked up the handset, at the same time giving a dismissive wave of his free hand to the hostess at his side. The call from New York was brief and he signalled to the hostess to return and refill his glass. The final business of the day was done. One of the two possible reasons why the share price of Tundra Corp had risen in London could now be safely ruled out. Discus Petroleum had no intention, according to his informant, of increasing their bid for Tundra Corp. The British must, therefore, know something the Americans didn't. The hostess passed him the glass of whisky. He sprawled out on the sofa and held his glass between his thighs. Sadly for you, Beaumont-*san*, I think your time is running out.

The main party, to celebrate three years of highly successful trading by Wajiki International in London, was being held in the computer room. Meryl Stewart winced as she stepped out of the elevator. A tidal wave of noise swept towards her as she walked along the corridor. The European acquisitions and mergers department, the 'boys' as they were called, were really letting rip. Pushing open the door of the computer room, she was met by an instant barrage of cheering and whistles. She raised her hand to quell the noise. The room suddenly became very quiet, the silence only broken by remnants of exaggerated shushing sounds. She waited patiently by the door until the very last man stopped stage-whispering to everybody to be quiet. She suppressed a smile. They were not called the boys for nothing. 'Gentlemen.' She gestured with her hand. 'I use the term loosely, of course. May I be the last to congratulate you all on your success.'

Shouts and cheers broke out even louder than before. The senior A & M got to his feet and walked a little unsteadily towards Meryl. He placed his hands together in front of him and gave a very low bow, as if offering the most deferential of Japanese greetings. 'O, beauteous Stewart-*san*,' he raised his eyes towards the ceiling, 'what draws you down from your celestial palace to this, our humble abode?'

'A glass of champagne, Micky.'

He straightened up. 'At once, beauteous Stewart-*san*. At once.'

'And, Micky, a message from JJ. Time to wrap the party up.'

He shook his head sadly. 'Why should one as fair as you always be the bearer of unwelcome tidings?'

She patiently pushed back the uninvited hand that had slipped round her waist to administer a gentle squeeze.

Someone appeared with a foaming plastic cup of champagne. Micky took it and presented it with a flourish to Meryl. He raised his own cup to hers. 'To us.'

She smiled. 'To us.'

The toast was taken as a signal to the rest of the party to demand the opening of more champagne. Meryl touched Micky's arm lightly. 'I really think you should start winding down the feast, Micky.'

'Sure.' Micky looked at her for a moment. It was worth a try. 'Ah, a few of us are going on to a venerable sushi bar. Want to come along?'

'Sorry, Micky. I have a dinner engagement.'

He shrugged. 'Nothing lust, nothing gained, as they say.'

When Meryl returned to the top floor suite of offices, many of the guests had already left. She glanced around and saw JJ standing by the window being earnestly addressed by the senior accountant. JJ caught her eye then adjusted the bracelet of his watch, to indicate he would join her just as soon as politely possible. She walked across to the buffet table and helped herself to a delicately carved square of vinegar flavoured rice and tuna, wrapped in seaweed. Meryl turned round and leaned against the table, facing the remaining occupants of the room. Her affair with JJ had begun over a plate of sushi.

Wajiki of Japan had set up its British banking arm, Wajiki International, in London three years previously.

Meryl Stewart, born Marylin Alice Stewart Beaumont, and late of Edmonton in the province of Alberta, had joined the Japanese merchant bank one week after she had arrived in England. The run-up to the City of London's 'big bang' had turned the world into Meryl's oyster.

After majoring in law at Toronto University, she had taken her tutor's advice and had gone on to specialise in corporate law, and to study what he called 'the most important language on earth: Japanese.' A stint at the Royal Bank of Canada had provided her with a glowing reference to present at her interview with Haruki Kushida, joint head of Wajiki International. A brief introduction by Haruki Kushida to Joseph John Reynolds, his British counterpart, clinched the interview. Within an hour of arriving at Wajiki International she was walking out again with a new title: Senior Lawyer in the soon to be set up Compliance Department. Her brief was to ensure rigorous compliance with the rules for foreign bankers, laid down by the equally new Securities and Investment Board in London. Scorning the London underground, now that her salary was to be miraculously quadrupled, she hailed a taxi and returned home in a state of excitement. She had left Canada in deep despair. That was now in the past. The future? Well, that couldn't look brighter. She startled the taxi driver by shouting out loud, 'London, Wajiki, here I come!' The taxi driver shook his head. These Yanks were all the same.

Three days later Meryl found herself installed in a luxurious suite of offices one floor beneath the corporate heads of Wajiki International. Although Haruki Kushida forever remained *Mr* Kushida, Joseph John Reynolds quickly became JJ.

A junior clerk walked across the banqueting suite to where Meryl was standing. 'Excuse me, Miss Stewart.'

'Yes, Jeremy.'

'Message from Micky Knight for you, Miss Stewart. He asked me to tell you that the pack has dispersed quietly.'

'Thanks.'

He glanced around the room, as if not quite believing how he had managed to find himself in such exalted company.

'See you tomorrow, Jeremy.'

He stared at her for a moment, before realising it was his cue to leave. 'Oh. Yes. See you tomorrow, Miss Stewart.'

Meryl gave an amused smile and helped herself to another portion of sushi.

She turned at the feel of gentle pressure on her elbow. JJ stood at her side. 'Sorry, darling. Couldn't get rid of the man.'

'That's O.K.'

'See you downstairs at the car in ten minutes?'

'Fine.'

He squeezed her elbow discreetly.

Their affair, although known about in Wajiki International, was conducted strictly after-hours and had long since ceased being a source of gossip. A pleasant, friendly business relationship altered course on the first anniversary of Wajiki International's operations in London. At the party, Meryl had watched JJ struggling to eat with a pair of chopsticks and, although he was very much her senior in age and position, had cheekily offered him a quick lesson in the art of eating Japanese food. Pleased that his rather unsubtle ruse to gain her attention had worked, he graciously accepted her offer. Having taken longer than was strictly necessary to weave his chopsticks with confidence, it seemed natural enough, later in the evening, for JJ to insist that he take her on to a nightclub. The old-fashioned petting in his car in the early hours of the morning was not the tiresome groping she had anticipated, and it wasn't difficult for Meryl to convince herself that JJ was a very sweet man. Next month they discovered what JJ described as a perfectly charming pied-à-terre, and made it their base in town.

The private clinic in Edmonton specialised in the treatment of emphysema and other bronchitic ailments. The night nurse massaged the small of her back while waiting for the day nurse to complete her update on the night's events. The day nurse slipped her pen back into the top of her overall. 'That's it. How's old Mr Beaumont?'

'Not good. He's still in heart failure. Mr Jacques attended to him during the night. Said he will try to come and see him again as soon as he can after breakfast.'

The day nurse nodded.

Charles Franklin Beaumont lay back against the pillows. His eyes were shut, but he wasn't asleep. Somehow, seeing the early grey light filter through the venetian blinds had brought relief. The effort to breathe had become less of a battle between fear and exhaustion. He opened his eyes at the squeaking sound of rubber soled shoes on the polished floor. The day nurse smiled at him. 'How are we this morning, Mr Beaumont?'

Before he could answer, even if he had intended to, she popped a thermometer in his mouth and took hold of his wrist. He stared straight ahead, as if looking through the window, although without his spectacles he couldn't see beyond the foot of the bed clearly. Out there, on the skyline, was the tower block that literally stood for everything he had worked for. Tundra Corp.

The day nurse lowered Charles' wrist gently down on to the bed cover. 'Mr Jacques is coming to see you soon, Mr Beaumont.'

Charles raised a hand and lifted the oxygen mask away from his mouth. 'Don't want to see him. Know what's wrong with me.' The few words left him panting for breath.

The day nurse leaned over him to re-position the oxygen mask, but he grasped her hand with surprising strength. 'Do something for me. Get my lawyer, Edwin Reece. Tell him to come straight away.' He raised one shoulder up from the pillows. 'Do it. I'll see you right, if you do.'

The day nurse pressed him back against the pillows. 'You know that isn't necessary, Mr Beaumont. I am here to help you in any way I can.'

'Then get my lawyer.' Charles' head lolled back. The effort of talking had drained him of almost all that was left of his strength.

'I'll have to get Doctor's permission, Mr Beaumont.'

Charles fluttered his fingers in acknowledgement. He listened to the shoes squeak their way across the floor to the door, then opened his eyes and stared across to the half-shuttered window.

Charles' father, Franklin Reeve Beaumont, had been a drunken, whoring bastard, from what Charles could glean. In the late eighteen-hundreds his father had joined the Klondike Stampede, but never made it as far as Dawson. He died when Charles was still a young boy, leaving his widow and child nothing except a stretch of useless land not even fit for grazing cattle.

There was some mystery as to how Charles' father came to be in possession of the land in the first place. Charles' mother was always vague when questioned, but it was generally assumed that he had accepted the land in payment of a gambling debt. In the middle of the nineteen-forties, when Charles was nearing his twenty-fifth birthday, the Leduc and Redwater oilfields were discovered. Within days the worthless piece of Beaumont land was as valuable as any gold find. Charles, with his mother's blessing, formed a partnership with a young English geologist.

The bank manager in Edmonton, who seemed anxious to loan Charles and his partner every last dollar in his safe, suggested naming their company Tundra Corporation. Within two years the company lived up to its important sounding title and had bought out its smaller rivals to become one of the biggest upstream oil exploration companies in the province. By the time Charles was twenty-nine he was a millionaire twice over; had bought out his English partner; had built his mother a mansion on the outskirts of Edmonton, which regrettably she didn't live to see completed; had proposed to the daughter of the mayor and been readily accepted. By his thirtieth birthday he was grieving for a wife who had suffered a fatal ectopic pregnancy. Six weeks later he did the only thing he believed a man in his position could do and turned his whole attention to further developing the company he had founded.

Edwin Reece waited in a small room next to where Charles Beaumont lay, patiently waiting for the appearance of Charles' specialist. He stood up as Jacques entered the room. The doctor smiled warmly and held out his hand. 'Good morning.'

Edwin nodded and shook hands. 'How is Mr Beaumont?'

Jacques slowly rocked his hand back and forth.

'How long has he got?'

'Not long I'm afraid. We mustn't forget he is in his seventies, Mr Reece, and his condition is causing ever-increasing strain on his heart.'

Edwin picked up his briefcase. 'Well, I ought to go in and see him then.'

'Not too long. He tires very quickly.'

Edwin nodded.

When Edwin entered the sickroom Charles appeared to be asleep. He tiptoed across the room and stared down at the man who had been a good friend for over twenty years. Charles opened his eyes and gave a weak smile when he recognised who was standing by the bed. He beckoned to Edwin to pull up a chair and sit close to him.

'What can I do for you, Charles?'

Charles shut his eyes, as if he hadn't heard Edwin speak.

Edwin leaned closer to his head. 'What is it, Charles?'

A tear formed on Charles' eyelid. It seemed to hover uncertainly for a moment then trickled down the side of his face. His lips moved, but Edwin couldn't hear what he was saying. He put his face close to Charles'.

'Tell Marylin.' Charles moistened his lips. 'Tell Marylin I want to see her. Explain things to her, Edwin.'

Edwin placed his hand over Charles'. 'Sure. I'll get on to it right away.' He paused undecided whether to ask the question. 'Mary. Do you want to see Mary?'

Charles shook his head slowly.

'She would come to you, Charles. If you asked, she would come.'

Charles shook his head. He opened his eyes and turned to look at Edwin. 'Just Marylin.' As he spoke his breathing shortened and, even with the benefit of the oxygen mask, his mouth began rapidly opening and closing like a fish.

Edwin leapt up from the chair in alarm and rang for the nurse. Within seconds he had been bundled out of the room, to wait anxiously outside in the corridor.

Jacques' assistant came out of Charles Beaumont's room still wearing a stethoscope around his neck and was about to hurry off down the corridor, but stopped at the sight of Edwin Reece's anxious face. 'Mr Beaumont is resting quietly, but I cannot allow you to go in and see him.'

'I understand. Er, Dr –?'

'Morrisey.'

'Dr Morrisey, I have been asked by Mr Beaumont to fetch his daughter. She is his only child. Presumably she will be allowed to see him?'

'Yes, of course.'

'Good. I will make arrangements.' Edwin Reece looked around him distractedly, as if unsure what those arrangements were.

'Does she have far to come?'

'Yes. She lives in England.'

Dr Morrisey slowly pulled the stethoscope from around his neck. 'I think it wise if her journey is delayed as little as possible.'

Edwin nodded. 'I understand.' He pulled a handkerchief from his coat pocket and blew his nose. 'Excuse me.' His tear-bright eyes glanced briefly in Dr Morrisey's direction, then he hurried away down the corridor.

Charles Beaumont tried opening his eyes, but the effort

seemed too much. He felt the reassuring grasp of the nurse's hand holding his. The terrifying feeling of suffocating had passed. He was grateful for that. He felt thirsty, but was too frightened to ask for water. If he choked, his heart might not withstand the next spasm. He had to wait for Marylin. He moistened his lips with his tongue. He had to wait for her. He didn't care about Mary, but he had to wait for Marylin. He unconsciously tightened his grip on the nurse's fingers. Whatever had happened in the past, Marylin wouldn't let him down.

Charles Beaumont had been over forty before he seriously contemplated marrying again. By this time he was one of the wealthiest men in Canada and, as he said later, should have known better but he didn't, and set his heart on capturing a young woman almost twenty years his junior. Her name was Mary Stewart. She was from England. He first saw her gazing at him from the front cover of *Vogue* magazine, on a newsstand in Paris. She was very beautiful. By chance they met at a party several days later. At first, he couldn't make out where he had seen this stunning blonde before. When he did, he quickly got his host to introduce him.

Mary Stewart was a very successful fashion model and was used to men buzzing around her. She turned Charles down flat when he proposed. He consoled himself in thinking that perhaps he had been a little too fast off the mark. They had only met the previous day. She laughingly dismissed claims that she had broken his heart, but did promise to show a bewildered, unsophisticated Canadian the sights of Paris. He willingly walked his feet off in the Louvre; steeled himself against incipient vertigo and looked out from the top of the Eiffel Tower; even managed to eat a steaming bowl of onion soup at Les Halles, although he detested onions. Throughout, he never let Mary forget for a single minute that his enthusiasm for Paris could never match his enthusiasm for her. She accepted his ninth proposal of marriage having come to the conclusion that his open, rather touchingly boyish, admiration would be the beginning of love.

A week later, they married in London and honeymooned at Niagara Falls.

Eighteen months later, Mary produced a baby daughter. Charles hid his disappointment that the baby was not a boy and when he saw his daughter for the first time, claimed he had fallen head over heels in love with her. She was beautiful, just like her mother. She just had to be called Marylin.

A year later, Mary knew that she had made a serious mistake in marrying Charles. No longer able to stand his autocratic, possessive behaviour, she left him, taking her daughter with her. The man she fled to was the second mistake she made. He turned from a sympathetic lover into a raging bully whenever Marylin cried. Whenever Mary cried. The men who came in the night when Mary was alone and defenceless and took Marylin away, also took away her sanity. She knew who had sent them. She knew she could never fight him. She had never won a battle with Charles, even over the most trivial of things. The next day her lover packed a bag and left, claiming that her sobbing was driving him out of his mind. The sobbing stopped two nights later.

Mary's suicidal drug overdose and her ensuing breakdown was the official reason for the Beaumonts' divorce. Charles claimed, and was believed, that Mary was emotionally unstable and unfit as a mother. For him, Mary no longer existed. He could ride out the 'I told you so' voices, the knowing looks. He had made a fool of himself over her, but it wasn't the end of the world. He had his beloved daughter back where she belonged. That was all that mattered.

JJ flung out an arm and fumbled in the dark for the light switch, as the sound of the telephone ringing penetrated his sleep. Meryl snuggled further down into the bed, shielding her face from the sudden light from the bedside lamp. The call was probably some hapless drunk wanting them to provide a late night cab. It happened at least once a month.

JJ listened to the hesitant voice then sat up in bed. 'Sorry, I didn't quite catch what you said?'

Edwin Reece cleared his throat. 'My name is Edwin Reece. Am I connected to Miss Marylin – to Miss Meryl Stewart's number?'

'Yes, you are.'

'Can I please speak to her.'

JJ scratched at his chest. 'Do you know what time it is?'

'I am sorry, but I am calling from Canada. I must speak to Miss Stewart. It's her father. He is gravely ill.'

JJ glanced down at the body next to his and silently raised his eyebrows.

'Hello. Are you still there?'

'Yes, Mr Reece. Just a moment.' JJ was on the verge of saying that he would wake Meryl up, but decided that sounded a little indiscreet. 'I will get her to come to the telephone. Hold on.'

'Thank you.'

JJ shook Meryl's shoulder. 'Darling, wake up. An Edwin Reece wants to speak to you. It's urgent. It's about your father. Apparently he is seriously ill.'

'Hang up.'

'Meryl!'

'Hang up. There is nothing I want to hear from Edwin Reece or anyone else about my father.'

'I think you should.'

She flung the covers from her and sat up in bed. 'I do not want to know. If you don't hang up, I will.'

'All right, darling. I will tell him.' JJ sighed and spoke into the handset. 'Ah, Mr Reece, this is rather difficult, but Meryl doesn't want to speak to you. You will understand the reasons why, I believe.' JJ sighed more heavily as he listened to the almost pleading voice of Edwin Reece. He swung his legs out of bed and searched for a piece of paper and something to write with. 'Look, Mr Reece, give me

your number and I will call you back. I will talk to Meryl.'
He knew Meryl was glaring at him, but pretended he didn't
see her. 'Yes, yes. I will do my best. Goodnight.' JJ
replaced the handset and drew in a very slow breath. He
walked round to Meryl's side of the bed and sat down. The
last time the name of Meryl's father had been mentioned,
she had slung a crystal vase across the living room. He took
her hands in his and held them firmly. 'Meryl, your father is
dying. He wants to see you. He begged Edwin Reece to call.'

She tried to pull her hands away. 'I don't want to
see him.'

'Meryl, your father is dying.'

'I don't care. I don't want to see him. Not after what he
drove my mother to. Not after what he did to me.'

JJ curled his fingers around hers. 'I understand how you
feel.'

'You don't.'

'I have tried to, Meryl. All that I ask is that you don't do
something that you might regret for the rest of your life.'

She wrenched her hands free and leapt out of bed.

When Teriyaki Iwano's flight from Tokyo arrived at
Osaka, the heartland of Japan's chemical and heavy
industries, three members of the delegation were there to
greet him, reflecting the esteem in which he was held by the
consortium. It was no less than he deserved. A skilful
operator in his middle fifties, he was held in similar esteem
by his employers, Wajiki of Japan. Chief of the corporate
foreign acquisitions division, Teriyaki was fond of
describing himself to his Western associates as a marriage
broker. A *business* marriage broker. A very successful business marriage broker. Teriyaki sighed inwardly at the sight
of his welcomers. This particular groom was being unneces-
sarily nervous in approaching the intended bride.

The Osaka consortium comprised five companies sharing
one common interest: the supply of crude oil. Two were
involved in the downstream activities of primary oil

refining and marketing. The interests of the remaining
three centred on basic petrochemicals: polymers, acetyls;
materials vital in modern manufacturing technology. The
consortium had grown out of a prudent vision of the
twenty-first century, based on an unanswerable question.
For how long would the price of crude oil remain so
advantageously low?

As a non-oil-producing country, Japan's future eco-
nomic and financial growth lay, in part, in the continuing
and stable supply of oil. As visionaries, the consortium
were unable to say which non-Western oil-producing
countries in the twenty-first century could, or would, be
willing to supply crude. Memories of the Arab 'hike' of oil
prices in the nineteen-seventies prompted the visionaries to
look to the West and not to the East to attempt to resolve
the dilemmas of the future. There were vast, as yet to be
profitably exploited, oil fields in the West; particularly in
North America and Canada. The consortium approached
Wajiki, one of Japan's leading banks, and Teriyaki Iwano
was invited to advise the consortium on how best to acquire
a future and participating interest in oil exploration/
producing ventures by their Western allies.

Teriyaki's advice was unequivocal. Relations between
Japan and America would always suffer from a certain
volatility from time to time. It was extremely unlikely that
any United States government would countenance whole-
sale investment by Japanese companies in a domestic and
strategic raw material such as crude oil. Fortunately, the
Canadians took a less stringent view of things. It was probable that the Canadians would look more favourably on a
'back-door' approach by means of a friendly business ally.
The United Kingdom would prove more than suitable. The
consortium studied the broad brush strokes of Teriyaki's
ideas and liked what they saw. It was agreed that he should
seek out British interests in sympathy with those of the
consortium.

Six weeks after that initial meeting Teriyaki returned

from his journeyings and met with the consortium. He had found what they were looking for in the Tundra Corporation. Still controlled by its ailing president, Charles Beaumont, it had become embroiled in a bruising takeover battle launched by Discus Petroleum of America. Tundra Corp had vast undeveloped upstream potential, which would last well into the latter half of the twenty-first century, but it lacked the financial resources to sustain a continuing programme of expansion. It was common knowledge in Canada that Beaumont left the day-to-day running of the company to his chief general manager, David Barclay. Barclay was a young, thrusting man known to be a financial whizz-kid and widely expected to take over the reins when Beaumont was forced to step down as president. However, what would be of particular interest to the consortium was the fact that Tundra Corp still retained a strong British influence in the shape of institutional investors, strongly opposed to any American takeover of Tundra, but showing signs of growing concern at the limited growth prospects of the company. Teriyaki's report was studied enthusiastically by the consortium. He had found a most suitable bride. They gave unanimous approval to the courting of Tundra Corp's institutional shareholders.

As the limousine swung into the paved courtyard, Teriyaki pondered yet again on the response from the consortium to his latest proposals. It was still something of a mystery why Tundra Corp's share price had risen on the London Stock Exchange. The Toronto Stock Exchange had not shown a comparable rise. Neither had Discus Petroleum extended the battle lines against Tundra's resistance to a takeover.

The chauffeur opened the rear passenger door and Teriyaki stepped out. He smoothed the front of his jacket and followed his welcomers across the courtyard. Stalemate. That was what he had to report to the consortium. Stalemate. The Tundra/Discus affair was hanging in some kind of limbo. A mutually agreed limbo? The British institutional investors seemed to be sitting on the sidelines. Why? Discreet enquiries in Canada as to the health of Charles Beaumont had been met with bland assurances. True? Teriyaki shifted his briefcase into the other hand. A bold move was required. It was time the consortium made itself known, but it was unlikely that it would reach total agreement to do so.

The express train from London to Weymouth, on the south coast of England, conveniently stopped at Bournemouth where Meryl's mother, Mary Stewart Beaumont, now lived. Taking the train had been JJ's idea. He had said it would give Meryl time to compose herself before meeting her mother to discuss what Meryl should do about her father, Charles Beaumont.

Meryl glanced around the half empty railway carriage then turned back to looking out of the window. She had been staring out of the window for the last hour and a half. Taking the train had not been one of JJ's best ideas. Inaction made her feel more fidgety, more depressed. If she had driven down, at least she would have had something to concentrate on. She picked up the magazine in her lap and flicked through the pages. On the other hand, driving two hundred and fifty odd miles after a sleepless, troubled night wasn't such a brilliant idea, either.

The call from Edwin Reece had begun a chain of events that had driven Meryl and JJ to quarrel and then to make love. The implications of the telephone call defeated JJ's promise that making love would soothe her to sleep. It had done the trick for him, but Meryl had spent the ensuing hours until daylight pacing up and down the living room, arguing with herself. Anger. Guilt. Regret. The feelings had somehow solidified themselves into a stone-like mass in her stomach.

When JJ had woken up, he had forgiven her harsh words of the previous hours. He understood perfectly what had triggered her angry backlash. Edwin Reece's final words on the telephone, that it would be greatly to Meryl's advantage to go to Canada, were of course an affront to her integrity. If she chose to see her father, it would not be motivated by thoughts of gain, material or otherwise.

Meryl slapped the magazine down on the seat beside her. She picked up the plastic beaker from the little shelf under the carriage window and stared down at it. Even the buffet steward had for a moment seemed a little unsure as to whether he had poured tea or coffee into it. She took a mouthful of the liquid. Tea or coffee. What did it matter? It was hot. She raised her eyes as a man opened the far door and swayed towards her along the carriage. She stared at him for a moment. He bore a slight resemblance to JJ. She took another mouthful of coffee. She was being ridiculous. Close to, he didn't look anything like JJ. She put the beaker back on the shelf. JJ was an elegant man. Not just sartorially. In every way, in every thing he did, he was elegant. It was one of the things that had attracted her to him.

When she had first arrived in England she quickly became conscious of a need to tone down her act. Even by City standards she was considered too upfront, too brash. Her irritation at continually being mistaken for an American knew no bounds when she met with the always polite English 'what does it matter anyway?' response. JJ had resolved the problem in a flash. He taught her to explain that she had lived in Canada for many years, but that her mother was English. Explanations were not exactly her forte, but she did have to admit it worked like a charm.

JJ was also a generous man. Generous with his knowledge. Generous with his time. When he first made his interest in her very obvious, she had thought the interest in her career was just part of the come-on. It had been genuine. Unlike younger men, JJ was already successful, wealthy, secure. He didn't compete with her; wasn't jealous of her own success; didn't undermine her. Always ready to listen, *really* listen, to her problems. In the early months at Wajiki International, when she was struggling to make the Compliance Department the dominant voice she knew it had to be, JJ had given her backbone. He had encouraged her to stand in front of the board of directors and tell them that if they wanted her to be their watchdog, she must have teeth. If she didn't have their absolute support, she would resign. She had got her way. She had also been credited with the growing esteem in which the Securities and Investment Board held Wajiki International; as a model of good financial practice.

Meryl turned her attention from the window at the second prompting by the guard to produce her rail ticket. He checked the ticket and politely informed her that they would reach Bournemouth in just under forty minutes. She carefully slipped the ticket back into her purse. She briefly glanced around the carriage. She had been day-dreaming. Instead of thinking about JJ, she should have been going over what she was going to say to her mother. She shifted into a more comfortable position on the seat and looked out of the window again. She smiled to herself, remembering the first time she had hesitantly told her mother about JJ. Explaining, with the nervousness of a schoolgirl, that the relationship suited her. Suited JJ. They were both professional people, with demanding jobs. Neither of them wanted to cope with the demands of a complicated personal life. Her mother's response had surprised and also saddened her. Mary had said she was relieved that Meryl wasn't losing either her head or her heart. No man was worth either.

Mary Stewart Beaumont looked anxiously about her. She spotted a porter approaching, pushing an empty trolley. She stopped him and asked if she was on the correct platform for the train from London, quite forgetting that he was the same porter of whom she had asked the same question five minutes earlier. Reassured that she was, she turned and looked down the track and caught the eye of a smartly dressed middle-aged man staring at her. She glanced away, as if faintly irritated by his open admiration.

Although in her late forties, Mary was still strikingly beautiful. The fine bone structure of her face was less prominent, her body more rounded than at the height of her career, but that only added to her attractions. She unconsciously relaxed the grip on her bag at the sight of the train entering the station. The porter had been right after all.

Both women were tall and waved to each other over the heads of other passengers alighting from the train. Meryl smiled as cheerfully as she could and forced her way to her mother. 'Hi, mom. I'm so glad to see you.'

'Meryl, darling.' Mary held out her arms and hugged her daughter to her.

They walked quickly to the station car park. Mary slowed down at least twice to check that she had put her car keys in her pocket. On any other occasion Meryl would have teased her and asked if she was sure she remembered where she had parked the car, but today she didn't. Mary turned to smile at Meryl. She conveyed the vague nervousness of someone who felt they had good reason to doubt their own abilities. She put her hand into her coat pocket again and this time decided to carry the car keys in her hand for safety.

As they drove along the coastal road out of Bournemouth, Meryl kept up what she hoped was normal, light hearted conversation. Only once did she have to remind her mother that she was signalling right when she was actually intending to turn left. Mary turned into the driveway of the apartment block overlooking the sea, and stopped the car. She half turned in the driver's seat to look at Meryl.

'It's Charles, isn't it? I was dreaming about him last night.'

Meryl stared at her. It always irritated her when her mother spoke of her father as if over twenty years of divorce didn't separate them. But the question left her dumbfounded. 'Has Edwin Reece been in touch with you?'

Mary shook her head. 'No. Is he someone I should know?'

'No, Mother. I just thought –'

'It *is* Charles, isn't it?'

Meryl placed her hand on the door handle. 'He's dying.'

'Mm. I thought the dream must mean something.' Mary got out of the car. She turned and looked across towards the sea. 'I didn't love him, but I could never forget him. No one could ever forget Charles.'

Meryl slammed the car door shut. 'I have.'

'Perhaps, darling, that's because you weren't married to him.'

Meryl followed her mother to her apartment. The interior was immaculately kept. Little vases of fresh flowers were scattered around the living room. Without them the place would have looked curiously bleak, unlived in. Meryl didn't offer to help her mother to make tea. The kitchen was really only big enough for one person to comfortably move around in. Instead, she went to the french windows and looked out through the pine trees, towards the sea. She resisted looking out of the corner of her eye at the photograph of herself, as a baby, which sat on top of the writing desk. She didn't remember the photograph being taken, but she knew *where* it had been taken.

The Beaumont residence stood in a very exclusive suburb of Edmonton. As a child, Meryl had been too young to remember a time when her mother lived in it. She could only remember Nanny. Nanny McClaren, the kind but strict Scotswoman employed by Charles Beaumont to care for his daughter. Meryl's world had been happy, uncomplicated, until the day she discovered that her mother wasn't dead, that her father had lied to her. She was just thirteen. At first her father had been angered by her questions. For the first time in her life he had raised his hand against her. Nanny McClaren had intervened. She was the only person to whom Charles Beaumont deferred. Later, in her sitting room, over mugs of hot chocolate, Meryl listened to Nanny

McClaren's quiet reasoning. Her mother had betrayed her
father, wounded him. He deserved Meryl's love. He had
not abandoned her. He loved her too much to do that.
Ashamed by the hurt she had caused her father, calling him
a dirty, stinking liar, she rushed downstairs and flung herself on his lap, crying for forgiveness. Miraculously, or so it
seemed at the time, he did forgive her and the incident was
never to be mentioned again. Ever.

Although Meryl had told herself she wouldn't, the urge
to look at the photograph overcame her. She glanced at it. It
was difficult to pinpoint exactly when her father's love, his
possessiveness, became intolerable; when feelings of anger
and oppression overcame her guilt at questioning all that
he had done for her, all that he had unstintingly provided.
Meryl went to the writing desk and picked up the photograph. How do you complain to the person who has given
you everything and anything you wanted? She placed the
photograph back on the desk. She had been given everything but her freedom.

Mary brought a tray of tea and set it down on a small
table then realised she had forgotten the spoons and hurried
out in a flurry of apologies. Meryl sat down on the sofa and
began pouring the tea. To have offered to fetch the spoons
would have only increased her mother's confusion. Mary
returned and sat down next to Meryl. She pulled a plate of
cake to her and began slicing it.

'I'm afraid this is only packet-mix cake, darling, but the
cream is fresh.'

Inexplicably, Meryl felt tears springing to her eyes.
'Don't worry, Mom, I wouldn't know the difference anyway.' She picked up a slice of cake and crammed half of it
into her mouth. No wonder her mother had suffered a
nervous breakdown. Life with her father must have been
one long nightmare. He had expected, and got, efficiency,
perfection, from everybody around him. She gulped down
the cake. It had been easy for her. She had been born to it.
Her mother hadn't.

'Meryl.' Mary put her cup and saucer down. 'You don't need to protect my feelings. I don't have any. If you want to see your father, I think you should.'

'No. I have no intention of going to Canada.' Meryl pushed the remains of the cake into her mouth.

Mary delicately cleared her throat. 'I know the last time you saw him, he said some hurtful things, but that was just in the heat of the moment. Charles always had a ferocious temper.'

'I do too. We both meant exactly what we said.' Meryl washed the cake down with a mouthful of tea.

Meryl and her father had stood opposite each other in his study, each trying to out-shout the other. He had won, but the victory had been pyrrhic. The need to find her mother, to see her, talk to her, was not something Meryl could explain even to herself. It was just a need that had grown stronger every year she had avoided doing anything about it. She needed to know both of her parents. It was natural. He must understand that.

Meryl wiped a crumb from the side of her mouth. She looked across at the photograph again. He hadn't understood. He only understood that she was betraying him. Meryl was prepared to sacrifice years of love for curiosity about a woman who had abandoned her; a whore who had been unfit to be her mother. She remained unmoved. If nothing else, her father's fury only served to strengthen her determination. She wasn't a child. She was twenty-four years old. She would make her own decisions. This time, there was no Nanny McClaren to intervene. The open-handed slap across her face sent her reeling. He strode across the study and almost wrenched the door off its hinges. She could go to her mother. Perhaps she should, because she no longer had a father. She was disowned.

Faint sounds from the kitchen startled Meryl. She glanced around in surprise. She hadn't noticed her mother getting up from the sofa and removing the tea tray. She lay back against the cushions and shut her eyes. Despite the freezing, lashing rain, her father had pushed her bodily out of the house. She spent the night at a friend's apartment. When she returned home the next morning the expression on her father's face vanquished any thoughts she had harboured about a reconciliation. It was as if she was a stranger – an unwelcome stranger. It was the last time she entered the house. A week later she received a letter from her father's lawyers, delivered at the Royal Bank of Canada, where she worked, informing her that her monthly allowance was henceforth terminated and requesting the early return of any keys to the Beaumont residence still in her possession. Three months after that she had discovered her mother was living in England and made contact with her. It was the most wonderful moment of her life. One week later she was on a plane to England. She would disown her father, as he had disowned her. Somewhere over the Atlantic, she decided to shed the name of Beaumont and take up her mother's maiden name. She had years before changed her hated first name, Marylin. When the plane landed at Heathrow, Meryl Stewart stepped off.

The telephone rang out. Meryl jumped at the sudden noise. She waited a couple of seconds wondering whether she should answer it, or wait for her mother, then picked it up. Mary poked her head around the sitting room door. Meryl beckoned to her. 'It's for you, Mom. Simon.'

Mary hesitated. Meryl got up from the sofa and held out the telephone to her mother. 'I must go and unpack. Don't forget to give my love to Simon.'

Mary looked relieved.

The guest bedroom was small and cramped. In Victorian times it would have been used as a box room. Meryl slung her travel bag on the bed and unzipped it. She hoped Simon wasn't staying out of sight on her account. He was good for Mom. She could never understand why she didn't marry him. Meryl hung her bathrobe up on the bedroom door. When Simon was around, Mom lost her edgy nervousness. She smiled to herself. Even if Mom somehow managed to contrive to bring the ceiling crashing down on his head, she doubted if Simon would do anything other than pat Mom's hand and murmur that it wasn't important. Meryl picked up her washbag and took it into the bathroom. Simon attributed his patience to being a landscape gardener. People, like trees, need time to grow, to flourish, he said.

Mary tapped on the bedroom door as she walked in.

'Everything all right, darling?'

'Yes, fine.'

'Meryl.' Mary sat down on the edge of the bed and patted at the space beside her. 'Come and sit down. I want to talk to you about your father and I don't want you to get angry.'

'O.K., Mom.'

Mary clasped her hands in her lap. 'Have you considered that your father has asked to see you, because he wants to ask your forgiveness?'

Meryl raised an eyebrow.

'I believe, darling, when a person is dying, whoever they are, whatever they have done, they have a right to ask for forgiveness. We should not deny them that.' Mary twisted her fingers together. 'Sometimes, forgiveness is for ourselves, too. It frees us. Frees us to fulfil our own lives.'

Meryl looked at her mother. That sounded like Simon talking. She got up from the bed and went to the window. 'Do you really believe that?'

'Yes, I do, darling.'

Meryl turned and looked at Mary. The voice was strangely decisive. Certain. She turned to the window again. 'Do you want me to go and see him?'

'Yes. Whatever he has done, I wouldn't want to think of him dying alone. I wouldn't want that for anyone.'

Meryl nodded quietly.

Just the desk lamp illuminated the office of the chief general manager. David Barclay stood at the window, his hands in his pockets. He whistled soundlessly to himself. It wouldn't be long now. Beaumont had no more than a few hours to live. He turned round as his secretary gave a light tap on the office door.

'Is there anything else, Mr Barclay?'

'No. You can get off home now, Josie.'

'Thanks, Mr Barclay. By the way, I gave Mrs Stimpson a copy of the marketing analysis, like you said, but she didn't know whether she should send it on to Mr Beaumont, or put it on one side until he comes back.'

'Tell her to leave it on his desk. He should be back by tomorrow afternoon.'

'O.K., Mr Barclay, I'll tell her. Goodnight, Mr Barclay.'

David turned away from the window and went to the door connecting his office with that of the president. 'Going anywhere special tonight, Josie?'

For a moment she stared at him, her eyes bright with anticipation. 'Er – I'm not doing anything you'd call special.'

He smiled wolfishly at her. 'A girl like you should, Josie.'

The light faded from her eyes as he entered the president's office and closed the door behind him.

David snapped on all the lights in Charles Beaumont's office and looked around. Only the directors of Tundra Corp knew that Charles lay dying in hospital. It was considered vital that Discus Petroleum didn't find out and it was unanimously agreed that as far as Christopher Mallory was concerned, his adversary was fighting fit and ready to bloody his nose. David walked across to the gilt framed blow-up displayed on the wall opposite the president's desk and stared at it. Two gold prospectors posed self-consciously, each with a foot on a spade; their faces scarcely visible between their low-brimmed hats and their long beards. They were part of the Tundra Corp legend. The man on the left of the photograph was the great Franklin Reeve Beaumont. David began whistling soundlessly again. Charles Beaumont had once confided over a bottle of rye that he had found the photograph in a junk shop in Calgary. He had no idea who the two prospectors were. He had laughed so hard over his own joke he almost gave himself a seizure.

Simon Colefax waited for Mary Beaumont to catch his eye then gave an encouraging smile. She stopped pushing a piece of lettuce around her plate in a half-hearted attempt to appear to be eating. 'Oh, Simon, I'm sorry. This is a delicious salad, but I don't think I can manage all of it.'

He smiled again. 'Just eat a little. You haven't eaten all day.'

She placed her fork on the side of the plate. 'You think I'm being silly, don't you?'

'No. It is natural that you are concerned about Meryl, but,' he reached across the table and gently squeezed her hand, 'she is a big girl now. A grown woman more than capable of making up her own mind.'

Mary glanced downwards. 'I meant about Charles. After all these years, why should I worry about him? He has never worried about me. Not for one tiny moment.'

Simon leaned back in his chair. They had been through this conversation many times since Meryl had left, but still Mary remained concerned. 'Mary, dearest; Charles is the father of your child. Whatever happened between you and him doesn't alter that fact. You are worried because you fear that Meryl might be influenced by your feelings, your unhappy memories.' He squeezed her hand again. 'I, personally, don't think she is. I have a strong feeling that it is her own feelings towards her father that are influencing her attitude.'

'Do you really think so?'

'I really do.'

She looked across at him. Her face lost some of its tautness as his quietly spoken words of reassurance calmed her troubled thoughts.

Simon removed Mary's uneaten salad and his own plate and carried them to the sideboard. He switched on the coffee percolator and set out two cups and saucers. He glanced over his shoulder at Mary. She sat with her hands clasped in her lap like an obedient little girl awaiting permission to leave the table. He turned back to the sideboard and watched the first trickle of coffee drip into the jug of the percolator. Mary's emotional frailty hurt him as much as if it existed within himself.

He had met Mary almost ten years previously and, strangely, exactly five years to the very day his wife had died. Business in his landscape gardening company was booming, mainly through what had started off as a sideline in supplying plants to hotels and offices in London and major towns in the south of England, and he desperately needed an assistant secretary and general office help. Mary Beaumont had been the first applicant he interviewed for the job and although he saw a further fifteen people, he couldn't have possibly forgotten her. It was not just her beauty that had registered itself firmly on his mind, it was a certain look; a 'please don't reject me' plea in her eyes that touched him more than he would allow himself to admit.

Mary joined the firm of Colefax Landscape Gardeners the following Monday. Inside three days, Simon was seriously convinced that by the end of her first week she would bring the office to a state of total chaos. He had overlooked the problem of the photocopier becoming so blocked up with paper as to be rendered inoperable, as something that could happen to anyone. When Mary managed to jam a new daisy wheel into the electronic typewriter in such a way as to require a complete replacement printing head, he did take in a very deep breath and slowly counted to ten. When he opened his eyes the desire to wipe away the misery etched on the white face staring back at him seemed more important than either the photocopier or the typewriter. As the days passed he quickly schooled himself to remember that a kindly word, a friendly smile, produced dedication and efficiency; a frown, an unintentionally brusque response would produce errors on a scale that he feared to even contemplate. Gradually he got to know Mary better; was able to piece together the often hesitant revelations about herself, her past. He concluded that, like a neglected plant, she needed tender loving care.

Simon switched off the percolator and carefully removed the jug of hot coffee. He sighed unconsciously as he placed the jug on the tray. There were times over the ten years when he wondered if it would ever be possible for Mary to cast off the shadows of the past; for his tender loving care to be freely reciprocated.

Haruki Kushida, the joint head with JJ of Wajiki International, was a small, chunkily built man. Outwardly, he appeared very anglicised, urbane, but fifteen years of living in the West had not changed the Japanese character within. He stood up when Meryl entered his office. She greeted him and sat down as quickly as possible. As he was several inches shorter than she was, she had long ago evolved this polite, Japanese way of redressing the embarrassing physical imbalance.

'Meryl, please let me say first how sad I am to hear about your father. Also I want you to know that we hold you in much esteem. Please take whatever time you feel is necessary in the situation.'

'Thank you very much, Mr Kushida, but a week's leave is probably all I shall need.'

'Take as long as you like, Meryl. Ian has said he is happy to cover for you.'

Meryl nodded. She had no intention of staying away longer than necessary. Her assistant, Ian Fellowes, coveted her job too much. 'I can assure you, Mr Kushida, I shan't be staying long in Canada. I am only going to see my father and –' She couldn't quite bring herself to say, and bury him.

'Of course, of course.' Haruki patted her shoulder. He perched himself on the corner of the desk then folded his arms and stared down at them. 'I would like you to know, Meryl, if there is anything I can do to help you in any way at

all, you must let me know immediately. Your father's
financial interests are many.' He paused for a moment. 'It
is unfortunate for your father, at a time like this, to be
beleaguered, if that is an appropriate word to use, by
Christopher Mallory.'

She gave a quiet laugh. 'Tundra Corp's problems with
Discus Petroleum aren't my problem, thank goodness. I
understand my father's chief general manager, David
Barclay, is very much on the ball and in control of things.'

Haruki raised his head and looked at her. 'Good, good,
but the services of Wajiki International are at your disposal
should you need them.'

'Thank you very much, Mr Kushida.'

He nodded and gave her an almost fatherly smile. She got
up from the chair, realising that the interview had come to
an end.

Meryl walked slowly to the elevator. At least Haruki
Kushida had been unambivalent in his attitude. She leaned
against the wall and pressed the elevator button. She wished
she could say the same of JJ. When she returned from
Bournemouth and told him she had agreed to go and see her
father, there had been a momentary flicker of something in
his eyes. Disappointment? The elevator doors slid open and
she stepped inside. Something had been wrong when he met
her at the station. A faintly distancing disapproval that she
should have decided to do the very thing he had proposed.
She rubbed at her eyes as she stepped out of the elevator.
Stop being so stupid. You're letting the situation get to you.
JJ had been his usual self at the station.

The graveyard was neatly kept, although it was situated in a
poorish suburb of Edmonton. David Barclay walked along
a small path to a corner site. When he saw the upturned urn
and scattered flowers he gave a harsh gasp of rage. He
hurried to his mother's grave and righted the urn, cursing
under his breath at the vandals responsible for the foul
desecration. His rapid, angry breathing quietened as he

squatted on his heels and stared at the inscription on the gravestone. 'Maria Cane. September 1989. Blessed is thy memory.' He gathered up the petals around the headstone. 'Don't worry, Momma, it won't happen again. I'll see them punished for what they've done.' He picked up the bunch of flowers he had brought with him and began arranging them in the urn. Only four other people had known that Maria Cane was David's mother. Her mother, her sister and brother-in-law, and Charles Beaumont.

Maria had been the daughter of an Italian immigrant. Unlike her mother, who never learned to speak more than a few words of English, Maria was bright and determined to improve herself. During the day, she helped out in her father's tailoring business, but that meant that she was also under his constant surveillance. Her mother was the one to overcome her father's resistance to Maria going out to work. Maria was a good girl, she wouldn't bring them trouble; besides, the wages she would bring home every week would be welcome.

Maria was sixteen when she found employment at the Beaumont residence. While Maria was waiting to be served at the local butcher's she overheard the woman in front of her tell her neighbour that there was a maid's job going at the Beaumonts'. Maria rushed home with the chicken for her mother, then put on her smartest frock and hat. She counted the coins in her purse and discovered she had just enough money for her fare across town and back to the Beaumont place.

The butler burst out laughing when she rang the bell and announced she had come to be interviewed for the vacancy, and asked her if she always scrubbed floors in her best clothes. Maria blushed until she thought she must be red all over, but she stood her ground. She needed work. She needed the money. The housekeeper questioned her thoroughly about her morals and gave her the job on account of the fact that she attended Mass every day. No one who went to church every day was likely to make eyes at the under-gardener instead of getting on with her work, as the previous girl had done.

Maria came to Charles Beaumont's notice after she had been in his employ for about two years. He had returned home earlier than usual and found Maria spinning gaily around the hall. It took him a few seconds to realise that she had dusters wrapped around her feet and was polishing the marble floor as she danced. He watched quietly, taking in the full breasts, the rounded, swaying bottom. She caught sight of him and froze in horror. He didn't say anything and went into his study. Her image stayed in his mind until he realised he was going to have to do something about it. Since his divorce there had been women in his life, sometimes very frequently, but he had the innocence of a young daughter to protect, and they could never be there when he really wanted them. But the young maid was, and she had a body that cried out to be enjoyed.

The following Sunday morning when Maria went upstairs to make his bed, he followed her and laid out a handful of dollars on the dressing table. They were hers if she wanted to earn them for doing something she probably did for free already. Just a couple of times a week before his breakfast was served. He went downstairs again leaving the dollars on the dressing table. She left them where they were and spent the rest of the weekend sick with worry that she might lose her job. She had even greater cause to worry about losing her job the following week, when she accidentally dropped one of a pair of matching vases on a table in the corridor outside Charles' bedroom.

Charles had completely forgotten about the offer made the previous weekend, but when he found Maria on her hands and knees outside his bedroom, clutching a broken piece of vase to her chest and rocking to and fro in floods of tears, his interest in her was re-kindled. He helped her to her feet and listened rather impatiently to her story about the vase seeming to suddenly fly from her grasp, then took her into the bedroom and sat her down on the edge of his bed, gave her his handkerchief and went to fetch her a glass of water.

Maria smoothed the handkerchief. She would have to run away. The vase was probably priceless. Everything in the Beaumont residence was valuable. Charles returned with the glass of water and sat down beside her. Having blown her nose, as instructed, and taken a small sip of water, she felt a little better. The friendly arm around her shoulders was also a comfort, as it must mean that Mr Beaumont was not as angry with her as she had imagined. It didn't trouble her too much at first when the arm slid down her back and fingers undid her apron ties. When they eased themselves underneath her jumper to the hooks in her bra, she attempted to wriggle away from Charles' grasp, but hesitated when he reminded her of the broken vase and asked her how on earth she could ever repay him, except in kind?

When she became pregnant she wasn't sure who she was more frightened of, God or her father. Charles laughed when she said they would have to marry; he was prepared to help her but he wouldn't do that. He gave her money and the name and address of a doctor who could be relied upon to be discreet. She almost fainted with shock. Abortion was a mortal sin. Charles remained unmoved by such a claim.

Maria prayed fervently to St. Anthony to help her. A week later, her father suffered a stroke, rendering him speechless and barely able to move. Maria felt a certain unease at the manner of St. Anthony's intervention, but took the opportunity to confess first to her married sister, Bianca, then to her mother. The hysterical reaction to the dishonour she had brought down on her family was no more than she had expected, but reason eventually prevailed. Her mother decided on the plan. Maria would go and stay in Regina, with a friend of her mother's second cousin, while she was confined. When the child was born it would be adopted by Bianca and her husband Tony Barclay. Tony was an honest, hardworking man, but they

wcrc still childlcss aftcr ninc ycars of marriage. Bianca
would persuade Tony to adopt the child. It wouldn't be as if
they were adopting a stranger's child; Maria was, after all,
her sister. Maria wept bitterly, but it was agreed that as soon
as the child was born Bianca and Tony would take it back to
Ottawa and love it as if it was their very own.

Maria reported the family's decision to Charles
Beaumont. He shrugged and told her to do whatever she
liked, provided she didn't even *think* of causing him trouble. He could give her a lot more trouble than she could ever
dream of. How was he to know that it was his child anyway? If she slept with him, how many other men had she
slept with? He had the grace to look shamefaced when she
burst into floods of tears. Her undoubted virginity had
caused him at the time of coupling to reconsider his
determination to have her, if only briefly. Wearied by her
hysterical sobbing, he allowed himself to be assured that she
was a good girl and that there wouldn't be any trouble. Her
sister and brother-in-law in Ottawa would adopt the baby
straight away.

There remained one further problem for Maria to mull
over. Bianca was as dark as Maria, and Tony had mid-
brown hair and rather pale blue eyes. Charles Beaumont
had almost reddish blond hair and was almost a foot taller
than Tony. For the ensuing six and three-quarter months
Maria prayed very hard every night that the baby would not
be born with Charles' colouring, nor grow too tall. Three
weeks earlier than expected, Maria gave birth to a baby
boy with dark downy fuzz covering his head. The nurses
thought Maria was crying because she had to give up her
baby, but she was crying with relief that once again her
prayers had been answered.

Bianca and Tony took the baby back to Ottawa and he
was christened David Anthony. The next time Maria saw
her child he was a sturdy four years old, just slightly above
average height for his age, with slightly curling black hair
and bright blue eyes. The fact that Tony Barclay had lost his

job in Ottawa and could only find work, through a friend of the family, in Edmonton, required a further family conference. Bianca was fearful that Maria would change her mind and demand to have her child back. Their mother settled the matter by forcing Maria to swear on the holy bible that she would keep forever silent. To David, she must always be Auntie Maria.

David placed the flowers that had been scattered on the ground into the florist's wrapping paper and rolled it up. He looked around as twilight began to fall, casting shadows over the gravestones. 'Next time I come and see you, Momma, I will be president of Tundra Corp. Think of that. Remember how you always used to say to me, patience is always rewarded. I guess you must be right, Momma.' He got to his feet. 'Don't you worry, Momma, they are all going to pay for what they've done. Every last one of them.'

Meryl's stomach knotted as an artificially cosy voice advised Pan Am passengers intending to board Flight 896 to proceed to the embarkation lounge. JJ stood up. 'Time to say goodbye, darling.'

'JJ, *au revoir* please. I am coming back.'

He brushed his mouth against hers. 'I shall be waiting.'

Meryl walked to the embarkation entrance and stopped at the sign forbidding visitors to proceed beyond that point. She turned and waved to JJ, at the same time filled with a sudden urge to rush back to him.

The stewardess presented a posy of flowers to Meryl. 'Miss Stewart, these are for you. Mr Reynolds especially asked me to give them to you as soon as we had taken off.'

Meryl gave a little cry of surprise. 'Oh, how lovely!'

'I think the flowers are wrapped in moss. They shouldn't wilt too quickly.' The stewardess drew out the shelf in the seat facing Meryl.

'Would you like to keep them there, where you can see them?'

'Yes, thank you.'

'Is there anything I can get you, Miss Stewart? A drink perhaps?'

'Nothing for the moment, thanks.' Meryl pulled out the card that was tucked in the base of the posy. It just read 'JJ'. She put the flowers to her nose and sniffed them. Freesias. They were the first flowers he had ever bought her. Masses and masses of freesias.

David Barclay stood at the foot of the bed watching the inert figure of Charles Beaumont. He had been summoned to the clinic half an hour previously. A nurse sat quietly at Charles' side, her hands clasped loosely in her lap. Edwin Reece sat on the other side with head bent. David looked down impassively at Charles' hands resting on top of the bed cover. Under the wrinkled, papery skin the veins showed dark indigo. When David had been formally introduced to Charles, Beaumont had still been a strong, vigorous man.

The year Charles disowned his daughter was David's first year at university. Having seen one dream come true for her son, Maria became more ambitious. Not yet forty, she still remained an attractive woman and gave Charles every ounce of nightly comfort she could think of to help him blot out the anger and pain he felt about Meryl's defection. He had become used to confiding in her more than he realised and could only nod glumly when, after agreeing with everything he said, which she always did, she confessed relief that she had had a son and not a daughter. Daughters were trouble. Always.

At first, Charles was more than reluctant to meet the son he had never before set eyes on but, undeterred, Maria arranged an accidental meeting. After the initial shock of seeing David, he was relieved that the young man did not bear a strong resemblance to him. Introduced to David as Mr Beaumont, his mother's employer, Charles found himself warming to the very polite but intelligent, sharp-witted young man. After a couple of glasses of beer and a heated discussion as to which team would win the ice hockey championship, Charles decided that Maria had done a very good job.

Maria's prayers were answered, but as always not in full measure. Charles did not, as she had fervently prayed, claim David as his long lost son. He had certainly felt a twinge of regret for the son he had never known, but he was now too old to run the risk of further suffering at the hands of another offspring. Meryl's betrayal was hurt enough to last a lifetime. Maria contented herself with Charles' promise that David would join Tundra Corp, if he did well at university. She trusted Charles. He was a man of his word. He was also a man without an heir. It was not too much to dream that David might one day become head of Tundra.

David shifted his gaze to Charles' face. There was no peace. No calm acceptance. The face was flushed, the forehead creased into a frown. David glanced away. The man was fighting a losing battle with death.

As a child, on the rare occasions he happened to see Charles, David always felt strangely frightened of the burly man with the loud voice and was made more anxious by his mother's shame. Her stern warnings not to forget to address her as Auntie Maria, as otherwise she would lose her job, still rang in his ears. Charles Beaumont was a very respectable man. An important man. He wouldn't employ an unmarried mother in his house for one single second.

His childhood fear of Charles was something David, as he grew older, would laugh about when he remembered it. He laughed even more when, in his final year at university, he became the envy of his peers. It was rumoured that he had been unofficially headhunted by Charles Beaumont himself. It was a rumour David didn't contradict, thinking it unnecessary to explain the role his mother had played in his obtaining a coveted position in Tundra Corp. He could still remember clearly the very first day he stepped into the heart of Charles Beaumont's empire; could still clearly

Crackerjack

remember standing in the presidential suite feeling as vulnerable and exposed as if he was stark naked. Charles hadn't even offered to shake hands. He had called David 'boy', as if he was addressing a servant, although David had been better educated than Charles himself could ever be.

'Come over here, boy. Your mother wants me to give you a job, boy. Should I, boy?' Charles had roared with laughter at his embarrassed, mumbled response.

David swallowed as the remembered humiliation brought bitter-tasting fluid to his mouth. He glanced at the uneven peaks of light almost hesitantly crossing the monitor screen. Do you know I am watching you die, Beaumont? Do you? At that moment, the peaks of light straightened out into a continuous line. The shrill sound of bleeping filled David's head. Edwin Reece looked up at the nurse and she nodded to him. She stood up and carefully covered Charles Beaumont's face with the sheet. David turned on his heel and left the room. He walked swiftly down the corridor, a smile hovering around his mouth. Tomorrow, he would be president of Tundra Corp.

PART 2

Christopher Mallory kept a penthouse suite in the smartest apartment block in Manhattan, exclusively for his in-town entertainment. He also financed a three hundred acre property in Westchester County for his wife and two children. Chris, as he preferred to be called, kept a deliberately high business profile and the name of Discus Petroleum was rarely off the front page of the business newspapers. Whenever he was asked the secret of his phenomenal success, what drove him, he would shrug and claim to be an unambitious man who just happened to be good with money and people.

Tracy posed in the doorway of the bedroom, knowing that the light from the hall would shine through her semi-transparent negligée.

'Chris, honey, do you feel a little hungry?'

Chris propped his hands behind his head and made a not-too-serious attempt to consider the question. 'How about you coming over here and –' He was interrupted by the telephone ringing out.

Tracy scowled. Whoever the caller was, he or she was interesting enough to make Chris swing his legs off the bed and sit up.

'No problem, David. You weren't interrupting anything.' Chris half-turned to look at Tracy and shot a pointed finger at the doorway. Tracy retreated sulkily and shut the door behind her.

Chris felt a momentary twinge of regret when David Barclay told him Charles Beaumont was dead. In a strange kind of way he had admired the old bastard. He reached over to the chair and slung a bathrobe over his shoulders, content for the moment to allow David to lead the conversation. He had, at the start of his campaign to take over Tundra Corp, homed in on David, believing, correctly, that David would not be content to wait forever to step into the old man's shoes. The offer was irresistible. If David could swing the vote of the institutional shareholders in favour of Discus Petroleum and away from Charles Beaumont, then David would be installed as president of Tundra Corp with a not insubstantial stake in the company. As Chris had anticipated, David received the offer coolly and talked at great length about loyalty to Tundra Corp, his personal loyalty and great debt of gratitude to Charles Beaumont. Precisely the kind of shit, as Chris told one of his attorneys, that Barclay always handed out to the press. Believe it, and you were capable of believing anything.

Chris padded softly up and down the bedroom, his mind quietly registering the growing tension in David's voice. He sat down on the bed again; if he didn't wind the conversation up the guy would be yacketting on all night. 'David, your assuming presidency of the company doesn't change the offer, if that's what you are working up to. Tundra Corp needs an injection of capital if it's going to capitalize on its growth potential. I know that. You know that. A change of presidency doesn't alter that fact.' Chris rolled his eyes up towards the ceiling. 'O.K. OK. Look, get back to me, will you, when you've seen Edwin Reece. You know assumptions are all very fine, but the old guy could have had a change of mind and left everything to some little floozy. Get back to me when you've seen the will and we'll get down to some real business. OK? Fine.' He put the telephone back on the bedside table and slowly shook his head from side to side. If he didn't know Barclay better, he could easily believe the guy was cracking up. He went to the bedroom door and pulled it open. 'Honey? Honey, you there?'

There was no reply. He swore under his breath.

Tracy was sitting cross-legged on the living room floor watching television. Chris bent down and wrapped his arms around her.

'Did you say something before about being hungry?'

She stared pointedly at the television screen. He stood up. 'O.K. If you want to watch television, do it someplace else.'

She reached forward and switched the television off.

Meryl sat in silence alongside Edwin Reece in the back of the limousine. She had taken an immediate liking to the somewhat weary, pinch-faced man who had welcomed her to Canada. He appeared almost to crucify himself in his efforts to break the news of her father's death as gently as possible. He couldn't know and she couldn't tell him that the news came as something of a relief to her. During the long flight from England she had churned over in her mind again and again what she would say to her father; what he would say to her. By the time the plane had landed she would have given anything to be able to take the next flight back home.

Meryl had sighed heavily without being conscious of having done so. Edwin glanced at her anxiously. 'Are you sure you're feeling all right, Meryl?'

She summoned up an encouraging smile. 'Just feeling a little weary. I wouldn't say no to a cup of tea when we get to the hotel.'

'Yes, of course.' He looked quickly out of the window before speaking again. 'Meryl,' he shot her a sideways glance. 'You're sure you want to stay in a hotel rather than go straight home?'

'Yes, Edwin.' Her voice took on a firm note. 'For the time being, I would prefer to stay in a hotel rather than my father's house.'

He looked across at her. Again she had used that phrase 'my father's house'. He rubbed his hands together as if they were cold. It was natural, he supposed. Father and daughter had suffered a bitter estrangement.

The Four Seasons hotel not only had accommodation available, but also managed to provide a private suite at short notice. Meryl took a quick shower. Edwin had said that he had most important matters to discuss with her that really shouldn't wait. She dressed hastily and ran a comb through her hair. She looked at herself for a moment in the mirror. It's getting closer by the minute. You can't put it off much longer. She put the comb down on the dressing table. Decisions. Decisions conquered uncertainty. She would visit the house first thing tomorrow morning. She nodded to her reflection. Tomorrow. No excuses.

Edwin rose to his feet when Meryl entered the sitting room. 'I told the maid we would serve ourselves. What we have to discuss is very personal.'

Meryl nodded. 'Shall I be mother?'

'Yes, please do.'

She picked up the teapot and began pouring. Edwin pulled out a sheaf of papers from his briefcase. 'Here is your father's will, Meryl. Obviously, as a lawyer yourself, you won't need me to explain it to you, but perhaps you would like me to quickly summarise the pertinent points?'

'Please, Edwin.'

He put his spectacles on and cleared his throat. 'Your father's entire estate has been left to you absolutely.'

Meryl stared at the teapot still held poised in mid-air. She had fully expected him to say she had not been mentioned at all. He cleared his throat again. 'I am appointed as executor.' He pushed his spectacles higher up on his nose. 'The will contains a "gift over". If you should predecease your father or fail to survive him for more than twenty-eight days after his own demise, then the estate is to be put in trust; whereupon all your father's shares in Tundra Corp are to be vested absolutely in David Barclay.' He paused for so long that Meryl began to wonder if there was a special significance that she had overlooked. 'The remainder of your father's estate is to be held in trust, the income from which is to be distributed to various Canadian and British charities.' He passed the will across to her. 'Perhaps you would like to look at it yourself?'

Meryl took the will and began reading. As her trained eye skimmed through the formal wording, her mind was filled with just one question. Why? Why had her father left everything to her? She handed the will back to Edwin.

'Is there anything you wish to ask me about, Meryl?'

She hesitated, unsure how to phrase the question. 'You have been my father's attorney for many years. You know about what happened between my father and myself. He disowned me. Why did he change his mind? My father never, ever, went back on a decision once it was made.'

Edwin got up from the sofa and walked to the windows. 'You don't know this, but when you went to England he asked me to keep track of you. Once, I showed him a cutting from a British newspaper profiling the young high-flyers in the City of London. It had a photograph of you and said you were one of the new breed of dynamic, corporate lawyers. He didn't say anything, but I could tell by the expression on his face that he was very proud of you. When he asked me to draw up the new will a couple of weeks ago, he told me he wanted you to have everything he owned. You hadn't come crawling back. You had guts.'

Edwin removed his spectacles and studied them for a moment. 'He said you were the only person who could save Tundra now. You were his flesh and blood. You wouldn't allow the effort of two generations of Beaumonts to be wiped out.'

'I see.' Meryl slung the will on the table. 'He was only concerned about Tundra. Even at the end, all he could think about was his precious company.'

Edwin turned away from the window and looked at her. 'You're wrong. He loved you. He was a proud, often difficult man, I know, but I believe he loved you very much. The last thing he said to me was, "Take care of my girl for me, Edwin".'

Meryl pressed her lips together. Don't cry now. It's too

late. She got up from the sofa. 'Well, I shall be very grateful for your help, Edwin. Very grateful. For the moment though, I would like to rest, recharge my batteries. Perhaps we can make a start on things tomorrow morning?'

'Yes, of course. I appreciate that none of this can be easy for you.'

She nodded.

David paced up and down his office. He stopped and glanced at his watch then continued pacing. Something was wrong. Edwin Reece had deliberately put off seeing him until this afternoon, claiming that the Beaumont family should be acquainted of the will first. He balled his fist and punched the air in front of him. Nothing was wrong. It was just a ploy on Reece's part to keep him waiting as long as possible. The stupid old bastard had always resented him.

He stopped pacing at the sound of the outer office door opening and closing, and hurriedly sat down at his desk. He stood up again as Edwin Reece came through the door. 'Edwin! Good to see you.'

'David.' Edwin briefly inclined his head.

'Come and sit down. Can I get you a drink?'

'Not for me.'

David sat down again. He rested his arms on the desk and clasped his hands together. 'You know, Edwin, I still can't believe he's gone. A great man. A truly great man. He was like a father to me, you know.'

Edwin nodded. David paused, as if waiting for him to speak, then rubbed his hands together. 'Well, we mustn't dwell on things: Charles wouldn't have wanted it.'

Edwin placed his briefcase on the corner of the desk and opened it. 'Under the terms of Mr Beaumont's will his daughter, Marylin Alice Stewart Beaumont, commonly known as Meryl Stewart, inherits his entire estate. I have been appointed his executor.' He glanced across at David and noted with quiet satisfaction that the man looked as if he had just been turned to stone. 'It is also Mr Beaumont's express wish that his daughter, as majority stockholder, takes up a board directorship in Tundra Corp.' He took the will out of his briefcase and held it out to David. 'Miss Stewart has given me to understand that she has no objection to your having sight of the will.'

David stared at the document Edwin held out to him. 'Is this some kind of joke?'

'No. See for yourself.'

David grabbed the will and hastily scanned it. He flung it down on the desk. 'What about me?'

'What about you?'

David wrenched his chair away from the desk and stood up. 'You goddam know what I mean. Beaumont promised me the presidency. He promised to leave me a controlling interest in the company.'

Edwin shrugged his shoulders.

David came round to where Edwin sat and grabbed at the lapel of his jacket. 'Don't think you will get away with this. This will was only made a couple of weeks ago. I will contest it. Beaumont was in no fit state to make a new will.'

'Take your hands off me, or I will have the police lay a charge against you for assault.' Edwin spoke quietly, but firmly.

David looked at him for a moment almost as if he hadn't heard him. He let his hands drop to his sides.

'I took the precaution of having two independent medical witnesses testify that Charles was of sound mind when he made his will. Contest it if you wish, but you will be wasting your time.'

David walked, trance-like, to the drinks cabinet and took out a glass and a bottle of whisky. He carefully poured a shot of whisky into the glass. The measured slowness of his actions gave him time to control his rage. He walked back to the desk again. 'I must ask you to forgive me, Edwin. I have behaved badly. You must understand this has come as a shock to me. I looked upon that man as a father. I have given everything to Tundra Corp. Everything. And this is how I am repaid.' He took a mouthful of whisky. 'Sorry; did you want a drink?'

'Er- yes, I think I will. I'll help myself.'

David waited until Edwin returned with a glass of whisky then put his head in his hands. 'You know, I stayed with that man until his very last breath. I loved him. I trusted him.' He looked up at Edwin. 'What am I going to do, Edwin?'

Edwin stretched his legs out in front of him and crossed them. 'I suggest you prepare yourself to meet your new majority stockholder.'

David dragged his hands down his face. 'When is she coming?'

'She's here already.'

David gave a bitter laugh. 'Didn't waste much time, did she?'

'Her father asked for her to be fetched. He wanted to see her before he died.'

David stared at him. 'Why wasn't I told of this?'

Edwin shrugged. 'Why should you be? Family matters are not your concern.'

David resisted the very strong urge to get up and throttle the man sitting opposite him. He picked up the whisky glass and drained it then set it down on the desk again. 'Am I to assume that you have already met her?'

'You may. And now, if you will excuse me, I have a meeting to attend.'

David watched Edwin put the will back in his briefcase and lock it securely.

'Goodnight, David.'

'Goodnight.'

David waited until Edwin had left the outer office then slammed both fists down on the desk. You tried to out-wit me, didn't you, you old bastard? While you were lying on your stinking deathbed, you thought you had outwitted me.

The men's washroom was deserted. David turned the

cold tap full on and splashed his face with water. He grabbed a handful of paper towels and mopped his face. He looked down at the soggy, crumpled towels and crushed them into a ball. No one cheats on David Barclay. Ever.

The cream-painted facade of the house, the gnarled sprawling limbs of wistaria hugging the walls, looked exactly as Meryl remembered. The cherubic bronze figure was still urinating vulgarly into the ornamental pond, in the centre of the driveway. She stepped out of the car and waited for Edwin.

The front door of the house opened and a butler came out and hurried down the steps. Meryl stared at him, but didn't recognise him. Edwin touched her arm. 'Marsh, the butler. Shall we go in?'

She nodded and walked slowly up the steps. Edwin stood aside to allow her to pass in front of him and into the hall. She glanced slowly round then let Edwin guide her into the study as if she was a stranger to the house.

'If you will excuse me a moment, Meryl. I need to fetch some papers. Why don't you sit down. I won't be a moment.'

She nodded, and heard the door close behind her. She glanced around quickly. Nothing had been changed. No. The computer on the desk was new. There hadn't been a computer when . . . She took in a deep breath. Meryl could feel the presence of her father as strongly as if he was standing next to her. Sitting down in a leather covered chair, she gripped the arms. He would always be here. She raised her eyes to the portrait of herself hanging on the wall opposite his desk. He had had the painting specially commissioned for her eighteenth birthday. He had called her his golden girl. She got up and rushed into the hall. She had intended to run out of the house, but Marsh stood in her way.

'Can I get you anything, Miss Beaumont; perhaps some tea or coffee?' Meryl stared at him bemused. She couldn't remember the last time she had been addressed as

Miss Beaumont. She licked her lips. 'Thank you, Marsh, but my name is Stewart not Beaumont. And tea would be fine.'

'Right away, Miss Stewart.'

She felt a ridiculous sense of relief that he had accepted the name of Stewart without question.

Edwin Reece had been most meticulous. Draft accounts of her father's estate had already been prepared. Meryl sipped at her tea. She had always taken for granted the fact that her father was a rich man, but until now she had had no idea how rich. She carefully set the cup down in its saucer. Now it all belonged to her. She had become a multi-billionairess overnight. At least on paper.

Mrs Kemp, the housekeeper, trotted in front of Meryl like a small enthusiastic dog, occasionally turning her head to make sure Meryl was still following. She had offered her condolences with genuine sincerity and had shyly expressed a hope that Meryl would want her to housekeep for her, as she had done for her late father.

Mrs Kemp stopped at the door at the far end of the corridor. 'This is your bedroom, Miss Stewart.' She clapped her hand to her mouth. 'Oh, silly me. Of course, you know that.' She opened the door and stood to one side.

Meryl stepped through the doorway then paused. Nothing had been moved. Nothing had been changed. She gripped the door knob tightly and took in a deep breath in an unconscious effort to stop herself being swept helplessly back in time. Bobby sat on her pillow as he had always done. Her silver-backed hairbrushes still lay on the dressing table.

Mrs Kemp cleared her throat. 'Well, I will leave you, Miss Stewart. If you need me, I shall be downstairs.'

Meryl nodded almost absentmindedly. She went to the bed and picked up the teddy bear. She ran a finger across his mouth. Poor Bobby. He had fallen victim to her puppy. Nanny McClaren had embroidered a new mouth for him in brown thread, but it had left him looking sad, reproachful. She clutched Bobby to her chest and went to look out of the window. The ornamental cherry trees looked bare and lifeless. She turned quickly away.

The decision not to return to the Four Seasons but to remain in the house was prompted by a small knot of press reporters who had gathered outside the wrought-iron gates of the house, and by Edwin's suggestion that it might arouse speculation if Meryl insisted on staying in a hotel instead of residing in her own home. The news of Charles Beaumont's death had been released to the press that morning. Inevitably, there would be curiosity about Meryl, about the future of Tundra Corp. Being in the public eye would be something she would have to learn to live with from now on.

Chris Mallory spun the swivel chair round to face the window. He ran his fingers through his hair. He knew as soon as he had woken up that the day was not going to be a good one.

'O.K. O.K. David. So Beaumont's cheated on you. So the guy is a bastard. You're not going to change any of that. No one can. Just keep your head.' He swung round to face the desk again. 'Will you listen to me for a moment. Please. The offer still stands. O.K., you face an additional problem. You not only have to convince the British institutional stockholders to accept my offer, you have also to convince Meryl Beaumont to do the same. What? O.K. Meryl Stewart. Just get to it, pal.' He raised his eyes to the ceiling and drew in a slow breath. 'You're not thinking straight, David. I would advise you to do so right now. The daughter, Meryl whatever-she-calls-herself, has been estranged from her father. She has not appeared to express the slightest interest in Tundra Corp. She may just decide to take the money and cut and run. So get off that goddam high horse of yours and go and see her. Talk to her. And above all, persuade her to accept the Discus offer. That's all you have to do, David.' Chris looked up and beckoned to a young attorney standing in the doorway.

'David, I have to go. Call me again when you have some good news for me.' He sighed heavily as he put the telephone down. 'I am beginning to regret using that guy Barclay, I really am.' He rubbed at the side of his jaw. 'O.K. Frank, what've you got for me on Beaumont's daughter?'

Frank handed him a two page report. Chris skimmed through it. He swore loudly. 'Wouldn't you just believe it. A lawyer. Beaumont's daughter has to be a corporate lawyer for chrissakes.'

'Sorry to have to disappoint you, Chris.'

Chris raised both hands into the air. 'I know, I know. Don't say it. I was naive in thinking she might conceivably be a dumb nightclub singer or something.'

Frank grinned.

'OK. So she's a lawyer. She works for Wajiki. So.' Chris ran his fingers through his hair. 'So what are we looking at, Frank?'

'A tough cookie.'

Chris puffed his cheeks out. 'Have you a number she can be reached on? I think I should talk to her myself. I don't trust Barclay not to screw the whole thing up.'

Frank flicked the report open on the last page. 'Our sources say she is staying at the Beaumont residence. The number is on the bottom of the page.'

'OK, Frank, that will be all for now.' Chris sat down at his desk and picked up the telephone. He swung around in the chair and faced the window at the sound of Meryl's voice. 'Good morning, Miss Stewart. Chris Mallory. I hope I am not inconveniencing you.'

'Good morning, Mr Mallory.'

'I really just wanted to call and say how sorry I am to learn about your father. We didn't always see eye to eye on things, but I want you to know that I admired your father very much. And I'm very sorry.'

'Thank you, Mr Mallory.'

'Ah, Miss Stewart, I don't really know how to say this, but I hope you don't consider that the ah- pressure of negotiations between Discus and Tundra was in any way a contributory factor in your father's death.'

'No, I don't think that, Mr Mallory.'

Chris grimaced at the coolly polite voice. He tapped his fingers on the arm of the chair. It was no more than he could expect under the circumstances. 'Well, I won't take up any more of your time, Miss Stewart. I'll be in touch with you.'

'Goodbye, Mr Mallory.'

Meryl returned to the uneaten breakfast that had been carefully prepared by Mrs Kemp. She pushed the plate of scrambled egg to one side and picked up the coffee pot. The call from Christopher Mallory had been unexpected, but she had decided to take it at face value. The sentiments had sounded as if they were genuinely expressed. She refilled her coffee cup and took a sip. A restless night's sleep had left her head feeling as if it was stuffed with wet cotton wool.

It had been a mistake the previous night to call her mother last. The conversation had wiped out the positive feelings Meryl had felt after talking to JJ. Mary Beaumont had been very upset to learn that Charles had died before Meryl arrived. She had so wanted him to be at peace with himself, and he had been denied that. Mary's uncontrollable weeping disturbed Meryl and she decided to call Simon and ask him to go and see her mother. If anyone could comfort her, it would be Simon. Surprisingly, Simon had suggested that Mary needed to be alone. She needed to come to terms with certain aspects of her life. It was the best therapy for her.

Mrs Kemp bustled into the breakfast room. 'Oh, Miss Stewart, you haven't eaten even a morsel.'

Meryl was suddenly reminded of Nanny McClaren, except that Nanny McClaren had always addressed a situation from a mutual viewpoint. We have not drunk our hot milk. We have not cleaned our fingernails very well, have we?

The arrival of Edwin Reece diverted Mrs Kemp's attention from the untouched food. He accepted a cup of coffee and sat down opposite Meryl, not liking what he saw. She looked even more tired than she had done the day before.

'I had a call from Christopher Mallory just before you arrived.'

He looked enquiringly at her. 'What did he want?'

Meryl shook her head. 'Nothing. For the moment. He said he wanted to say how sorry he was about my father. That's all.'

Edwin looked down at his hands. 'There is something you should know before we go to the office. I should have raised it yesterday, but I didn't want to pressure you with too many things. Your father discovered that David Barclay had accepted an offer from Chris Mallory to make him president of Tundra Corp if Barclay could swing the institutional stockholders' vote in Discus Petroleum's favour.'

Meryl stared at him. 'Interesting. How did my father find that out?'

'You know what your father was like, Meryl. There was little he couldn't find out about.' Edwin rubbed at his hands. It wasn't prudent to tell her that her father had had David Barclay's telephone illegally tapped. 'Understandably, Charles was extremely angry. He decided to keep the information to himself for the time being. Then when he became ill, he asked me to keep a check on Barclay for him. I have no doubt whatsoever that Barclay has a foot in both camps.'

Meryl silently gathered up the mail she had been opening. So that was why her father had changed his will. She tossed the discarded envelopes into the waste bin. Events, not a change of heart, had forced him into a reconciliation. Typical. She looked across at Edwin. 'Tell me about this man Barclay. What's he like?'

'There's something about him I have always found a little odd, but he is very capable. Has the knowhow, the experience.' Edwin rubbed his hands together again. 'The situation is a rather delicate one. Your father had latterly left the day to day running of Tundra to Barclay. No one is indispensable, but he comes pretty close.' Edwin cleared his throat. 'He was under the impression that he would assume the presidency of the company if anything should happen to your father. There is some justification for him thinking that. Charles often said there was no better man than Barclay to run the company.'

Meryl picked up a sheaf of letters and tapped them into a neat shape. 'So David Barclay has tried to ensure whichever way the coin drops he wins. He is indispensable to Tundra. His own future is secure should Discus Petroleum take Tundra over.' She placed the pile of letters neatly in front of her. 'We are, are we not, Edwin, looking at an ambitious man?'

'I believe we are.'

'Good. Now I know everything I need to know about Mr Barclay.' Meryl flashed a smile at Edwin.

Edwin stared at her. When she smiled she was truly beautiful. Her mother must have looked like that when she was her age. Charles couldn't have stood a chance.

Josie stared in dismay at the tall, elegantly dressed blonde. No one should look as good as that. It wasn't fair. Edwin motioned to her.

'Tell Mr Barclay that Miss Stewart has arrived please, Josie.'

'Yes, Mr Reece.' She turned to speak into the intercom. 'Miss Stewart and Mr Reece are here, Mr Barclay.' She turned round to stare at Meryl again.

David swept the door open then stopped for a second, startled by what he saw. Instinctively his eyes swept over Meryl from top to toe and back again, taking in her sophisticated, discreet sexuality. The last time he had seen her she had been nothing more than a little cocktease, spoilt and indulged beyond belief by her father. That memory stifled the sudden, strong, sexual urge. He stepped forward and held out his hand, schooling his voice into disinterested politeness. 'I am David Barclay, Miss Stewart. How do you do.'

'How do you do, Mr Barclay.' Meryl smiled in amusement. She was used to men behaving at first sight as if they had just been let loose in a sweet shop and he had been no exception, but she would give him nine out of ten for a quick recovery.

'I am delighted to meet our new majority stockholder, Miss Stewart, and I hope very much you will come and have lunch with me. In the meantime, may I show you around Tundra Corp? I think you will find it very interesting.'

'Thank you, Mr Barclay. What will be of interest to me is to meet with Tundra's Financial Director. Perhaps you will arrange that. Shall we say in half an hour?'

The smile on David's face remained in place, but only just. 'Of course, Miss Stewart, if that is what you wish.' He turned to Josie and told her to ask the Financial Director to report to the presidential suite immediately. As he did so, he noticed Meryl and Edwin exchanging glances. He frowned to himself. They were both horses from the same stable, but it was more than natural affinity between two lawyers. He would have to be very careful. 'If you would like to follow me, Miss Stewart, I will take you to the presidential suite.'

'Thank you, Mr Barclay.'

Much to David's annoyance Meryl gestured to Edwin to accompany her. So far David had managed to totally ignore him.

Meryl studied the back of David's head as she followed him through his office. He was very attractive in a dark, rather moody, sort of way. Not as tall as JJ, but tall enough.

The Financial Director, believing in safety in numbers, was accompanied by the company lawyer. Meryl declined to sit in her father's chair and suggested they should all sit around an oval conference table at the far end of the room. Edwin sat next to Meryl and David ensured that he sat opposite her as if in the role of antagonist. The Financial Director and company lawyer positioned themselves impartially in the middle of the group.

David settled back in his chair. His urges had not remained stifled for long and he now stared overtly at Meryl. Someone had taken her further education well in hand. He wondered who the lucky bastard was.

She wasn't wearing any rings. Not that that in itself was significant. He stared at her hair. The long tresses and the fringe from behind which she used to view the world had gone. Now it was all coiled on top of her head and firmly kept in check. That mouth hadn't changed, though, it had always been a dead giveaway. A bit sulky and capable of creating physical havoc in any red-blooded male. David spread his thighs and rested them against the sides of his chair. She had to be about three years older than he was, but he still reckoned he could teach her a thing or two.

Meryl was highly conscious of David looking at her and twice had to mentally chastise herself severely before the lawyer gained control over the naive schoolgirl. She raised her head and looked across at David. 'Mr Barclay.' She used what she liked to believe was her courtroom voice. 'Perhaps you would like to start.'

His eyes flickered for a moment. She sucked her cheeks in slightly at his silent, grossly sexual, misinterpretation of her words. His gaze shifted slightly and his expression returned to that appropriate to a businessman dealing with a serious question. He leaned forward and rested his hands on the table in front of him. 'I guess you will want me to brief you first on the hostile bid by Discus Petroleum.'

Meryl's features settled into the bland objectivity of a lawyer listening to the evidence of a condemned man. She gave a slight nod and relaxed a little more into her chair. David Barclay had been very, very fresh. All the time they had talked, his dark gaze had swept openly up and down her body, lingering on the bare flesh of her throat, the swell of her breast beneath her formal suit.

Thoughts of David Barclay faded and, after spending over an hour going through the company's books, Meryl also found her initial unease at being so close to the heart of her father's empire dissipating. Professional curiosity also overtook her and she quite unconsciously took control of the meeting; asking questions, challenging received truths. David's initial predatory attitude towards her had dissolved into a more or less sullen silence, unless she asked him a direct question.

Meryl placed her hands together and rested her chin on the tips of her fingers. 'Very well, gentlemen, I think we should summarize what we have been discussing. Tundra's assets are considerable.' She ticked a finger. 'Number one. Its petrochemical business. There is great potential, running to the end of the next decade. Number two. Its share in a North Sea exploration bloc, with prospects of further finds. Number three. It's exploration rights in the Athabasca tar sands. In terms of human resources, its workforce is maintaining a high degree of productivity and flexibility. Now, turning to the question of Discus Petroleum; Tundra is facing a counteractive time-limited scenario.'

The Financial Director and company lawyer straightened up and trained their eyes on Meryl, like two retrievers waiting for their master to raise the gun that would bring their quarry down to earth. Meryl glanced across at David as he appeared to be about to say something. He gave a slight shake of his head to indicate that he had abandoned such an idea. She rested her hands on the table in front of her.

'I am a lawyer, gentlemen, not a financial advisor, but I feel that part of the weakness in Tundra's defence to Discus's bid is its shyness. Tundra appears not to have told anyone just how really exciting this company is and can be in the future, in terms of growth and profits. I think we must commend our Financial Director for the excellent profit forecast he has produced.' She gave a brief smile in his direction.

'However, and perhaps this is my father's fault, Tundra has adopted an ostrich-like attitude to Discus, thinking that if we keep on ignoring its presence it will stop being a nuisance and go away.' She paused to allow her words to sink in, not realizing that she had used the word 'we' for the first time.

This time David did speak out. 'Meryl, this is rather embarrassing for me to have to say, but may I suggest that part of our defence at Tundra has been the special relationship your father had with certain institutional stockholders in Britain.'

His words brought quick affirmative nods, even from Edwin Reece.

'I take your point, David. I think it is very relevant.' She glanced around the table. 'Gentlemen, following my father's death, Tundra needs a change of tactics against Discus. Time is not on our side in this. Discus' bid closes in less than a week. David, as acting president, I am sure you have ideas of your own regarding Discus.

David looked at her sharply. Something in her tone of voice gave him the distinct feeling that the statement was less innocent than it sounded.

Meryl briefly scanned the faces around her. 'But, there is only one question to be answered. Why should Tundra Corp remain an independent company? Answer that question and you will have won the battle against Discus.' She gave a brief smile. 'As majority stockholder, I can assure you that I shall be more than interested to hear your answers.' She rose from her chair. 'Thank you for your time, gentlemen.'

Both the Financial Director and the company lawyer shook her hand enthusiastically, as if the meeting had imbued both of them with new spirit. When the meeting finally ended, Edwin took Meryl to one side and patted her shoulder. 'I think you've just won round one. You had them eating out of your hand.'

'I don't think that can be said of David Barclay. Yet.' She gave him a conspiratorial smile.

David returned to his own office and told Josie to take an early lunch. She looked at him nervously. He was in a foul mood about something. He went to the water cooler and filled a plastic beaker with water. Shaking with rage, he gripped the beaker so hard it cracked, sending a spray of water down the front of his trousers. He cursed and flung the remains of the beaker at the water dispenser.

Fucking bitch. She had treated him like an office boy asked to account for a missing cent from the petty cash. He stormed into his own office and slammed the door shut. He leaned against it and shut his eyes. Fucking bitch was just like her father. He rubbed a hand across his brow. He had thought it had all ended with Beaumont's death. Now she was here, it was beginning all over again. He half stumbled across to the drinks cabinet and poured himself a double shot of whisky.

The restaurant offered the latest nouvelle cuisine. Meryl studied the menu carefully. 'Canadian food has certainly improved since I was last here.'

'You must let me take you on a guided tour sometime. A lot has been happening in Edmonton over the last couple of years.' David waved the menu at the wine waiter. 'I think you'll be surprised at some of the changes around here, Meryl.'

She grinned. 'But Sundays surely are the same. Edmonton wouldn't be Edmonton if there was actually something to do on Sundays.'

He laughed.

The wine waiter appeared at David's side and took his order. 'Would you like another aperitif, Meryl?'

Meryl thought for a moment. 'Yes, if you are having another. Why not?'

David ordered two more aperitifs. The anger of the previous hour had died away, leaving an even greater sense of determination to charm Meryl Stewart into selling her Tundra shares. A forceful, charismatic man, he was confident that he had a way with women. Enough of them had fallen victim to his charms to prove it to be so. The waiter appeared with their drinks. David leaned back in his chair. The first glass had encouraged the use of first names, perhaps the second would encourage her to discuss Tundra's future.

'I understand, David, that it is a foregone conclusion at Tundra that you will take on the presidency.'

His eyes flicked open wide. Once again, she had uncannily pre-empted his thoughts. He gave a modest smile and tried very hard to appear embarrassed by the statement. 'I will admit that I would consider it an honour to follow in Charles' footsteps. A great honour. I also like to think that my track record at Tundra will allow me to say in all humility that I believe I am the ideal candidate.'

Meryl suppressed a smile. The man definitely had a way with words. She picked up her glass as if about to make a toast. 'I believe your appointment as president will be made very shortly. Congratulations.'

He stared at her for a moment, hardly daring to believe what he had just heard. He picked up his own glass. 'Thank you. Thank you, Meryl. I can't tell you how delighted I am to receive your vote of confidence.' He waited until the waiter had served the first course before speaking again. 'I would be very interested to know your views about the Discus offer for the company. Your father was set against it and that is a natural reaction. However, as much as one would like, one cannot run away from the fact that Tundra needs outside capital if it is going to survive in the future.'

Meryl pursed her lips. He began talking quickly again. 'We must consider the position of the British institutional investors. I think you should know, Meryl, that the British stockholders have been unhappy about Tundra's growth potential for some time. Their position is understandable. Two of them are pension fund managers employed by large companies. While they have remained loyal to Tundra, their first and foremost duty is to ensure continuing capital and income growth of the monies they are responsible for investing. You must see the truth in that.'

She laughed. 'I well understand the workings of pension funds, David. You really don't have to explain such things to me.'

'I'm sorry, I wasn't trying to preach to you. However, it does have to be said that they will accept whatever is in their interests to accept. The Discus offer being a case in point.'

'Where do you stand on this, David?'

'Me?' He shrugged his shoulders. 'I suppose I have very ambivalent feelings. Obviously, I would like to see Tundra Corp remain totally independent, but I wouldn't see the company's future sacrificed to that end.'

She laughed again. 'You do have very ambivalent feelings.'

'I think that is understandable under the circumstances, but my feelings are unimportant. It is what the majority stockholder thinks that is important.'

Meryl ignored the indirect question and concentrated on her food. 'This veal is excellent. What's your duck like?'

'Great.' David stifled his growing irritation. 'Forgive me, but I don't think you answered my question, Meryl. What do you, as the majority stockholder, think about the Discus offer?'

'Why is it so important to you to know?'

'Come on!' He rested his fork on the plate. 'Of course it is important to me. If I am going to be president of Tundra, if I am to function properly, I must know the views of all the stockholders, majority or otherwise.'

'I know.' Meryl clasped her hands beneath her chin. 'I have a lot of things to deal with at the moment. A lot of things. I haven't really made my mind up about anything at the moment.'

'Have you come back permanently to Canada?'

'No. I hope to be returning home as soon as possible.'

He nodded, picking up his fork again. Perhaps it was enough for the moment to gain the admission that she was returning to England. She obviously wasn't interested in taking on a highly visible role in the running of the company, if she intended to go home. He chewed slowly on his food, feeling more confident that he could persuade her to dispose of her shares.

The Tundra Corp refinery was based at the aptly named Refinery Row to the east of Edmonton city centre, across the Saskatchewan River. The security officer at the gates raised the barrier when he spotted the dark limousine swing off the highway onto the short approach road.

Meryl's entourage was met with open curiosity as it swept through the main gates and on to the head office. She had quickly taken up David's invitation to visit the refinery. If she was going to be involved in Tundra's affairs, she should learn something about its business first hand. As she stepped out of the car and walked the few feet to the office block, one brave soul, working high up on a platform and partially out of sight, plucked up courage and gave a wolf-whistle. Meryl sensed the group of men standing outside the office, waiting to greet her, suddenly freeze at the sound. She glanced up at the platform then raised a hand in the air, and gave a brief waggle of her fingers in acknowledgement. That produced a faint cheer from up above. She laughed. 'Now that's what I call a real friendly welcome.'

The men on the ground took her laughter as a clear sign that their female VIP had not taken offence, and visibly relaxed.

After the introductions of senior personnel were completed, Meryl began to realize how the British Royal Family must feel. Her wrist was throbbing from a series of bonecrushing handshakes. She was also touched by the genuineness of the simple condolences offered by each of them on the death of her father. Face after face mirrored the deeply felt respect for Charles Beaumont, a respect that appeared to be freely carried over to her as well, except that it was tinged with unspoken questions in their eyes. What is going to happen? What are you going to do? Where do we go from here?

One exception to the questioning eyes was Lonny 'Panhandle' Jones. He was retiring at the end of that week and had none of the inhibitions of the other men. He doffed his hard hat and startled Meryl by giving her a smacking kiss on her cheek. 'Remember you, Miss Marylin, when you were just a little baby girl. Your pa brought you here once to show you off.' He took hold of her arm and squeezed it. 'I'm as sure as hell gonna miss him. I worked for your pa for fifty years now. No finer man I know. A hard man, but a fair man. Could hold his liquor, too.' He squeezed her arm again. 'You've grown into a fine lady, Miss Marylin. Your pa must be mighty proud of you.'

Meryl smiled politely then surprised herself by finding her eyes suddenly brimming with tears. She felt David grip her elbow as blurred, but anxious male faces loomed into view. Lonny Jones was tactfully drawn away. She blinked several times and quickly regained her composure. She smiled at her escorts. 'I suspect Mr Jones could tell a story or two about my father.'

There was a ripple of nervous laughter. Again there was palpable relief, this time because they had been saved from the fearful prospect of coping with a tearful woman.

Before being taken on a conducted tour of the refinery, David excused himself, saying he had a couple of urgent things to attend to, but promised Meryl that she would be left in the very safe hands of Jim Stanton. He was the senior maintenance engineer, known in refinery parlance as a 'crackerjack'. Jim was a tallish, fair-haired man with an instantly likeable easy-going manner. He helped Meryl clamber into overalls and non-slip boots. By way of conversation she told him about her meeting with Lonny Jones.

He burst out laughing. 'We usually ensure visitors see Lonny last and preferably not at all.' He gave her a hard hat emblazoned with the Tundra Corp logo. 'Hope this is going to be comfortable for you. Tried to find the smallest size we have.'

She put on the hat. 'Fine. No problem.' She reached down and grasped at the legs of her overalls and held them out, to invite inspection. 'What do you think?'

Jim cocked his head to one side then nodded. 'I have to say, Miss Beaumont, you do a lot for the outfit. You really do.'

She laughed. 'Just checking. Right, let's go.'

Meryl followed Jim across the compound listening intently to his running commentary on how they processed the 'liquid gold'. They stopped outside the No. 2 cat cracker. She craned her neck and looked up at the array of pipes and complicated steel structures. It looked like something out of science fiction. She turned to Jim. 'Why is it called a cat cracker? Sounds as if you do painful things to domestic pets.'

He smiled. 'Everyone says that. What we call cracking is just a technical name for breaking down large-molecule hydrocarbons into little ones. And, as we use catalysis for breaking down the petroleum into further compounds, the equipment is called a cat cracker. Nothing at all to do with our feline friends, I can assure you. We actually have two cat crackers. No. 1 is undergoing routine service at the moment and is quite old as cat crackers go. This,' he jerked his thumb, 'the No. 2, incorporates the most up to date technology.'

'How long have you worked here, Jim?'

He thought for a moment. 'Getting on for ten years. Something like that.' He paused as if struggling with some inner doubt as to what he intended to say next. 'Always had a lot of time for your father, Miss Beaumont. Knew what he was talking about.'

She nodded.

'You're very like him.'

Meryl looked at him in surprise. 'Am I?'

'Hope you don't mind my saying, but you are. You're direct, you get to the point. Your father was like that.'

'Thank you.' She didn't know why, but she felt flattered.

After forty minutes dutifully trudging around after Jim, the weight of the heavy boots began to tell on Meryl's ankles. She was relieved when he suggested she might like to take a break and they made their way back to the office building for a cup of coffee. They had almost reached the office compound when there was a sudden muffled sound like a clap of thunder. They both turned to look in the direction from where the sound had come. Thick smoke was pouring out of the No. 1 cat cracker. Jim pulled at her arm and dragged her to the door of the office. 'Go inside and stay there.' He pulled out his personal radio and began shouting instructions into it. 'Miss Beaumont is in Sector 5. Repeat. Sector 5. Get her to safety immediately. Repeat. Immediately.' He slammed the door shut in her face. At the same time klaxons began blaring out their staccato message of danger to every part of the refinery.

Meryl unconsciously held her hand up to her chest as she stared anxiously out of the office window. She had no idea what was going on, but whatever it was it was serious. She watched Jim running at full stretch across the compound. The next explosion was loud enough to rattle the windows. Meryl leapt back, fearing that they would shatter. She let out a small cry when she looked up and noticed a sheet of flame shooting straight up into the sky from a huge, tank shaped steel container that looked to be about a block away in distance. She craned her neck to see out of the window as far as she could. Men were running into and across the compound from every direction. One man flung himself to the ground as two fire engines, one after another, careered around the corner of the building opposite, almost running him over. Insulated from most of the noise going on outside,

Meryl could only stare out of the window as if transfixed. The scene outside took on an almost dream-like quality as she watched men rushing hither and thither like ants. She raised her eyes and stared up at the sky. The flames had disappeared. Only a plume of thick white vapour could be seen. Almost unconsciously, she began to realise that everything was gradually slowing down. One of the fire engines returned, but travelling at a much reduced speed. Men reappeared from doorways, clambering down access ladders, still talking into their radios, but with less apparent urgency.

A car sped up to the office where Meryl was waiting. Its tyres smoked as the driver made a handbrake turn and slewed the car round to face the way it had came. He got out and ran to the door of the office and pulled it open. 'O.K. Miss Beaumont. There's no panic. Everything is under control. Come with me, please.' He didn't wait for her to answer. He grabbed at her arm and hurried her out and into the car.

She managed to find her voice as they drove towards the main office building. 'What happened?'

'Just a small explosion in the No. 1 cat cracker.'

Meryl turned round in her seat to stare at the driver. That had to be the understatement of the century. He flashed a quick smile of reassurance. 'Everything is under control, Miss Beaumont, believe me.'

'Has anyone been injured?'

'Ah – I think a couple of the guys are receiving treatment for injuries, but nothing serious.' He braked heavily and pulled in to the side as a fleet of ambulances converged on the car then overtook it.

Meryl stared at the driver again. She had counted six ambulances. 'I thought you said only two people had been injured.'

He lifted his hand off the steering wheel, as if making a silent plea.

'Don't worry, please. It's standard procedure that all

fire-fighting appliances and medical services turn out
whether they are needed or not.'

When they arrived back at the main building, David ran
down the steps and opened the car door. 'Meryl, are you
O.K.?'

'Yes, I'm fine.' She stepped out of the car. 'Is everybody
else all right? That's the most important thing.'

'I think so. No serious injuries have been reported. A
few of the men have been overcome by fumes, but they'll
be O.K.'

Having seen Meryl settled in one of the offices with a cup
of tea, and a young secretary to tend to her needs, David left
her again to obtain a further and personal update from Jim
Stanton on conditions.

A little later a call came through to the office from David.
Much to Meryl's relief the news was not as bad as she had
feared. The explosion had caused serious structural damage
to the cat cracker, but fortunately, as had been earlier
reported, no one had suffered serious injury. The cause of
the explosion was as yet unknown. Meryl poured herself a
second cup of tea and waited for David to return. She
couldn't offer any real assistance and David was probably
better off doing whatever he needed to do without having
her under his feet.

Eager for an update on the press release from Tundra, the
waiting press and television reporters swarmed around the
car as soon as they saw it was Meryl pulling up outside
Tundra House. The chauffeur accelerated away from the
front of the building, almost knocking over one of the less
nimble-footed cameramen, and drove quickly to a rear
entrance.

The appearance of Meryl and David in the offices of
Tundra was greeted with relief. The staff had been
inundated with calls wanting to know who the next president of Tundra Corp would be. Was Marylin Beaumont
stepping into her father's shoes? How serious was the

explosion at the cat cracker? Had the battle with Discus Petroleum precipitated Charles Beaumont's death? It was Edwin Reece who calmly restored order. For once, David didn't object to Edwin's advice. Meryl took a little more time to be convinced that the way to deal with the press successfully was to appear to give them what they wanted, but not quite in the way they hoped. David would issue a formal statement, as acting president, confirming that the Tundra directors would shortly be convening to consider all matters arising out of the death of its former president. The press would be informed without delay of the outcome. Meryl would grant a television interview, strictly on a predetermined question and answer basis. The public relations department hurriedly got to work on David's statement and Edwin commandeered the president's suite to draft out the text for Meryl's interview.

By the time Meryl was ready to leave Tundra, the building was under siege. A nervous sounding Marsh had reported a similar situation outside the Beaumont residence. Determined not to be outwitted a second time, reporters were covering every possible entrance and exit. It was David who hit upon the idea of 'coptering Meryl out. As there was no question of Meryl returning home, the company helicopter would fly south as if heading for the international airport then fly in a curve around the western side of the city to the municipal airport. Even if someone could scramble a helicopter quickly enough they could still shake them off. A car would be waiting for Meryl at the airport and would take a circuitous route back to the Four Seasons hotel, where she would stay the night.

The mid-evening television news carried the chaotic scenes outside the Tundra building earlier in the day. Meryl peered at the television screen not quite believing that the strained, anxious face staring out of the besieged car was herself. She stared in horror at the television pictures of the explosion at the refinery. Half of the No. 1 cat cracker looked like a tangled mass of shattered metal. One of the refinery workers had suffered a broken leg after being blown off an access ladder by the force of the blast. Fifteen other men had been admitted to hospital suffering from the effects of toxic fumes. Speculation as to the cause of the explosion centred on a possible failure of safety standards that had allowed highly inflammable gases to build up in a section of the cat cracker; although it was stressed that Tundra Corp had a commendable safety record. There was, of course, the question of sabotage. Until a full investigation had been carried out, that must remain a possible explanation.

Meryl poured herself a third glass of wine. She needed some liquid anaesthetic. She was beginning to realise that a lot of what had actually happened at the refinery had been kept from her at the time. Perhaps they thought she would have hysterics. Rubbing a hand across her brow, she half listened to the television anchorman announcing that the funeral of Charles Beaumont would be strictly private, limited to immediate members of the Beaumont family only, but that the date for a memorial service would shortly be announced. She felt faintly sick as the anchorman's voice took on a positive, upbeat note and confirmed that Marylin Beaumont would be giving an exclusive interview, on this network only, the following day.

She glanced warily at the telephone when it rang out. The hotel switchboard had been instructed to take calls from a strictly limited number of people, but mistakes could be made. She answered the telephone and agreed to take an urgent call from David Barclay.

'Meryl?'

'Yes. Hello, David.'

'Hope I haven't inconvenienced you, but I have been suffering from the attentions of the press as well. A friend has let me bunk down for the night at his place and then I realised I should call and give you his telephone number, in case you had been trying to reach me.'

'I hadn't actually, but thanks for letting me know where you are. Have you any further news about the explosion? What caused it?'

'I don't have any further information. It will take a couple of days to do a full investigation. How are things with you, Meryl? Quiet, I hope.'

'Yes, mercifully.'

'Well, things should get better when the board of directors makes its statement and we can give the press some hard facts about the Discus offer. It's something that has featured very heavily in the press in recent weeks. Understandable, if you think about it. People are concerned about any rationalization plans that Discus might have. Fears about reductions in Tundra's workforce are bound to surface, aren't they?'

Meryl twisted the telephone flex around her fingers. A dark suspicion was forming in her mind as to the real reason for David's call.

'Hello? You still there?'

'Yes, I'm still here, David. I was just thinking it is rather premature to talk in terms of the Discus takeover being inevitable.'

There was a slight pause. 'Sorry, but it is difficult to see it otherwise. Tundra needs capital, period.'

'There are other alternatives to Discus.'

'What?'

'A rights issue.'

He laughed. 'Forgive me, but I don't think the British institutional stockholders would buy that one.'

'Why not?'

'Because, as I said over lunch, their job is to maximise earnings and growth on their investments. It is not their job to prop up an ailing company.'

Meryl gave an audible sigh. 'David, I think we should have this conversation some other time. I am rather tired.'

'Of course, it is just that while I sympathise with your personal situation at this moment in time, the business of running the company still has to go on. The Discus offer is not such a bad deal for the company. Like I said earlier, I want Tundra to remain an independent force, but I wouldn't sacrifice its existence to that end. I think you should consider the Discus Petroleum –'

Meryl rudely interrupted. 'David, I think I am clear as to your position. I will consider the question of Discus, but not tonight. Thank you for giving me a number where I can reach you, and now I will say goodnight.'

'Goodnight, Meryl.'

Meryl thankfully put the telephone down. She would have to do something about David Barclay, but first of all she had to decide what to do about her shareholding. She lacked her father's fierce, almost insane, devotion to the name of Tundra. Meryl took a mouthful of wine. Perhaps the name should die along with him. She banged the wine glass down on the table. Perhaps. In the meantime, she was not going to stay trapped in this hotel like a rat in a trap. She picked up the telephone and told the operator to get Edwin Reece for her. She drummed her fingers on the table. She would go and visit the refinery workers who had been admitted to hospital. As majority stockholder that was the least that she could do.

The director's assistant signalled to the cameramen then called out.

'Thirty seconds, everybody.'

Meryl's interviewer gave her a reassuring smile. 'I will lead with the fall in Tundra's share price following the death of Mr Beaumont.'

She nodded nervously, hearing a disembodied voice call out a second time that there were ten seconds left, and licked her lips. She was already running with perspiration from the heat of the studio lights and the sticky, heavy foundation the make-up girl had applied to her face.

The interviewer began speaking to camera, outlining the events over the last two days, then Meryl realised he had turned to face her and had asked her a question. She swallowed. It wasn't the question he said he would begin with. He gave her another prompt.

'You were christened Marylin Alice Stewart Beaumont. Why did you change your name to Meryl Stewart?'

She heard a strange voice replying. 'I have never particularly liked my first name. It used to confuse people. They always pronounced it as in Marilyn Monroe. My surname; well, I wanted to pursue my own career as a lawyer. I didn't want as it were a free ride on the Beaumont name.' She dug the fingers that were hidden from view into the palm of her hand.

'How did you become estranged from your father?'

Meryl felt a swift surge of anger. These were not the questions previously agreed. 'You use the word estrangement. Looking back, my leaving Canada was due more, I think, to a need for independence.' She shifted in her seat. Edwin had said only reveal as much truth as is necessary, no more. 'I -er, did feel at some stage uncomfortable at always being known as Charles Beaumont's daughter, rather than someone in my own right.'

'But the estrangement was a bitter one?'

'My father was certainly disappointed, yes, by my decision.'

'Why did you go to England?'

'I wanted to see my mother.' As soon as she uttered the words, she could have bitten her tongue off. That had been very stupid.

'Your parents were divorced when you are barely two years old, weren't they?'

'Yes.' She dug her fingernails into the palm of her hand again.

'Your father has left his estate, including his majority stockholding in Tundra Corp, to you. Can I now ask you, in the light of today's fall in Tundra's share price, what your intentions are regarding the company, with particular regard to the takeover bid by Discus Petroleum?'

A wave of relief swept over Meryl. She was on much firmer ground with the set question. 'As you know, David Barclay has been appointed acting president. He is a very able man and I have every confidence in his abilities. I do not regard the fall in Tundra's share price as anything other than a speculative response to the death of my father. The question of Discus Petroleum is irrelevant in this context.'

'But your father *was* Tundra, wasn't he?'

'Indeed, but the company has developed its own natural synergy. If my father were alive today, I am sure he would acknowledge the very dynamic role that the board of directors has always played in Tundra's affairs. That, of course, will continue to be the case.'

'Turning now to the takeover by Discus Petroleum, will you continue to fight it, as your father did?'

'The matter of Discus Petroleum, along with other matters, will be fully discussed by Tundra's board of directors when they meet.'

'As majority stockholder, do you intend to sell out to Discus?'

'As I said, the matter of Discus Petroleum will be thoroughly discussed and I shall be taking into very careful consideration what the board of directors feel is in the best interests of Tundra, its employees and its stockholders.'

'Can you now tell us the cause of the explosion at the refinery yesterday?'

'I am afraid not. It is hoped that a full report on the investigations which are being carried out to determine the cause will be available very soon.'

'Your father was a popular and respected employer, always concerned about the welfare and safety of his workforce, in what can be a dangerous occupation. Was that the reason behind your secret visit last night to the workers still detained in hospital?'

Meryl gave a surprised laugh. 'If you know about it, it can hardly be described as a secret.'

The interviewer allowed himself a small smile.

'I simply wanted to see for myself that injured members of Tundra's workforce were being well cared for.'

'Tundra Corp's historic, humble beginnings are well documented. Your grandfather, Franklin Reeve Beaumont, started out as a gold prospector in the Klondike. Your father turned Tundra into a multi-million dollar organisation. You are a lawyer with considerable corporate expertise, with a reputation in England for being tough and outspoken. Are we going to see a third-generation Beaumont in control? Are we about to witness a new and invigorating chapter in Tundra's history?'

Meryl smiled, as Edwin had instructed her to do.

'Meryl Stewart Beaumont, thank you.' The interviewer turned full face to camera one.

Meryl glanced out of the corner of her eye at the floor manager, who signalled to her to stay where she was. Within seconds the studio lights went up and Meryl rose to her feet, her knees shaking with relief. The interviewer held out his hand. She shook it perfunctorily. 'You didn't stick with the agreed questions. Why?'

'Sorry about that. We couldn't cover all the questions. We were running a little late. Don't worry, we managed to cover the human interest angle.'

Meryl stared open mouthed as he turned on his heel and crossed the studio.

Edwin Reece was waiting for her in the foyer of the television offices. A man rarely prone to displays of excitement, he hugged her and told her she had been absolutely wonderful. He had watched everything on a studio monitor. She hadn't put a single foot wrong throughout the entire interview. He had even more good news for her. For some reason the press-hounds had been called off. There wasn't a reporter to be seen outside the house or at Tundra's offices. It was safe to return home.

The following morning every newspaper had its version of the 'Beaumont' story. Meryl had slept better knowing the ordeal of the television interview was behind her and had woken up in a more cheerful mood. Her cheerfulness quickly evaporated as she flicked through the newspapers Marsh had presented. Nothing had been left out. The young, beautiful teenage wife, Mary; the handsome lover for whom she had forsaken a life of luxury with Charles Beaumont; the little baby girl abandoned by her mother. One newspaper had even managed to print a blurred photograph of Meryl, aged about three, dressed in a miniscule cowgirl outfit, holding on to her father's hand and staring up at him, as if he was God. Meryl felt sick. Her mother hadn't been a teenager and Meryl hadn't been abandoned. It was a gross distortion of the truth. Meryl flung the newspapers into the waste bin.

Mrs Kemp poked her head around the door, took one look at Meryl's face and quietly removed the plate of ham and eggs she had left for her. Meryl paced up and down. It was doubtful if the British press would run the Canadian stories. She reached the window and turned round and paced back to the table. Perhaps she should call Simon again. Resurrection of the past would only cause her mother anguish. Mrs Kemp returned with a glass of milk. 'Drink this, Miss Stewart; it's my special health drink. It's got an egg whisked up in it, with wheatgerm and honey. You need something to help you face the day.'

Meryl took the glass of milk and made an attempt to drink it down. Mrs Kemp fidgeted for a moment as if wrestling with her thoughts. 'I wondered, Miss Stewart, if you would object to my attending Mr Beaumont's funeral this afternoon. I would like to pay my last respects to him, that is, if you don't mind.'

'No, no, not at all, Mrs Kemp. There will only be Mr Reece and myself going. Would you like to travel with us?'

'Oh, Miss Stewart, thank you. I would like that very much.'

'Fine.' Meryl managed to finish all of the milk and

handed the glass back. 'I don't mind admitting, Mrs Kemp, I shall be glad when it's all over.'

Mrs Kemp smiled sympathetically. 'I know, Miss Stewart. I know how you must feel.'

Meryl nodded. She doubted whether Mrs Kemp could possibly even begin to understand how she felt. She checked her watch and composed a mental timetable of her tasks. She would ring her mother after the funeral. It would be a good excuse to find out if anything had been reported in the British press. Ask Edwin Reece to make contact with Tundra's British stockholders and find out if their attitude to the Discus takeover had changed. It had to be Edwin, she couldn't trust David Barclay to do it. Then she must call JJ. Just talking to him over the telephone would clear her head, help her to think straight.

JJ Reynolds finished chopping a handful of fresh herbs then cracked two eggs into a bowl. He didn't consider himself an accomplished cook, but prided himself on making a good omelette, decent spaghetti alla carbonara and a smoked salmon and quails' egg *salade tiède*. Very soon after he had moved into the apartment with Meryl, he had quickly grown tired of her cold meat suppers created from several purchases from the local delicatessen, followed by revoltingly sweet maple syrup poured over a block of ice cream, and he had taken over the task of cooking on the evenings they weren't dining out.

He was just about to uncork a bottle of wine when the telephone rang. The caller was Meryl. He managed to tuck the handset under his chin and and began to open the bottle of wine. It was doubtful if he would get back to his omelette in less than half an hour, but at least he could give himself a drink in the meantime.

'JJ, the line is terribly faint. I can't hear you.'

'Hello, darling. Is that better?'

'Yes, much better.'

He tucked the bottle of wine under one arm and gently

pulled out the cork, murmuring soothingly at regular intervals while he filled his glass.

'You know, JJ, I really don't know what to do.'

'It is not like you to be so indecisive about matters. If you don't make your mind up soon, events will make it up for you.'

'What do you mean?'

He took a sip of wine. 'Tundra's share price here has dropped as well. It is not actually in free fall, but it is causing concern in some quarters. I think it will remain depressed while this uncertainty about Tundra remains.'

He heard her give a heavy sigh. 'Meryl, you are the majority shareholder now. The lead must come from you.'

'I know that, JJ.'

'Well, what do you want to do?'

'I'm not sure.'

He took another sip of wine. 'You have two clear alternatives, Meryl. Sell your shares to Discus Petroleum and return to England and resume your life here. Or, stay in Canada and fight to save Tundra. Which is it to be?'

'It is not as simple as that.'

'It is, Meryl. If you think about it carefully, it is.'

There was a very long pause. JJ reached for the wine bottle and refilled his glass.

'You see, JJ, it's rather difficult to explain, but I cannot just abandon Tundra's entire workforce to the mercies of a takeover by Discus. Christopher Mallory has a reputation for asset stripping, and Tundra wouldn't necessarily be an exception. Remember his takover of Omega Oil a couple of years ago? He carefully filleted out the guts of the company and tossed the carcass aside the following year.'

'Loss of jobs happens all the time, all over the world, Meryl.'

'Yes, but many of the men have worked at Tundra for years. I have spoken to them. It wasn't the company they worked for, it was Charles Beaumont the man. They believed in him.

JJ propped himself up against the work unit. 'And they look to his daughter to protect their jobs, is that it?'

'In a way, yes.'

'I see.'

'What does that mean?'

'It means, I see your problem. Look, darling, I am happy to advise you in any way I can, I have always done so in the past, have I not?'

'Yes, JJ.'

'But this time, only you can decide what should be done.'

'Perhaps if I came home, distanced myself from the situation, it might help me make up my mind.'

'I think you should stay in Canada. You wouldn't be distancing yourself from the situation, you would be running away from it. I know the last two days have been traumatic for you, but forget about the past, forget about what happened with your father. Concentrate on the present. For as long as I have known you, you have never run away from anything. Don't you think, darling, it is a bad time to start now?'

Meryl laughed despite herself. 'Yes, you're right. Well, enough about me. What are you doing?'

'I was just about to make myself something to eat.'

'Oh, I'm sorry, JJ. You should have said.'

'No matter. Look, I'll go now and call you in a couple of days.'

'I do miss you, JJ.'

'Ah, that definitely proves the theory that absence makes the heart grow fonder. Carry on like this and I shall begin to believe you are in love with me.'

She laughed again.

Having said goodbye to Meryl, JJ returned his attention to the omelette. He glanced across at the copy of the London evening paper he had slung on the kitchen unit when he came in. The front page led with a story of the Anglo-Canadian lawyer who had inherited her oil tycoon father's multi-million dollar exploration and refining company. The writer of the article had faithfully copied the report from Canada, and referred to Meryl as Meryl Stewart Beaumont. Brief details were given of her glittering career as head of the compliance department at Wajiki International in London. The article ended by quoting reliable Canadian sources that she was certain to take over the presidency of Tundra Corp and revitalize its flagging fortunes.

JJ carefully slipped the omelette on to a plate and took it through into the sitting room. He poured more wine into his glass and began eating. He raised his head and gazed around the silent room. Meryl had already reached a decision, it was just that she herself hadn't yet realised. He picked up his fork and cut into the omelette. She would realise in time. She was intelligent, clever and not lacking in ambition.

Teriyaki Iwano placed a call to Osaka. He hunched over the telephone.

'Ah, Tatsuo? Teri, here. You are aware that Charles Beaumont has died? Good, good. I have been doing further investigation. Beaumont's daughter has inherited everything, including his shareholding in Tundra Corp. I have made some discreet enquiries and it would appear that this has come as something of a surprise, to put it mildly, to the British pension fund shareholders. The situation is confused by much rumour, unfortunately. Reports from Canada suggest that no one is ruling out the possibility that she will take over the company. The attitude in London is that she has little inclination to do that and will sell out to Discus Petroleum. There is one institutional shareholder, a Mr Graham Vose, who is senior portfolio manager of a major insurance company. He has always been sympathetic to the long terms plans of Tundra, but I do not know for the moment what pressure, if any, he may try to bring to bear to persuade her to hold on to her shares. However, I intend to approach both Miss Beaumont and the pension fund shareholders, discreetly of course. They might both agree to a deal enabling the consortium to purchase her shares and provide the financial backing to dispose of the Discus Petroleum bid.'

Teriyaki reached across the desk and pulled a cigarette from an already open packet. 'Yes, yes. I agree it is strange that David Barclay has not automatically become president. It is what makes me think there has to be a good reason why someone is playing for time. Possibly, Miss Beaumont herself. Tundra hold extensive rights to extract oil in the Athabasca tar sands. They also hold full patent rights on a process to extract non-conventional, high-sulphur crude. What they don't have is the capital to develop the process and exploit its potential use. Presumably Miss Beaumont is very aware of this and may just be holding out for a better deal from Christopher Mallory. He would dearly like to get his hands on Tundra. Its operations would marry nicely with Discus' own operations in the Utah and Kentucky oil shale deposits.' Teriyaki paused to light his cigarette.

'I think it is time the consortium took the initiative. No further moves have been made by Mallory. It could conceivably be as a mark of respect of Charles Beaumont, but I doubt that very much. However, I have a feeling that when things start to move, they will move very quickly. Very well, Tatsuo. I will be in touch.'

Teriyaki put the telephone down and leaned back in his chair. He drew on his cigarette before pulling his diary in front of him and made rapid entries. The funeral of Charles Beaumont had been held today. He flipped over the page of the diary. He would approach Miss Stewart Beaumont tomorrow.

Frank slipped a cassette into the video tape recorder and switched it on. 'Ready, Chris?'

'Is that the complete recording?'

Frank nodded.

'Then shoot.'

Chris Mallory leaned forward and watched the monitor

curiously. He gave a low whistle when Meryl appeared on the screen and watched the re-run of her interview on Canadian television intently. When it finished he nodded to Frank to switch the monitor off. He scratched at one eyebrow. 'What do you make of this guy Barclay, Frank? Do you think he's some kind of fag?'

Frank grinned.

Chris stood up. 'He could at least have warned me about her. She is beautiful. Really beautiful. A guy sure needs to get his act together for a woman like that.'

Frank grinned again.

'What do you make of the Mona Lisa smile?'

Frank's eyes flicked open in surprise. 'Mona Lisa? Don't follow you.'

'Wake up, Frank. At the end of the interview she was asked if the world was going to see a third-generation Beaumont at Tundra. She gave a funny kind of keep-watching-this-space smile.'

'May not mean anything in particular.'

Chris spun round on his heel. 'It could also mean a hell of a lot in particular. That guy she shacks up with at Wajiki International. She could have just persuaded him to find her a white knight. There's an awful lot of loose change floating about in Japan, Frank. We could be left with a lot of egg on the corporate face if she has Japanese funding and can get the British institutional stockholders to follow her.'

'Why should she want to do that? By all accounts she hated her father's guts.'

Chris ran his fingers through his hair. 'Precisely, Frank. Precisely. What better reason would she have for holding on very tight to Tundra?' He pushed his hands in his pockets. 'It may not have come to your notice, Frank, but women are perverse creatures. So she hated her father. Doesn't necessarily follow that she hates his money too.'

'You're right. It doesn't.'

'Thank you, Frank. Have you heard anything from Barclay? He's dropped out of sight too long for my liking.'

'Not heard anything further. Do you think he has gone over to her?'

'If he has, I fully intend that he should walk with a limp for the rest of his life.' Chris gave Frank a glowering look. 'You know, I think it is about time Miss Stewart, or Beaumont, or whatever goddam name she calls herself, and I got down to some serious business.'

'Shall I try and find out if there is a Japanese connection?'

Mallory rubbed a hand down the side of his jaw. 'How?'

'I'll work on it.'

'Thanks, Frank.'

The photograph of Meryl as a child in the previous day's newspaper had been obliterated by heavy strokes of a black felt tip pen; so heavy that in places the paper had torn. David laced his fingers together, loudly cracking his knuckles as he flexed them. Meeting Meryl again had disturbed him. When Charles Beaumont had died, David was filled with a healing calm. As if by magic, the clamouring voices in his head had left him. They came and went of their own accord. He would be left on his own for months, perhaps a couple of years, then the voices would return. Urging. Compelling. He first heard them when he was almost ten years of age.

Tony Barclay had agreed to adopt his sister-in-law's baby for his wife's sake. He reasoned it might stop Bianca weeping and wailing every month. He didn't concern himself with David's welfare; that was Bianca's job. She had got her longed-for child of sorts. The rest was up to her.

David had inherited quick intellect from his real father, Charles Beaumont, and quick tempered emotions from his mother, Maria Cane. As he grew up he learned to stay out of Tony Barclay's way. After two severe beatings for telling lies, he was careful always to be appeasing in front of Tony. Bianca and the woman he knew as Auntie Maria were different. He could do no wrong in their eyes, although he frequently did. Auntie Maria came to see him every month, bringing him what gifts she could afford. He quickly learned to be very affectionate with Maria, rushing up to her as soon as she arrived, demanding hugs and kisses. He knew very well that after her visit, Bianca would take him shopping and buy him anything he wanted, provided he assured her that he liked it more than Auntie Maria's gift.

By the time David was approaching adolescence, Tony had become increasingly irritated by what he took to be dumb insolence on the part of the child he had supported since birth, who wasn't even his own flesh and blood. He told Bianca more than once that the kid should be told the truth. His excuse was that the kid had a right to know. Privately, he thought it might teach him to be grateful; to show a little more respect.

The night that David spent locked up in the tool shed brought the truth out into the open. The previous afternoon he had accidentally broken a window playing handball. Tony lost his temper and began hitting him, calling him a clumsy son of a bitch. Bianca knew when not to protest too strenuously. She too could easily end up on the receiving end of Tony's temper. She contented herself by telling him he shouldn't call the boy names like that. Tony took hold of David's collar and shook him like a rat. He was more than a son of a bitch. He was the son of a whore. Maria did more than make Charles Beaumont's bed for him. Bianca screamed at him to stop.

David had been too frightened to protest at being shut up in the tool shed. He crouched by the door, his ear to the keyhole. He couldn't understand why his father had looked at him with such repugnance. He strained to hear what his parents were saying. Tony had stopped shouting. David felt sick as he caught the sound of his father's lowered voice and his mother's half-hearted giggle. He knew what that meant. He sat down in the gloom, thankful he was in the shed and not in the bedroom next to theirs, listening to their noises. He knew what his father did to his mother every week. He knew what a whore was, too. Those things he didn't know about, Tony told him the next day. David returned to the tool shed of his own volition. In the quiet darkness his mind slowly stopped spinning. His mother was his aunt. His aunt was his mother. He hugged his knees to his chest and rocked back and forth. His mother was his aunt. His aunt was his mother. He wanted to kill them both. He loved both women and both in their own way, by keeping the truth from him, had betrayed him, and he was incapable of forgiving.

Over the ensuing months, confused by anger and guilt, there were times when he wanted nothing more than to have Maria hold him tightly in her arms and weep for him. There were other times when voices filled his head with vile, bestial thoughts about her that left him sickened and ashamed. He took to walking for hour after hour until the voices faded. Only then could he calmly reason with himself. Maria had told him only that a bad man had made her pregnant. She didn't know who he was, not even his name. Tears would spring to his eyes at the thought of what she had endured, and, yet again, he would vow before God to protect her from all further evils.

Josie buzzed through to David's office. 'I have Mr Vose of Anglo-Allied Life Assurance on line one for you.'

'Thanks.' David picked up the telephone. What did the only major institutional stockholder loyal to Tundra want? 'Yes, Mr Vose. What can I do for you?'

'I'm actually trying to get in touch with Miss Stewart Beaumont. Have you got a telephone number where I could reach her?'

David tore the photograph of Meryl from the front page of the newspaper and screwed it up in his hand. 'I have, but can I be of any help in any way?'

'Not for the moment, Mr Barclay, except to say that I am pleased that you have taken over as acting president.'

'Thank you. Let me put you back to Josie and she will find the number for you.' David transferred the call then sat back in his chair. He tossed the piece of crumpled newspaper into the waste bin. One guess as to why Vose wanted to get in touch with the majority stockholder. An attempt to continue blocking the takeover by Discus. He pushed his chair back angrily and stood up. As acting president he knew less about what was going on than he did when Beaumont was alive.

Graham Vose was the senior portfolio manager of Anglo-Allied Life and wielded considerable influence in their choice of investments. He had been a strong supporter of Charles Beaumont's strategies for Tundra and had given his backing to mounting a defence against Discus Petroleum. Unlike pension fund managers, whose aim was to take as much profit in the short term as possible, Graham Vose's employers could also take into account the mid- and long-term views of an investment, a fact that was a distinct advantage to a company like Tundra operating in a highly volatile market.

Meryl reluctantly took Graham Vose's call. She had half expected an approach would be made by him, but would have preferred to put it off until she had made up her mind as to what she was going to do.

'Miss Beaumont, I am sorry to have to trouble you under such sad circumstances, but I am extremely anxious to discuss the Discus takeover with you, and indeed, what you yourself intend doing. I hope you will share my concern. Under the circumstances I can, if necessary, come to Canada to discuss matters.'

Meryl paused for a moment, then reached a decision that wasn't logical, but it was what she knew she wanted to do. 'I do share your concern, Mr Vose, and a visit to Canada will not be necessary. I shall be returning to England tomorrow.'

'I look forward very much to meeting you, Miss Beaumont.' The relief in his voice was undisguised. 'I think it is in everyone's interests to decide upon matters as quickly as possible. Tundra's share price has fallen this morning on the London Stock Exchange. I fear it will continue to do so, while so much uncertainty appears to surround Tundra's future.'

'Indeed.' Meryl bristled slightly at the veiled hint that somehow it was all her fault. 'Would you be prepared to support a rights issue?'

There was a very long pause. Vose was unsure whether the question indicated that she was planning to retain her share in Tundra, or whether she was simply leading him on; creating a smokescreen for her own convenience.

'I would first have to discuss that with my colleagues before I could answer that question, Miss Beaumont. An issue would have to be launched in the, shall we say, right climate. It would be damaging to the company if it was seen as a last ditch resort. The idea requires serious, in depth discussion.'

'Then I suggest you do just that. See you in London.' She put the telephone down and remained perfectly still for several moments, then on some strange impulse went to her father's study.

Meryl glanced slowly around the room as if seeing it for the first time. The expensively leather-bound books that were never read. The hunting trophies. The high backed leather chair behind the desk. It's people who make Tundra successful, Marylin. People. Never forget that. She walked slowly towards the over-sized desk. Whatever else one could say about Pops, he always looked after his employees. Always. Tears stung her eyes as she realised she had used her pet name for him. Slowly she opened the top left hand drawer of the desk and stared down at the bunch of keys. It had to be done some time. It might as well be now. She picked up the bunch of keys and picked out the one to the deed box Edwin Reece had left with her, which contained her father's personal and private papers.

PART 3

The security guard on duty at the entrance to Tundra's refinery turned his head quickly as he caught sight of the familiar white Cadillac turning off the highway. He gave a sharp intake of breath, before remembering that Charles Beaumont was dead. Someone else was driving his car.

Meryl pulled up by the booth. The security guard saluted. 'Good morning, Miss Beaumont.' He sounded slightly flustered. 'Can I be of assistance, Miss Beaumont?'

'Just point me in the direction of the main offices, if you will.' He crouched down by the driver's window and gave instructions to drive straight on, then turn left and first right. As soon as Meryl pulled away, he quickly ran into the booth and picked up the telephone to warn the occupants of the main office that Miss Beaumont had arrived completely out of the blue. Meryl drove slowly along the access road. From this direction the damage to the No. 1 cat cracker was clearly visible. Several workmen stopped and stared into the car as she passed them, then, realizing who was behind the wheel, raised their hands to their safety helmets in brief salute.

When Meryl pushed open the door to the reception area, it was clearly evident that the staff present had been put on full red alert. A dark haired girl behind the desk smiled nervously. 'Good morning, Miss Beaumont.'

'Good morning. I am meeting Mr Schmidt, the director of research and development, here. Has he arrived yet?'

The girl looked at her blankly then down at the appointments book in front of her. 'I'm sorry, Miss Beaumont.' She traced her finger down the page. 'There is no entry for Mr Schmidt.'

Meryl smiled. 'Don't worry. I wasn't expecting one. I arranged the meeting with Mr Schmidt myself.'

The girl gave a quick smile of relief.

'He's probably been delayed. The traffic is pretty bad this morning. Would you like to wait in the office, Miss Beaumont? I can fetch you some coffee.'

'Thank you; a cup of coffee would be very welcome.'

The office was decorated in the same marine blue, grey and brilliant white as Tundra's logo. Meryl settled herself in a chair by the window and took a sheaf of papers from her briefcase. Beginning the task of sorting her father's papers the previous day had been a watershed. Today, by first light, she understood the decision she had to make. It was not whether to sell her shares in Tundra, it was whether she was prepared to accept responsibility: the responsibility that her father had left to her and no one else. A responsibility that she could not and would not shirk.

By nine o'clock, after one of Mrs Kemp's gargantuan breakfasts, Meryl was starting to piece together a plan of action to meet the demands of that responsibility. A plan that, of necessity, must exclude participation by David Barclay for the time being, but that must convince Tundra's shareholders that the company had a future, independent of Discus Petroleum or anyone else. She began with a call to the financial director to procure the very best possible profit forecast and asset valuation from the accountants. The next step was to obtain the highest estimate of the North Sea exploration bloc's potential. Now, she was ready to meet Gerry Schmidt, the man who could give a current opinion on the value of the exploration rights in the Athabasca tar sands.

Gerry Schmidt was in his middle fifties, with a neck and head that seemed to merge into one heavy mass. He inclined his head towards the white Cadillac parked outside the office. 'Miss Beaumont?' It was a superfluous question. No one except Charles Beaumont's daughter would be driving it.

The receptionist nodded. He briefly raised both eyebrows.

'She's waiting for you in the office at the end of the corridor, Mr Schmidt.'

He grunted and strode away. The two girls behind the desk exchanged glances. It was routine to assess the capabilities of any man who walked through the door and Gerry Schmidt would have normally rated a zero. The fact that he had an extremely attractive wife and five daughters earned him a listing as ugly, but interesting.

Meryl got up from her chair as Gerry swept through the door. 'Sorry, I'm late, Miss Beaumont. Got held up.'

'Thank you for coming at such short notice, Mr Schmidt.'

He drew a chair up opposite Meryl's. 'Gerry, please. Only my bank manager calls me Mr Schmidt.'

She smiled. 'Right, Gerry, I need to pick your brains. Athabasca tar sands. We have a patent for the extraction of oil, but I understand it is for the moment not particularly viable, financially speaking.'

Gerry shot her a long hard look. He rested his hands on his torso and gently massaged it. He had been curious about her telephone call asking him to meet her at the refinery. He had been even more curious when he learned that David Barclay would not be in attendance. Why was the majority stockholder asking questions of him that could easily be answered by the acting president? He folded his hands across his chest. 'I shall do my best to answer any technical questions, but Mr Barclay would be in a better position to answer questions on financial viability, Miss Beaumont.'

'Shall we let me be the judge of that?'

Again, he gave her a long and hard look. The voice was softly spoken, but authoritative. He shrugged. 'As you wish. What exactly do you want to know?'

'Everything, but beginning with tar sands. What are they?'

He scratched at the side of his neck. 'I think possibly in Europe you would know tar sands under a different name. I think you call them heavy oil sands.'

Meryl nodded, although felt little the wiser.

'Simply, tar sands are, as the name implies, bituminous impregnated sands. Some belts of tar sands are conveniently close to the surface, others are not.'

'Athabasca?'

'Unfortunately that comes under the "other" category. The overburden is several hundred feet thick in places.'

'What is overburden?'

Gerry sighed to himself. If it had been someone other than Meryl Beaumont, he would have told them to go back to school. 'Layers of rock above the pockets of oil deposits.'

'I see. This patent specification for extracting oil appears to be based on tertiary phase techniques. I don't understand. Why can't a first or second phase be used, assuming that such techniques exist? What do all these terms mean, anyway?'

Gerry scratched at the side of his neck again. 'These terms apply mainly to off-shore oil drilling, but there are certain similarities with on-shore drilling. The so-called first phase is the easy option. You've got the oil welling up around your ankles, if you see what I mean. The second phase is when things get a little harder. When you have to start repressuring or flooding to get the oil to the surface. The third, or tertiary, phase is when you start scraping the bottom of the barrel, if you will forgive the pun. The tertiary phase is when your problems really begin.'

'How so?'

'Because you have to find the most effective method of reducing the surface tension of the oil. Usually, by micellar-surfactant flooding.'

Meryl laughed. 'Could I have a quick translation, please.'

Gerry's face broadened into a grin. It was the first time he had smiled since he had arrived. 'Let's see. I don't want to blind you with too much science, but I find it difficult to explain other than in technical terms.' He tilted his chair back and rocked it to and fro. 'A combination of water and chemicals is pumped down into the rock. This solution frees the oil adhering to said rock. Further flooding then allows the oil, plus water, plus chemicals, to be pumped to the surface for treatment.'

'I see.'

He sat the front legs of his chair down on the floor. The conversation was becoming an interesting problem. 'Ah, do you or have you ever used a dishwasher, Miss Beaumont?'

She stared at him in surprise. 'Frequently, but what's that got to do with extracting oil?'

'Not much, but do you know why you have to use a rinse-aid in your dishwasher?'

She thought for a moment. 'Er- yes. It aids the drying process, doesn't it? It makes the water run off the dishes and they dry better.'

'Good, good.' He smiled again. 'So, the rinse-aid in your dishwasher is a surfactant.'

'Ah, I see what you mean. In a similar way, surfactant flooding makes the oil run off the rock.'

He laughed softly. 'Not exactly *run* but you've got the idea.'

Meryl looked at her watch. 'Would you like some coffee, Gerry?'

'Love some.'

Meryl got up and went to the intercom on the desk. A young male voice answered her call and promised to have coffee sent in straight away. She turned round and leaned back against the desk.

'Earlier, you said after the oil is extracted from the rock it is pumped to the surface for treatment. What does that treatment entail?'

'Decanter centrifuges.' He paused and waited for her to ask what that meant.

She thought quickly. 'The spin cycle on an automatic washing machine is a centrifugal action, is it not?'

'Got it in one. So, the mixture of oil, surfactants, water, mineral deposits and God knows what, is transferred to the decanter centrifuges and is first milled, or perhaps a more descriptive word is pulverized, usually with ten per cent by weight of hot water. That is flushed with further volumes of water. The centrifugal action draws the particles of sand out to the edges of the decanter and they are extracted. The mixture is allowed to settle and the resultant foam which floats to the surface is then skimmed. The remaining water, etc., is removed from the foam leaving a residue of what is referred to as "synthetic" crude oil ready for distillation into fuel oil, kerosene and so on.'

Meryl tapped her fingers on the edge of the desk. 'The process sounds simple enough. Why isn't it widely used?'

He gave an amused laugh. 'Because, Miss Beaumont, as simple as the process sounds, it is an extremely lengthy and costly process. Look, it takes about thirteen tonnes of oil sands to produce one cubic metre of synthetic crude. Thirteen tonnes! Moreover, the treatment is extremely costly. The maintenance costs are a nightmare.'

She looked at him with total incomprehension. He stood up and hitched his trousers higher around his waist. 'Miss Beaumont, we are not talking about domestic washing machines here. We are talking about decanters measuring four to five feet by nine to ten feet. You need at least two hundred and fifty horsepower motors to drive them. Sand is a very abrasive element, particularly when it's being flung around at high speed. These decanters can only run for about five thousand hours before they need extensive overhaul.'

There was a knock on the door and the dark haired receptionist brought in a tray of coffee. Meryl gestured towards the desk. 'Thanks. Leave the tray there.'

'Anything else you want, Miss Beaumont?'

'No thanks.'

The girl cast a smile vaguely in Gerry's direction and walked to the door. Meryl waited until Gerry was no longer distracted by the receptionist's legs before speaking again. 'I am confused. If the process of extraction and treatment is so expensive, why did my father bother patenting it? Sounds as if he was less smart than I thought he was.'

'No. Just the opposite in fact. All major oil companies have similar ongoing R and D. It's like having a rainy day acount. It may not be useful right now, but it could be sometime in the future.'

'O.K. Let's have coffee. How do you like your coffee, Gerry?'

'Hot, strong and very sweet.'

Meryl smiled wryly. 'The usual rejoinder to that somehow escapes me for the moment.'

Gerry gave a loud laugh. Meryl poured a cup of coffee and handed it to him. 'You say other companies have similar research and development programmes for the extraction of oil from tar sands. Does that constitute an infringement of our patent rights?'

'No, no.' He rubbed at his forehead. 'You've got completely the wrong end of the stick.' He helped himself to four lumps of sugar.

'The patent, and I assume we are talking about the same patent, does not protect the process of extraction. No, the patent covers a design by a guy called Rufus Mackenzie that was supposed to upgrade the efficiency and durability of the decanter centrifuges.'

She clapped her hand to her head. 'I see, I see. I thought – forget that. So we have a patent for an improved design of the decanter centrifuges. Tell me about it.'

He slowly stirred his coffee. 'If I had known what it was you wanted to discuss beforehand, I could have looked up the required information.'

She didn't respond. He carefully shook the drips from his spoon into the coffee then rested the spoon in the saucer. 'Ah, these processes became the flavour of the month back in the mid-seventies. When the Arabs had us by the –' Schmidt stopped suddenly, almost forgetting for a moment to whom he was talking. He gave an embarrassed grin. 'Let's say, when you were still just a kid the price of a barrel of oil hit the roof and beyond, and we frightened the life out of ourselves. Everyone in the West was falling over themselves to find alternative sources of crude. As far as I can remember, Rufus Mackenzie hit on the idea of using the, then, newly developed ceramics in decanter centrifuges. These centrifuges are made of inches-thick steel. They have to be to withstand the punishment they take. Ceramics were supposed to be the greatest thing since sliced bread, allegedly capable of withstanding extremes of heat, vibration, you name it. Using these ceramics, the Mackenzie process, as Rufus liked to call it, would theoretically reduce the weight of the decanter centrifuges, and the amount of power required to run them, so extending their working life by almost double, and reducing maintenance costs. All in all, Rufus reckoned his design would reduce the cost of treating tar sands by fifty per cent.'

'Sounds too good to be true.'

He laughed. 'Funny you should say that. There were problems. Rufus had a nice idea, but that was all it was.'

'Why?'

'I recall the ceramics didn't actually live up to their reputation. Instead of using conventional steel, Rufus used aluminium lined with ceramic material. There were problems with the bonding. The ceramic material had a tendency to fracture and break away from the aluminium.'

'Who developed these ceramics?'

'The Japanese.'

'Were they told about these problems?'

'Sure. It sent them scurrying back to their drawing-boards. I guess there were other problems too, but whatever they were, the project was quietly put on the back burner by your father. Rufus was pretty mad at the time, but your father was right to do what he did. Even if the problems had been resolved, by the time the process could have come fully on stream, the price of conventional crude had dropped dramatically. The panic was over, at least for the time being.'

Meryl poured herself a cup of coffee and added just a dash of milk to it. 'Does Rufus Mackenzie still work for Tundra? I don't recall meeting him.'

'No, no. Your father fired him a long time ago.'

'Oh.'

'He had no choice. Rufus was a good engineer, but could get a little crazy at times. Particularly when he hit the bottle. He got involved in a brawl with one of the crackerjacks. Almost killed the guy.'

'Why?'

'I don't know. Rufus had some idea the guy was fooling around with his wife. It wasn't the first time he'd got himself into a fight. He had been warned once by your father. This time around he was fired.' Gerry placed his coffee cup on the desk. 'Oil is a tough business, Miss Beaumont. You've got to have discipline.'

Meryl glanced at her watch. 'Thank you for putting me in the picture, Gerry, and for answering all my questions.'

'Can I ask you a question?'

'Mm.'

'Why are you so interested in oil extraction from tar sands?'

'I am interested in everything that has to do with Tundra Corp, Gerry.'

He looked straight into her eyes, as if searching for an answer to an unspoken question. 'A certain company, whose name shall not cross my lips, is interested in oil extraction from shale deposits in Utah. A not dissimilar process.'

'Really?'

'Really.'

'Would you do something for me, Gerry?'

'Sure.'

'Get me an update on the latest ceramic materials. Improvements must have been made since the seventies. I also need an updated opinion on Rufus Mackenzie's process. Can you do that?'

'No problem.'

'Fine. If you need to get in touch, call me at home. If I'm not there Mrs Kemp will take a message.'

'Will do.' Schmidt held out his hand to her.

She braced herself for another crushing handshake, but the large, broad knuckled hand gently held on to her fingers for a moment, then released them.

'I meant what I said before, Gerry. I am interested in everything that involves Tundra's future. If I cannot convince myself that it can be a secure and independent future, none of the other stockholders will be convinced either.'

He pushed his hands into his pockets and stared down at his shoes. 'The workforce are kind of anxious to know what is going to happen. Will they still have jobs next week.'

'I'm afraid they are going to have to stay anxious for a little while longer.'

'I understand.'

Edwin Reece didn't usually drink at midday, but he allowed himself a small beer while he waited for Meryl. He looked up as she rushed into the bistro, stood up and raised his hand. She waved cheerily and came to join him. 'Edwin, sorry I'm late. Edmonton's traffic problems have got worse since I've been away.'

He smiled. 'I wouldn't have thought that possible. Would you like a drink before we see the menu?'

'Thanks, I think I need one. Edwin?'

'Yes, Meryl.'

'I have made up my mind. I am not going to sell my shares.'

He nodded quietly.

'You don't look very surprised.'

'I never thought you would, once you understood the situation.'

'Oh, I see.' She felt rather deflated. 'Anyway, I have had a very useful conversation with Gerry Schmidt at the refinery.'

'What about?'

'Tar sands at Athabasca.'

Edwin raised an eyebrow.

'Listen Edwin, I have arranged to see Graham Vose of Anglo-Allied Life in London. It is possible he will consider the question of a rights issue. I have to try and make it more than a possibility. To do that, I am going to have to come up with convincing and vigorous expansion plans. The accountants are preparing, shall we say, very optimistic profit forecasts. A review of the North Sea exploration potential should be available by this evening and, I know it's a long shot, but I have asked Gerry Schmidt to let me have an update on Rufus Mackenzie's process. If it is something that can be incorporated into our future development plans, it has to be a plus.'

Edwin pursed his lips. 'That one is a very long shot. The price of a barrel of oil would have to rise to something like $50, before oil extraction from tar sands became a viable proposition.'

'What is to say that won't happen someday?'

'True.'

'Edwin, is there anything I have left out?'

'Yes. David Barclay.'

Meryl rested her hand on Edwin's sleeve. 'Keep him quiet for me. I suspect you are very good at doing that.'

'It won't be easy. He's not going to like you going over his head and dealing with people direct.'

'I know, but I must hammer out something with Graham Vose in London before I let David in on anything. Please, Edwin; I just need a couple of days.'

'You've got them.'

'You are marvellous, Edwin.' She caused him acute embarrassment by suddenly reaching over and kissing him on the cheek. 'I will deal with David Barclay when I get back. Promise.'

'How?'

She widened her eyes provocatively. 'By charming him into submission, of course.'

'I am sure he will enjoy that very much, knowing David.'

'Is there someone special in his life, as they say?'

He looked at her strangely. 'Why do you ask?'

She shrugged. 'Just curious.'

Edwin finished the remains of his beer, while he considered broaching a question that he hoped would not set her thinking too hard. It would be disastrous for Meryl to become too interested in Barclay. He was her half-brother.

Charles had been a little the worse for drink when he had told Edwin that David Barclay was his son. The dumpy little maid with the big breasts, Maria Cane, was David's mother. Charles very often treated Edwin like a father-confessor when he was drunk. A condition he trusted Edwin never to turn to his own advantage. Edwin had been very alarmed, fearing that Charles was leaving himself open to blackmail. Charles had laughed. There was no chance of that. Maria was ambitious. Ambitious for her son. One day, David would become president of Tundra, but not if anyone tried to blackmail Charles. There was little chance of that happening. Even David didn't know who his real father was.

Edwin stared down into the empty beer glass. He would keep Charles' secret until the day he died. Even from Barclay himself. Barclay had done enough damage already. Charles might have lived to be reconciled with his daughter, if Barclay's treachery had not taken its toll of his already weakened body.

Meryl touched Edwin's sleeve again. 'What is it? You look a thousand miles away.'

He gave a gentle smile. 'Sorry. I was just wondering what you made of David Barclay.'

She grinned. 'Charming, but too ambitious, I'd say.'

'Do you remember when he was a little boy? He was so fat, he looked like a pudding.'

Meryl burst into giggles. 'I don't think so.'

'Do you remember his aunt?'

'Aunt?'

'Yes. Maria Cane.'

'Oh, Miss Cane.' Meryl laughed 'She of the heavily swaying bottom.'

'She was David Barclay's aunt.'

'Really! I didn't know that. I used to suspect Pops of quite fancying her.'

'Absolutely not, Meryl. A woman like that wouldn't be his type.'

She grinned again. 'Pops was never a snob. Certainly not where available women were concerned. Miss Cane was a very attractive woman in a, shall we say, rather blowsy way. Was she David's maternal aunt?'

'I believe so.'

'I must say David has inherited more than his fair share of the family good looks.'

He glanced sharply at her. 'Do you think so?'

'Mm. Bit of a rat, but very good looking.'

When Teriyaki Iwano asked to speak to Miss Stewart Beaumont, but declined to give his name, Mrs Kemp was a little suspicious; particularly of his accent. However, she informed him that Miss Stewart Beaumont was not in residence, but had returned to London. She was expected home in a few days.

Teriyaki was unable to decide whether the information was good news or not. He reasoned that it wasn't wholly bad news. To learn that she had gone to New York would have been very bad news. It would have indicated a deal with Discus Petroleum. Her journey to London could mean that she was conferring with the other major shareholders. He shuffled papers into his briefcase and snapped it shut. Initiative. That was what the situation required. But the consortium were reluctant to take his advice, preferring instead to wait until he could discover what Miss Stewart Beaumont's intentions were. He had failed to persuade them that by the time they knew that, it might be too late to initiate any dialogue with her.

* * *

Meryl travelled in grim mood to the appointed meeting with Graham Vose. At the start of trading on the London Stock Exchange, Tundra's share price had dropped to a new low. Although she and the institutional shareholders together held a massive block of Tundra's shares, there were still sufficient private investors, as well as arbitrageurs holding Tundra stock purely on a speculative basis, to cause fluctuation in the share price by selling. If Tundra's share price dropped any further, it would make the offer from Discus Petroleum look like a Christmas and birthday gift rolled into one. She was beginning to think perhaps it was Graham Vose who had been selling shares, to frighten her into action. She would have dearly liked to confer with JJ, but unfortunately, she hadn't been able to reach him before leaving Canada, and could only leave a message on the answering machine at their apartment. He in turn had only time to leave a hastily scrawled note on the hall table to say that he was sorry he hadn't received her message in time to call her before she left Canada, and was himself leaving that same evening to travel to Venice to attend a two day seminar. It was not an engagement he could cancel without good cause. Needing his moral support was, unfortunately, not a cause good enough.

Her spirits had been lowered even further by a politely measured article in the *Financial Times* regarding the crisis facing Tundra. While fairly pointing out her undoubtedly respected expertise as a corporate lawyer, it raised the question of whether that in itself would be the force to revitalize the flagging confidence of institutional shareholders, or would Christopher Mallory of Discus Petroleum win the day?

Graham Vose greeted Meryl and offered her a chair in front of his desk, then remained standing with his hands behind his back, like a schoolmaster.

'Miss Stewart Beaumont, I would like to begin by saying that I have always had the highest regard for your father:

something that has been a contributory factor in Anglo-Allied Life's continued investment in Tundra. I must now turn to matters of a more personal nature and trust that you will not be offended.' He paused for a moment as if expecting confirmation that she wouldn't, then continued. 'I was assured some time ago by your father that on his death his shareholding would be put in trust for you and that it would be managed by trustees with similar objectives to ourselves, thereby preserving continuity of aims. I was also led to believe that, on his death, the presidency would pass to David Barclay. A man, may I say, whom I consider to be more than able to run the company. However, it would appear that all this is not now the case.' He stared down at his feet. 'It is with regret, Miss Beaumont, that I have to say that I feel that our trust has been betrayed.' He lapsed into silence and continued looking down at his shoes.

Meryl stared at him in growing anger. Anger at his patronising manner, as if he was addressing a naughty schoolgirl, and at the implication that her father had deliberately betrayed him and his company.

Vose looked up at her then quickly glanced away. He went round to the other side of the desk and sat down. 'Of course, Miss Beaumont, I am aware of, indeed recognize, your competence as a lawyer and have no doubt that you will act responsibly.' He clasped his hands in front of him. 'You will appreciate, Miss Beaumont, that we must know what your intentions are without delay. We have the right to know what the majority shareholder intends and how that will affect our interests.' He glanced across at her. 'Have I made myself perfectly clear?'

'Perfectly clear, Mr Vose. Now allow me to make myself perfectly clear. Do not talk to me as if you are some provincial little bank manager and my account is overdrawn.' Her words were snapped out like machine gun fire.

He stared at her. He looked no less surprised than if she had slapped his face. 'Miss Beaumont, I trust that this meeting is not going to become acrimonious.'

'I share your sentiments.'

'Very well.' He formed his hands into a steeple and rested his chin on them. 'I believe it is essential that the majority shareholders form an alliance and agree immediately on a united approach to the Discus offer, if we are to protect all of us from major losses. I also believe that David Barclay should be made president immediately, and restore confidence in Tundra. I think I mentioned earlier that I consider him very able to run the company.'

'He is more able than that.'

Vose looked at her. 'What do you mean?'

'Exactly what I say. Barclay is so able he has done a deal with Mallory. Didn't you know?'

Vose didn't answer. He got up from the desk and walked to the window. Meryl watched him grimly. Take your time digesting that one, Mr Vose.

'How do you know?'

'My business.'

He turned to look at her. 'You have proof?'

'Yes.'

Vose looked out of the window again. 'Are you going to tell me?'

'If you wish. I am in possession of taped telephone conversations between Barclay and Mallory. They are absolutely genuine.'

He turned to stare at her. 'Please go on.'

'Mallory offered Barclay the presidency of Tundra and a stake in the company if Barclay persuaded you and the British pension fund managers to accept the terms of the takeover. Your vested interest in Tundra hinges on the fact that you will eventually need an overseas hedge when North Sea oil expires. That is why you have remained such loyal investors in Tundra.' Meryl couldn't resist allowing a little sarcasm to creep into her voice. 'It is common knowledge that you feel American interests would supersede British interests in any takeover of Tundra. Your influence would be greatly reduced, if not completely. But you trust Barclay.

If it was seen that Barclay was still very much in charge of Tundra operations you would be reassured and stay the little well-behaved investors that you are.'

Vose pushed his hands into his pockets. He could have done without the heavy sarcasm. She was as abrasive as her father. 'I suppose we should have anticipated this. Barclay is ambitious. That is a necessary quality in any successful manager. And it may be said that he has stood too long in your father's shadow at Tundra.'

Meryl made a quick interruption. 'And we all know that senior executives of a company that is taken over are the first to get the chop.'

'Quite.' He turned away from the window and walked slowly back to where Meryl sat. 'It is to be expected that Barclay will look after his own interests.' He glanced down at his chair for a moment, as if uncertain whether to sit in it or not. 'Would you like more coffee, Miss Beaumont?'

'Thank you, yes.' She noted with some satisfaction that his tone of voice had suddenly become softer, conciliatory.

He refilled her cup and passed it back to her. 'And you, Miss Beaumont. What about you? My decision must inevitably be affected by any decision you reach.'

'I do not intend to sell anyone down the river, Mr Vose, if that is what you are implying, and least of all my father's company.'

'Am I to take it that you will reject the Discus offer?'

'Yes. You have a duty to protect the interests of your company. I think I have a duty to protect the interests of Tundra's workforce.'

Vose nodded. 'It is what your father would have wanted, I have no doubt.'

'When I spoke to you on the telephone I mentioned the question of a rights issue. I believe we can fight Discus off by convincing our nervous block of floating shareholders that Tundra has the business will to go for vigorous expansion, with the prospect of healthy future profits. It will, however, need capital to do that. Would you support a rights issue?'

'I would, if it was also supported by the other institutional shareholders.'

'Good. That's problem number two sorted out.'

Vose smiled for the first time. 'You sound exactly like your father.'

Meryl had never made a financial presentation in her life, but had been involved often enough in the drafting of presentations at Wajiki International to feel fairly confident. As she outlined Tundra's vigorous expansion plans to take them into the twenty-first century, she fed him with a continuous supply of facts and figures.

She fairly pointed out that in the eighties, her father had wisely concentrated on expanding the company's downstream business as a hedge against the low-price environment of upstream activities. A policy that she believed should be continued.

Vose said little, contenting himself with the occasional nod. His face took on a look of expectancy when Meryl announced a plan to commission a cracked-naphtha etherification plant. She caught the expression on his face and felt a sudden surge of confidence.

'There will, I believe, be a continuing and growing demand for lead-free gasoline of high octane quality. The new plant will ensure that Tundra will be in the best possible position to take advantage of that sector of the market.'

'Indeed it will, Miss Beaumont. Can I see the projection figures again, please? I'm afraid I am not as young as you. Can't rely on the memory as much as I used to.'

She handed him the sheet of figures and he quickly made some notes on a pad by his side.

Meryl wound up the presentation by pointing out Tundra's strong contingency plans for alternative supplies of oil: the exploration rights in the Athabasca tar sands. Should global unrest create a sudden demand for synthetic crude, Tundra was well placed to meet that demand.

Meryl sat back in her chair. 'I hope you will agree, Mr Vose, that Tundra Corp should be viewed as a company with strong and profitable potential, and that a rights issue will mark a period of growing prosperity not only for the company, but also for its shareholders.' She rested her hands in her lap and tightly crossed her fingers.

'I must say, Miss Stewart Beaumont, that I am very impressed by your presentation. However, I shall, of course, need time to digest the information you have provided.'

'There are only a few days before the Discus deadline, Mr Vose. The matter is of some urgency.'

'Indeed.' He stood up and came round to her side of the desk. 'Miss Beaumont you do fully realize what you are taking on, don't you? Christopher Mallory is a formidable opponent and he always plays a rough game.'

'Good.' Meryl gave a tight smile. 'Makes it all the more interesting.'

Vose raised one eyebrow to indicate his more than mild disbelief. 'Very well, I will contact you tomorrow, Miss Beaumont, with my decision.'

'Thank you.'

Ian Fellowes greeted Meryl with great surprise when she appeared unannounced in her office at Wajiki International. 'Meryl, I didn't expect you back so soon. Hope I've kept your seat warm enough for you.'

'I must go to back to Canada, probably tomorrow, so don't move out just yet.'

His pleasure at seeing her increased visibly at the news. 'No problem. Everything is under control.'

'Good, because I'm going to need a little more time. I'm going to take on Discus Petroleum, Ian, even if it is a fight to the death.'

Ian slowly nodded his head. 'Doing the right thing, Meryl. No question about it.'

'I need a favour, Ian, and quickly.'

He spread his hands out in front of him. 'Say no more. It's done.'

'I need to know everything there is to know about Christopher Mallory and Discus. Everything.'

'Know just the chap for that one. He's a friend of mine. I'll get on to him now.'

'Thanks, Ian. By the way, is Mr Kushida in? I should put him in the picture.'

'Not a bad idea. He's been trying to get in touch with you urgently.'

'What!'

'Didn't JJ tell you?'

'I haven't seen JJ. We missed each other by about twelve hours.'

'Didn't he leave any message for you?'

'Not about Mr Kushida.'

Ian raised his eyebrows. 'I see. Er – did you get the message from a firm of solicitors called Dixon & Dixon?'

'No. What message?'

'They called and asked if you would contact them as soon as possible. I gave the message to JJ straight away, Meryl.'

'Don't worry, I'll sort it out. Have you got their telephone number?'

'Somewhere here.'

'While you're looking, I'll check with Mr Kushida's secretary to see what he wants.'

The offices of Dixon & Dixon were old-fashioned and rather gloomy. An equally gloomy looking man came out of the inner office to attend to Meryl.

'Good afternoon, my name is Meryl Stewart Beaumont. I called earlier. I understand that you have a deed box belonging to my late father, Charles Beaumont.'

The man stared at her suspiciously for several moments before asking to see her passport. He indicated that she should sit down while he fetched the deed box from the safe. Meryl checked her watch. She hoped he wouldn't take too long. She had an appointment with Mr Kushida at four o'clock.

The nameless man returned and placed a heavy tin deed box on to the reception desk. He handed her the key and stood back. She quickly opened the box and pulled out a bundle of papers. She flicked through them quickly. They seemed to consist of title deeds to a property in Scotland, and a handful of share certificates. The last document she stared at curiously. It was a patent specification with an uncompleted patents pending application form attached to it. The man gave a discreet cough. She hastily pushed the papers into her briefcase.

'If you would just sign this release form, Miss Beaumont.'

Meryl hastily penned her signature and handed the form back.

'May I wish you good day, Miss Beaumont.'

'Thank you.'

He opened the door to let her out. She raised an eyebrow. He seemed as anxious to be rid of her as she was of him.

Settled in a taxi taking her back to Wajiki, she had time to read the patent specification. It described Rufus Mackenzie's design improvements for decanter centrifuges. She checked the date again. It had been produced little more than two years previously. She pushed the specification back into her briefcase as the taxi stopped outside Wajiki International.

Meryl checked her watch. She had ten minutes before her meeting with Mr Kushida. She hurried to her office and let out a long sighing breath. Ian hadn't let her down. The report on Christopher Mallory was lying on her desk. She skimmed through the pages. It told her everything she needed to know about Christopher Mallory from the day he was born down to the last cent in his pocket that morning.

She buzzed through to Ian's office. 'Ian, this report is just what I wanted. Thanks. Can I buy you lunch sometime?'

'Yes, please. The Ritz?'

She laughed. 'I was thinking more of a smoked salmon sandwich at Kelly's.'

'Fine by me.'

Meryl put the report on Christopher Mallory into her briefcase. She could now formulate her next move. She did one last thing before going to see Haruki Kushida. She faxed the patent specification she had discovered in the deed box to Gerry Schmidt at Tundra, with instructions to check it out as soon as possible.

Rufus Mackenzie stumbled into a sleazy bar near the end of 96th Street. He had been thrown out of the previous one. He gave up trying to negotiate sitting down on a vacant stool and leaned against the counter, resting his arms on the edge. 'Gimme one of them.' He jerked his elbow in the direction of the drink in front of the man standing next to him.

The bartender shook his head. 'Shouldn't you be getting on back home, Rufus?'

Rufus uttered a string of obscenities. The bartender shook his head again and reluctantly served him a glass of rye.

David Barclay pushed the bar door open and looked quickly round. He saw the stooped figure of Rufus Mackenzie and stepped in. At last. He had visited four bars in the area trying to track him down. As he walked up to the bar, Rufus ordered another drink. The bartender slung a grimy towel over his shoulder and came to where Rufus was standing.

'Let's see your money, Rufus.'

Again Rufus hurled abuse at him.

'If you want a drink, let's see the money first.'

Rufus searched angrily in his pockets for money. 'I've been robbed. Someone's stolen my money.'

The bartender shrugged and walked down to the other end of the bar.

'Hey, I'm telling you. I've been robbed.' Rufus whirled round at the touch on his arm. 'Watch it, fella.' He raised a fist then stopped and peered at David. 'Mr Barclay. Mr Barclay from Tundra, isn't it?'

David smiled. 'That's correct.'

Rufus grabbed at David's arm. 'Let me buy you a drink. I owe you one. Aw, shit.' He stared around him in bewilderment. 'Someone just robbed me, Mr Barclay. Would you believe it?'

'That's O.K, Rufus. This one's on me.' David signalled the bartender to refill Rufus's glass.

Rufus spun round unsteadily to face the occupants of the room. 'This is my good friend, Mr Barclay.' He grabbed hold of David's arm again. 'A good and honest friend.' He looked up at David. 'I want you to know you're a good and –'

David gently removed Rufus' hand from his arm. 'I know, Rufus, I know. You told me before, remember?'

Rufus frowned. 'When did I tell you that?'

'Ooh, sometime recently.' David looked at the bartender with a smile and a shrug, indicating that he knew Rufus was completely stewed.

The bartender poured another shot of rye into Rufus' glass. 'I think this should be his last, friend.'

David nodded. 'Sure. Could you call a cab, please?'

'This is a bar, friend, not a taxi service.'

David took out his billfold and flicked a couple of notes on to the counter. 'I would appreciate the favour.'

The bartender scooped up the notes and pushed them into his trouser pocket.

David grabbed at the glass before Rufus could managed to raise it to his lips. 'Easy, Rufus.'

Rufus rocked gently on his feet. 'Wassamatter, Mr Barclay?'

'You're going home now, Rufus. I've called a cab for you. Take that slowly. It's your last one.'

'It is?' Rufus stared up at him with a puzzled expression on his face.

'It is.'

Rufus looked down at the glass in his hand. 'Anything you say, Mr Barclay. Anything you say.' He tried to turn round to face the room again, but thought better of it. 'You're a good, honest friend, Mr Barclay. The only friend I've got in this goddam world.' He stopped and lapsed into silence, as if considering what he had just said, then raised his hand to his eye and brushed away a tear with the cuff of his sleeve. 'Yes, sir, the only friend I've got in this rotten, stinking world.'

David took a slow intake of breath. At least while the old fool was talking, he wasn't drinking.

The taxi driver reluctantly helped David to push Rufus into the back seat. Rufus sprawled out and began singing loudly about a girl from the Isle of Rum with a rather peculiar anatomy. David shot a grin at the taxi driver. 'He's harmless.'

The driver slammed the rear door shut. 'He'd better be.'

'Here's his address. Make sure he gets home, will you.'

The driver took the piece of paper and the hefty dollar tip. 'Take him anywhere you want, mister.' He opened the driver's door and climbed in.

David waited until the taxi had pulled away from the kerb before turning on his heel and walking swiftly down the street. He cursed silently at himself, his language no less salty than Rufus'. He should have kept tabs on Rufus. The stupid bastard was in no fit state to even remember his own name now. He hailed a passing taxi and told the driver to take him to Jasper.

When Rufus Mackenzie was fired from Tundra he became an embittered man, blaming all his problems on Charles Beaumont. No one took much notice of his drunken ramblings. He had related his story in every bar in Edmonton without arising much interest, until the day David Barclay sought him out on the instructions of Charles Beaumont. Charles hated to see a good man go to ruin and by all accounts Rufus was sinking fast. Re-employing him was out of the question, so Charles did the next best thing.

Using David as a go-between, he ensured that Rufus received a regular monthly allowance from Charles' own pocket, in cash, and no questions asked.

The first time that David met Rufus, Rufus had just been released from a drying-out clinic and was more clear headed than usual. That was how David came to learn of a second, but unfiled, patent specification concerning the use of ceramic materials in decanter centrifuges. The process was a much improved version of the original idea. It would dramatically reduce the cost of producing synthetic crude. Rufus claimed Beaumont stole it from him. Beaumont had promised to have it filed at the patent office, but never did. It would have made Rufus' fortune. At first, David didn't believe him, but Rufus explained his revised design sufficiently for David to begin to take him seriously. Seriously enough to check at the Patent Office. Rufus was right about one thing. No second application had ever been filed.

David laughed quietly to himself as he stared out of the taxi window. Too bad you never made your fortune, Rufus, but you are going to make mine for me. David had planned to do more than accept Christopher Mallory's offer. When he found Rufus Mackenzie's missing patent specification, and it was just a question of time, he would be calling the shots both at Tundra and Discus.

Haruki Kushida was standing by his desk when Meryl entered his office. He walked swiftly to her and took both her hands. 'Meryl, it is very good of you to come and see me under the circumstances.'

'I'm sorry I didn't get your message earlier, Mr Kushida. I hope it hasn't inconvenienced you.'

'Not at all.' He adjusted the angle of the chair by his desk and invited her to sit down. 'I shall come straight to the point, Meryl, I believe you would wish me to.'

She shot him a quick glance. Sounds very much as if you are due for the chop, Meryl.

'My colleague at Wajiki in Tokyo, Teriyaki Iwano, is

acting on behalf of certain clients of the bank and he has asked me to discuss with you certain matters that will prove to be of mutual interest.'

She stared at him in some surprise.

'These clients, and I shall refer to them for the moment as the Osaka consortium, may be in a position to assist Tundra Corp to rid itself of the threat of Discus Petroleum.'

Meryl suddenly felt her heart give an extra fluttery beat.

'I can assure you, Meryl, that the intentions of the Osaka consortium are in the most excellent faith.'

She suppressed a smile at the quaint Japanese attempt at English idiom.

Haruki Kushida lightly clasped his arms across his chest, allowing a few seconds for the implication of what he had just said to sink in. Meryl glanced at him. She thought by remaining silent she might force him to continue speaking, but he obviously was not intending to. She smiled. 'I am most interested in what you have to say, Mr Kushida.'

He nodded gently, as if her interest was a foregone conclusion.

'And I shall be interested to learn a little more about the Osaka consortium.'

'Quite so. The Osaka consortium have interests in the petrochemical industry. I am convinced that those interests are greatly compatible with those of Tundra. Our clients are looking to the long rather than the mid-term in their wish to ensure secure supplies of oil sufficient for their future needs. They consider investment in a company such as Tundra would adequately fulfil this requirement.'

Meryl sucked in her cheeks. That was a polite way of taking over Tundra.

'There would, of course, be very clear benefits to Tundra, if such an investment was made. Tundra lacks the financial resources to either increase its downstream activities or to continue necessary upstream exploration. I am instructed to make it absolutely clear to you, Meryl, that the Osaka consortium do not wish now or in the future to launch a takeover of Tundra. Nor is it their intention to influence action that would prove detrimental to the company.'

Meryl relaxed slightly in her chair. That was good news, if it was true.

'The Osaka consortium are prepared to negotiate terms which should make Tundra a much less attractive proposition to Discus Petroleum. They are prepared to back a ten year funding operation in return for a 50% stake in Tundra's ownership of the Greywolf field in the Athabasca tar sands.'

Meryl's eyes widened. 'Why a stake in Greywolf?'

'If at some time in the future, Middle Eastern oil becomes too expensive; heaven forbid, but if there is serious war in the Gulf involving both East and West; if supplies of oil from the Gulf are interrupted for any reason, no doubt non-Gulf oil producing nations, like Venezuela, Nigeria, would immediately raise the price of their crude. If any of these situations should occur, then the extraction of synthetic crude from the Athabasca tar sands will become an economically viable proposition.'

'The Americans produce oil. None of the scenarios you have raised would necessarily be the end of the world.'

'Not the end of the world, no, but it would have an extremely disruptive effect on trade. As to the Americans, their oil deposits are now considered mature. Our clients are looking to the very long term, Meryl. The middle of the twenty-first century and beyond.'

'I understand.'

'I said earlier that the interests of the Osaka consortium and Tundra are compatible. You hold patent rights for improved tertiary techniques for the treatment of tar sands. I believe one of Tundra's engineers, a Mr Rufus Mackenzie, was instrumental in its development.'

Meryl stared at him. Somebody had done their homework very well.

'Our clients believe that the development has great potential in the light of the great improvements made in ceramic materials; ceramics being an area in which one of the Osaka consortium has a major interest.' Haruki Kushida got up from his desk. 'Naturally, you will need time to consider what we have discussed, but I think you will not find the offer unattractive.'

'I shall need to discuss this with my colleagues, but I should make one matter perfectly clear now, Mr Kushida. It is my intention to keep Tundra a truly independent company.'

'I understand perfectly. I trust you will also take into account that the Osaka consortium's offer provides more than your wish to preserve Tundra's independence. It provides for future expansion on such a scale that it will make Tundra a leader in the Western world.' He smiled. 'Who knows? One day you may be making a bid for Discus Petroleum.'

Meryl laughed. The idea had its attractions.

After the meeting with Haruki Kushida, Meryl returned to the apartment she shared with JJ, feeling mentally exhausted but strangely exhilarated. She had a feeling she would get a favourable response from Graham Vose and it looked as if, through the good offices of Wajiki of Japan, she had just found herself a Japanese white knight.

Meryl checked her watch. She was tempted to contact JJ in Venice, but decided to go and have a shower first. Italy was about an hour ahead in time. JJ was probably just about ready to be sumptuously wined and dined. It was the reason, she suspected, why he attended so many international conferences.

She was just about to get up from the sofa when the telephone rang again. The caller was Graham Vose. In view of the great urgency, he thought he should let her know that he had discussed the question of a rights issue informally with some other British pension fund investors and they would be prepared to give favourable consideration to it. Meryl stifled a sigh of relief. Vose suggested that they had a further meeting tomorrow morning to discuss the presentation of Tundra's proposals to the pension fund managers, and to discuss the situation regarding Discus Petroleum. He stressed it would be up to her to convince the fund managers to stay with Tundra. No rescue attempt could be launched without their backing. She was about to mention her meeting with Haruki Kushida, but thought better of it. It was something that was better discussed with Graham Vose face to face.

Meryl went to take her shower. Without JJ being on hand to cook, she decided to indulge in her favourite pizza with double cheese topping from Gina's dial-a-pizza service and watch something undemanding on television; neither of which would have earned JJ's approval. She methodically smoothed body lotion up her arms. One of the first things her mother had done when Meryl arrived in England was to rush out and buy a large bottle of moisturising lotion for her. One could never begin to pamper fair, sensitive skin too soon. She crooked one arm and dutifully massaged extra lotion on her elbow, as instructed by her mother.

JJ Reynolds had just settled down comfortably with a cigar and a post-prandial glass of cognac when a bell boy approached and whispered that there was a personal call for him from London. JJ swore under his breath and excused himself to his two colleagues. The bell boy led him to a small ante-room.

JJ picked up the telephone. 'JJ Reynolds.'

'Darling, it's Meryl here.'

'Meryl, lovely to hear from you. How are things? Have you managed to settle everything?'

'No, but I have settled the most important thing. I have decided to hold on to my shares in Tundra and fight Discus every inch of the way.'

JJ didn't reply immediately.

'You sound surprised.'

'Very. What made you change your mind, Meryl?'

'Oh, hard to say really, but I had a very constructive meeting with Graham Vose. I also had something of an eye-opener of a meeting with Haruki Kushida. He has clients in Japan who may just turn out to be Tundra's white knight and . . . hello, are you still there, JJ?'

'Yes, I'm still here.'

'Is something wrong?'

'No, I'm just very surprised to hear about Haruki Kushida. He didn't say anything to me about it.'

'Didn't his secretary ask you to give me a message from him?'

'No. If she had, I would have done.'

'How odd. Perhaps Ian Fellowes got hold of the wrong end of the stick. Anyway, although I feel absolutely mentally exhausted, I think I am just beginning to see a light at the end of the tunnel. This morning I felt so depressed, but now, although I've only got four more days to beat Discus' deadline, I think we might just do it.'

'Good.'

'What's the matter? You don't sound very pleased about my news.'

'Forgive me if I don't share your excitement, darling, but I too, have had a particularly busy day. In fact, I was just about to have an early night, actually.'

'Oh, I see. Well, I just thought I would tell you my news.' As she spoke Meryl's voice lost some of its original brightness.

'How long are you staying in London?'

'It depends what transpires really. Twenty-four hours, maybe longer.'

'Well, I will try to see you, if I can, darling.' JJ put the telephone down and walked thoughtfully back to the hotel lounge.

The American delegate who had attached himself to JJ at dinner grinned at him. 'Wifey been checking up on you?'

'No. Just a social call.'

'Ah, *that* kind of call.' The man thumped his shoulder. 'You old dark horse.'

JJ gave a faint smile.

'Serious?'

JJ looked puzzled. 'Is what serious?'

'The lady who made the social call. Is it serious?'

'No. It was pleasant while it lasted.' There was a hint of disinterest in JJ's voice, as if he found the subject boring.

JJ's interest in Meryl had begun on a purely sexual level. He hadn't pursued her, believing himself to be just a little too old for her, but was flattered enough by her obvious admiration and awe of him to make a slightly inebriated pass at her. Much to his surprise it hadn't been rebuffed. He was a little disappointed to find her less sexually experienced than he had assumed. He found women who didn't know what they wanted rather tiresome, but enjoyed the role of tutor more than he had anticipated.

Six months before they met, JJ's life had experienced unaccustomed turmoil. The firm of stockbrokers he had founded was merged, against his wishes, with a powerful American securities house intent on establishing a trading base in the City of London. Realising that he was in a minority of one in voicing objections to the merger, he bowed out of the proceedings gracefully and took early retirement. JJ was a very highly respected City broker and observers were not surprised when he was quickly headhunted by Wajiki of Japan to jointly head up their new merchant bank operation in the City. It was a change of direction in his career that many envied. What did surprise them was that he accepted Wajiki's offer. He was seen as being very much the old style broker; public school education, a belief in the gentlemanly way of doing business. When asked why he had accepted the offer, he somewhat wryly explained that at least the Japanese were polite to your face. What he didn't make public was the fact that he found the changes going on in the City deplorable. A fact of life that he laid fairly and squarely at the feet of the Americans. Working for the Japanese was simply the lesser of two evils.

JJ's renaissance began when Meryl entered his life. The envious looks of men half his age, when he and Meryl went out together, was an undeniable fillip to his ego. His newfound energies were not just confined to the bedroom. They were also directed towards some behind-the-scenes management of Meryl's career. She was a willing protégée eager to learn, trusting in his shrewd business instincts without question. He in turn took a quiet pride in the success of his pupil. He was old enough and wise enough to accept that there would be times when she found younger men as attractive as they obviously found her, but was content to relinquish sole rights to her body in return for her complete dependence upon him.

A waiter appeared by the side of JJ's chair. 'Excuse me, *signore*, the gentlemen at the bar wish to know if you would care to join their party?'

'No. I shall be retiring in a few minutes.'

'Very good, *signore*.'

JJ got up from the chair and rubbed at his forehead, feeling suddenly very weary. Meryl was slipping away from him. It had been pleasant, very pleasant, while it had lasted, but the party was over.

The next day, Meryl's second meeting with Graham Vose was on a more positive, upbeat note than the first. Vose had little doubt that the pension fund managers would support a rights issue, providing that certain conditions were met. They were not, as far as Meryl was concerned, going to be too difficult to comply with. The real problem was the timing of the rights issue. The markets had had to swallow too many in the recent past. Finding someone who had the stomach to underwrite the issue would not be easy.

Graham Vose raised his hands to his shoulders and stretched. 'Time for some coffee soon, I think.' He leaned back in his chair. 'So. We have agreed that David Barclay

must be offered the presidency. Admittedly he has been a
bad boy, but he is exceptionally capable and it would be
damaging to Tundra at this stage to bring in a new face. Do
you think he will take it?'

Meryl laughed. 'With both hands. I know David. He isn't
a fool. He will quickly decide where his fortunes lie.'

'What about the offer from Mallory?'

'David knows, I think, that he wouldn't last more than
about three months in the Discus empire.'

'Why do you say that?'

'Because I think that he and Christopher Mallory are too
alike to tolerate each other for any length of time.'

'You're probably very right. Now, to the question of
your appointment to the board of directors.'

'Mr Vose, you will have in me, you have my word, the
strongest possible voice in expressing the wishes of the
shareholders in the running of the company. After all, as
majority shareholders, we have a vested interest.'

'Good. That's what I wanted to hear. That just, now,
leaves the offer from the Japanese to be discussed. I must
say, Miss Beaumont, that I think it should be viewed with
great caution. A white knight usually carries a two-edged
sword. They come to your rescue. All well and good. But,
you know, something like eight times out of ten, when the
dust has settled and the hostile bid has been defeated, the
targeted company is usually taken over by the so-called
white knight.'

'Haruki Kushida did stress that was not the intention of
the Osaka consortium, although I agree we would need
more than just assurances. I still feel very strongly, Mr
Vose, that we must seriously consider entering into negotiations with the Japanese. It would take the immediate
pressure off us as regards a rights issue.'

Vose leaned back in his chair and stared up at the ceiling.
'Indeed it would. Look, shall we agree for the moment to
continue the dialogue with the Osaka consortium. May lead
somewhere, may not.'

'Agreed.'

A young man brought in a tray of coffee at exactly half past ten and for ten minutes or so, Meryl and Graham Vose abandoned the topic of Tundra. It gave Vose the opportunity to probe gently into the real reason why Charles Beaumont had suddenly changed his will.

Meryl's answer was unequivocal. 'Father saw everything in monochrome. You were either for or against him. If he believed you were against him you instantly became a non-person. David Barclay made the mistake of falling foul of that edict, Mr Vose. I have some sympathy for him, having made the same mistake myself. Not for the same reasons, but the results were the same.'

Vose looked momentarily embarrassed. 'I presume you are referring to your mother.'

'Yes. I assume you have read the sensational rubbish in the newspapers.'

'Not really. I don't pay much attention to the gutter press.' Vose lapsed into silence and contemplated the contents of his coffee cup. What she had said about her father was very true.

'See me as the prodigal daughter, Mr Vose.' Meryl spoke softly as if to herself.

'Sorry? I missed that.'

'I said see me as the prodigal daughter.'

He gave a quiet laugh of amusement. 'Actually, there is something I must ask you. How are you going to manage two jobs at once, so to speak? Your interests in Tundra will take up a great deal of your time. You also have a very demanding job at Wajiki International.'

'Yes, I know.' Meryl made no attempt to deny it. Again, she realised almost with a sense of surprise that another unconscious decision had been made. 'I shall probably resign from Wajiki. It would be less than fair to pretend I could go on giving them of my best.'

'I think that is a very wise decision. May I say that Tundra needs you more than Wajiki International?'

'Yes. I am beginning to realise that.'

Vose looked at her with a frankly open gaze. She had inherited her mother's undeniably good looks, but she got her temperament from her father. Several times when they were in deep discussion he had the uncanny feeling he was listening to Charles Beaumont.

The presentation to the pension fund managers, as Graham Vose had predicted, went down well. As he had presumed, Meryl's attractions ensured she was given a fair hearing. An unfair tactic, but a useful one.

Meryl took in every face sitting in front of her before making her final statement. She settled her gaze on the man directly in front of her, who had stared at her chest, as if mesmerized, throughout the entire presentation. 'As you will see, gentlemen, from the figures before you, Tundra's assets have historically been undervalued. Its intrinsic value is substantially higher than the bid by Discus Petroleum would suggest. To accept the Discus offer would be to give Tundra away.'

In less time than it took Meryl to take a deep breath and pour herself a glass of water, the fund managers gave their support to the package of measures she proposed to implement against Discus Petroleum. There was, however, some division regarding the offer from the Osaka consortium. Some were for, some against it. It was finally agreed to adopt Graham Vose's suggestion that Meryl should continue the dialogue with Haruki Kushida and see what transpired.

By twelve-thirty the final details of the package were hammered out. David Barclay was to be made president of Tundra immediately, on condition that he remove both feet from the Discus camp and on condition that he supported the call for Meryl to be made a director. A statement would then be issued by the majority shareholders, stressing their confidence in Barclay as president of the company, and their equal confidence in the continuing profitability of Tundra as an independent company. Finally, Tundra would throw the gauntlet down as far as Discus Petroleum was concerned. There would be no holds barred.

Each of the measures proposed would play an important part in restoring the City's confidence in Tundra Corp. The financial press would also have a part to play in the confidence-building exercise. As they usually took their lead from the reactions of leading analysts, Meryl would ensure, through her many contacts, that she had the ear of every oil analyst in the City.

At one o'clock precisely, Meryl hosted a sumptuous lunch for the pension fund managers. It was designed to show them the esteem in which they were held by Tundra Corp and no more than they had expected. By four o'clock, a further and slightly inebriated agreement was unanimously reached. The majority shareholders should meet much more often. Privately, Meryl and Graham Vose agreed that he should be the one to contact David Barclay and invite him, on behalf of the majority shareholders, to take up the presidency. Regarding David's dealings with Christopher Mallory, Vose suggested it might be more appropriate if she raised it with David. Meryl resisted the temptation to point out that it was appropriate merely because it allowed Vose to very conveniently sit on the fence.

David Barclay poured out a single shot of whisky and tossed it back. He refilled the glass. The call from Graham Vose had brought both welcome and unwelcome news. To be invited to take up the presidency was no more than he had expected. To learn that Meryl would be expected to take a seat on the board was much less to his liking.

He cupped the glass in his hands. His present position did not allow him much room for manoeuvre. He had lost his chance to convince the British stockholders to accept the Discus offer, if, in fact, the chance had ever existed. He took a mouthful of whisky. His slowness in approaching Vose had in fact worked to his advantage. If he had pushed the Discus deal, now that Meryl and Vose had obviously joined forces, it would have left him in a very ambiguous position. As it was, there was nothing, as far as they were aware, that could connect him with Discus.

David drained the whisky glass. Better get it over with. He picked up the telephone and dialled Meryl's London number. 'Hello, Meryl. How are you?'

'Fine. You?'

'Never better. I have just had a very constructive conversation with Graham Vose. I believe you both met earlier today.'

'Yes, David. He did say he would get in touch with you.'

'I just wanted to call and say that I am delighted to be offered the presidency and even more delighted to accept.'

'I'm so glad, David.' Meryl paused, then decided to go for the jugular. 'I felt sure somehow that you would prefer to work for me rather than Christopher Mallory.'

'I'm sorry. I don't quite understand.'

'I think you do, David. I know about the offer Christopher Mallory made.'

He remained silent for so long that Meryl burst out laughing. 'Don't worry. I'm not going to slap your wrist this time.'

Anger rippled through David's body at the sound of her laughter. He clenched his fist around the handset. 'I trust I am forgiven.'

'Yes. You have stood in my father's shadow for too long, perhaps, and he could be a difficult man. That you chose to make sure your own position was secure once the Discus takeover bid was announced, was predictable.'

The muscles around his mouth tightened leaving a rim of white around his lips. Condescending bitch. He took a deep breath. He had to control himself; otherwise he might lose everything. 'I hope you will forgive me, Meryl, if I say that your assessment of my situation is not entirely inaccurate. I don't mind admitting that there have been times over the last few months when I have found it extremely difficult to carry out my job as I believed it should be done. May I ask how you found out about Mallory's offer?'

Meryl smiled to herself. Now perhaps was the time to muddy the waters slightly. 'Let's just say that Christopher Mallory has enemies as well as friends.'

'But that's –'

'David, it is unimportant. Put it behind you. As far as I am concerned the matter will not be held against you. Now, are you going to fight the good fight with us?'

'You mean Discus Petroleum?'

'The very same.'

'Meryl, I want very much to assure you that I sincerely regret the situation with Discus. It came at a time when I was experiencing many difficulties on various levels.' He deliberately lowered his voice to create a tone of deep seriousness. 'I also want to assure you of my absolute loyalty to you. I know only actions and not words can prove that, but I shall do everything in my power to keep Tundra Corp independent.'

'That's what I wanted to hear, David. It is vitally important that we work closely together on this one.'

'For me, Meryl, it will be an honour and a pleasure.'

'Thank you. That reminds me of something I have been meaning to ask you. Talking to Edwin Reece recently, he said you and I must have met years ago when we were children. He said you had an Aunt Maria who worked for my father at one time, as a maid. I believe she was known as Miss Cane. She used to bring you up to the house occasionally. I must confess I don't remember. Do you?'

He shut his eyes. Damn Reece for trying to humiliate him.

'Hello, David. Are you still there?'

'Yes, yes. I was just trying to think. I don't recall our ever meeting. I think Edwin must be confusing me with someone else.'

'Quite possible. Well, I'll say goodnight, David.'

'Yes. Goodnight, Meryl.' David put the telephone down and rested his head in his hands. God rot Edwin Reece. He picked up the whisky glass. And God rot you, you sneering bitch. He gripped the glass so hard he cracked the rim, swearing as a sliver of glass cut into the flesh between his thumb and forefinger. He pulled a handkerchief from his pocket and wrapped it around the cut. Tony Barclay's rough laughter echoed in his ears. *He's not a son of a bitch. He's a son of a whore.* David picked up the glass and flung it into the waste bin. He wrapped the handkerchief more tightly around his hand. No, Meryl, Edwin Reece has got it all wrong. It wasn't my aunt your father fucked. It was my mother.

When Maria Cane had handed over her baby to her sister, Bianca, and returned to Edmonton, she found certain things had changed in her absence. Her father had died while she was living in Regina. As she was eight months pregnant at the time, there had been absolutely no question of her attending the funeral. Now, her Uncle Tito had taken over the family tailoring business and there was no work for her. He had made it very clear that whilst he would never see his brother's family starve, his own sons and daughters were given preference when jobs were available. As her Uncle Tito had thirteen children, Maria decided not to wait her turn to work in the business. She eventually found a job in a diner near Refinery Row, but walked out after three days when the owner made it very clear that he expected her to put in extra time with him in the storeroom late at night, doing things that Charles Beaumont had never made her do.

She needed a job, she needed to support herself and her mother, and it wasn't such a difficult decision in the circumstances to pluck up her courage and once again seek a job in the Beaumont residence. This time, she didn't don her best dress, but one that was now just a little too tight around the bodice and showed her figure off to its best advantage. She examined herself critically in the mirror then smiled to herself. Giving birth had left her with even more of what Charles Beaumont liked.

Once again St. Anthony granted her prayers in a fashion.

She arrived at the Beaumont residence just as Charles was stepping out of his car. A sudden gust of wind flattened the fabric of her dress against her body. She let her breath out slowly as the stern expression on Charles' face when he set eyes on her was replaced by an expression of lust as his gaze travelled compulsively over her body.

The following day Maria returned to her old job as a maid. Charles' benevolence was prompted less by altruism than a disenchantment with the lady friends who quickly believed it to be their right to make demands upon him in return for their favours. Maria was different. A simple woman, she was content with the fact that he very much liked what he saw and could be a generous man in his way. This time, he didn't lay even so much as a finger on her until she had followed his orders to go to the doctor and to get herself fixed up. There must be no more mistakes.

For the next few years Maria felt life was as good as she could ever expect. She worked hard at her job. She felt no shame at picking up the extra dollars occasionally left on Charles' dressing table. The money bought welcome extras for her mother. Sometimes, Charles would not require her services for weeks, and she would find herself wistfully wondering when they would be required. Other times he would occupy so much of her time, she would worry as to how she would ever catch up with her other work.

It was in the summer of the following year that the storm broke. Maria's long kept secret was no more. David now knew that she was his real mother. Maria took him back with her to her mother's house. She had been given little choice in the matter by Tony Barclay. At night and sometimes during the day she would weep for her beloved baby. Although David was ten years old she still thought of him as her little baby. Sometimes he would collapse sobbing into her arms. Sometimes he would stare at her and her flesh would creep in fear, but that fear was not as great as her fear of what Charles would do if he knew what had happened. She managed to keep David's presence in Edmonton a secret. One of Uncle Tito's daughters was happy enough to look after him during the day, taking him to school, giving him a meal when he came home; while Maria secured herself extra work at the Beaumont residence, helping out with the washing and ironing, assisting Miss Marylin's own personal maid. What money Maria managed to save was put into a savings account for when David went to university. It was her dream that her son should go to university. She was determined he would one day become an important man. Just like Charles Beaumont. Someone people would look up to.

Meryl had just finished taking a leisurely bath when she thought she heard a key being turned in the front door of the apartment. She hurried out into the hall and gave a sigh of relief when she saw the figure of JJ.

'Oh, you gave me such a fright. I thought it was a burglar. Why didn't you call me to say you were coming home?'

'The last day of the seminar wasn't of particular interest. I went to the airport and managed to get the last seat on the next flight to London. Didn't have time to call you.' He closed the door, presented her with a small gift-wrapped parcel and kissed her cheek. 'You smell deliciously warm and desirable.'

'Missed me?'

He laughed. 'More importantly, have you missed me? I doubt it!'

'I have missed you very much. Really.'

He slipped his arm around her shoulder and walked with her into the sitting room.

Over a dish of JJ's spaghetti alla carbonara and a bottle of wine, Meryl enthusiastically gave him all her news; asked his advice about everything under the sun; demanded to know what he thought of her plans; until over coffee he couldn't contain his irritation any longer. 'Meryl, darling, please don't think me rude, but ever since I arrived you have done nothing else but talk about Tundra.'

She looked at him with a hurt expression. 'I'm sorry. I thought you would be interested.'

'I am, up to a point, but I am more interested in you.' He got up and pulled her to her feet. 'Come and make love.' He quickly ran his hands over her body, as if checking that nothing had changed since it had last been in his possession.

Meryl slipped her arms around his neck. The Venetian air had definitely done something for JJ.

Bobby the bear was propped up against several lace-trimmed pillows on the bed. JJ walked to the bed and picked up the bear.

'This yours?'

'Mm. That's Bobby. I never used to be without him when I was little.'

JJ propped the bear up on the bedside table. 'I trust he is discreet.'

'Oh, absolutely.'

Meryl slipped her clothes off and left them in a heap on the floor. She was always the first to undress. JJ ritually laid out his clothes neatly and in unvarying order; apart from the first night they had spent together when the urge to make love was fulfilled on a velvet-covered chaise longue in his apartment. She sat down on the edge of the bed and watched him carefully ease his underpants down over his erection. Swinging her legs up on to the bed, she lay back. Occasionally, he needed what she jokingly referred to as a little helping hand before they made love, but not tonight.

JJ came to the bed and sat on the edge. 'You're not too tired, are you, darling?'

Meryl shook her head. He scooped his hands beneath her shoulders and raised her up into a semi-upright position and began removing the pins from her hair. It was a ritual that stemmed from their initial love-making. A reversal of roles had JJ bellowing in pain when he fell back on an upturned and sharply angled hairpin embedded in the chaise longue. He had recovered enough to gallantly carry her to the bedroom, but refused to allow her into his bed until every last pin had been safely removed from her hair.

Meryl stared up at JJ as his fingers expertly searched her heavy coil of hair. Excitement made his eyes look darker than they were; the irises just a rim of cold light surrounding the dilated pupils.

'What did you do in Venice?'

He curled his lip dismissively. 'It was really rather boring. Second class speakers mouthing half-baked ideas.'

She ran a finger down the sparse covering of hair on his chest. 'I thought perhaps you might have stumbled across a glamorous contessa and been swept away to her palazzo for nights of unending, unbridled passion.'

He burst out laughing. 'Darling, I am always deeply flattered by what you think I get up to when I go away, but,' he pushed her back against the pillows and lowered himself down on to her, 'nothing could be further from the truth, I can assure you.' He kissed her, then pressed his mouth to her breast. She giggled when he mumbled that if such an extraordinary thing should ever happen to him, he would not make the same mistake twice. Unbridled passion notwithstanding, he would make sure the bloody woman could cook.

He raised himself away from her and slid a hand down over her stomach, following the shallow curve of pelvis to her thigh. 'You have lost weight.'

'Don't think so.'

'You have. I can tell. I shan't desire you so desperately if you become skinny.'

She shut her eyes as gently caressing fingers slid between her thighs and parted them.

JJ climaxed at the precise moment the telephone began to ring. He rested his forehead on her shoulder. 'Did you put the answering machine on?'

'Yes.'

'Thank God.' He pressed his mouth into her shoulder then raised his head. 'My darling, you are very beautiful and one of these nights you will be the death of me.'

She smiled to herself. *But it will be a glorious way to go.* He kissed her shoulder again. 'But it will be a glorious way to go.' She stroked the back of his head. The words, the gestures, never varied.

JJ reached down the bed and dragged the duvet up and covered her shoulders. 'What was Canada really like?'

'I thought you didn't want me to talk about it.'

He slid an arm beneath her neck and pulled her closer to him. 'I said I didn't want to discuss business matters. That doesn't mean I'm not interested in how things went for you personally.' He lay on his back and flattened the area of duvet in front of him with his free arm. 'I worried about you when I left you at the airport. You looked so pale and tense.'

She sighed. The earlier urge to confide everything had vanished. It seemed too much of an effort now to collect her thoughts. He crooked his fingers and reached up to caress the side of her head. 'Do you want to talk about it, or would you like to make love again?'

'I think I feel too sleepy to do either. Do you mind?'

'No.' He inclined his head sideways and brushed his mouth against her cheek. 'Sweet dreams, darling. You deserve them.'

Meryl stared up at the ceiling, listening to JJ's breathing quietly fading into the rhythm of encroaching sleep. There was nothing to tell. Nothing to say that could reach beyond JJ's superficial understanding of things. He had had a normal upbringing in a normal family, untrammelled by destructive emotions. She stifled a yawn. Even his divorce had been so civilised he and his ex remained on friendly terms. The Beaumonts were different. Everything that had happened had been like . . . She yawned again, then smiled ruefully to herself. JJ had once likened her description of family life to a Verdi opera. She turned on her side and snuggled up to him. He drew his arm around her and sleepily mumbled an endearment.

* * *

David Barclay sheltered in the porch of the church, waiting for the heavy shower of rain to stop. He looked up at the scudding clouds and imagined for a moment the shape of Beaumont's head in one of them. He gave a quiet laugh. Beaumont wasn't up there. He was where he belonged.

The rain eased off and David stepped from the porch and hurried to his mother's grave. He crouched down and remove the now wilted flowers, left on his previous visit. 'Hello, Momma; sorry I haven't been to see you, but things at Tundra have been pretty hectic these last few days.' He removed a fresh bunch of flowers from their wrappings and arranged them in the urn. 'Things are turning out better than I expected, Momma. Your son is going to end up running an organisation even bigger than Beaumont had and he's going to make himself a pile of money, too. What do you say to that, Momma?' He dropped the dead flowers into the wrapping paper and screwed it up.

'By the way, Momma, saw Rufus Mackenzie the other day. He looked in a bad way.' David brushed a few fallen leaves away from the base of the urn. 'Thought you'd like to know that, Momma. Reckon it won't be long before he follows Beaumont. Before he does though, I'm going to find what I'm looking for. That second patent specification has to be somewhere.' He pushed the cuff of his overcoat back and checked his watch. 'I've got to go now, Momma. But don't you worry about a thing.' He stood up and tossed the parcel of dead flowers into a receptacle beneath a tree near the grave, and made his way out of the churchyard.

Business sections of both British and Canadian newspapers carried formal statements made by Tundra and its shareholders. Reporting on the statements was generally favourable. Only the *Financial Times* cast slight doubt on the wisdom of launching a rights issue in the present financial climate.

By mid morning, Tundra's share price had recovered from its previous low and rose 120p on the London Stock

Exchange. When the Toronto Stock Exchange opened for business, Tundra's share price showed an even greater gain. The gains made the Discus Petroleum offer look seriously undervalued and dealers were confidently predicting an improved bid.

News that Tundra's share price had risen sharply both on the London and Toronto Stock Exchanges became hot gossip on Wall Street. Tundra's publicity department had burned much midnight oil and were ready to hand out quotes from its stockholders and management to anyone who cared to ask. Many did and faithfully reported them. David was quoted as saying, 'Mallory's bid is preposterous. The man is just not serious.' The quote from Meryl was equally contemptuous. 'Mr Mallory appears to be totally out of touch with reality and is therefore entirely unfit to run a corporation like Tundra.'

Sensing a battle was in the air, news reporters camped outside Discus Petroleum's headquarters. It was rare for any of Christopher Mallory's victims to be in a position to fight back.

Christopher Mallory chaired a meeting of his advisors with less than his customary good humour. The call from David Barclay informing him that he was no longer interested in his offer was expected. To be told that Meryl Stewart Beaumont had obtained information about the offer from someone inside Chris' own company, was not. Chris thumped his fist on the table. 'I want the person who leaked the information found. There are only four people who knew about the offer to Barclay. Isn't that right, Frank?'

Frank nodded glumly. He was one of the four. Until the culprit was found he was under as much suspicion as anyone else. 'Could be she's just trying to wind you up, Chris. Barclay could have told her.'

Chris stared at him. 'Give me one good reason why he would risk doing that?'

Frank shook his head.

'O.K. Leave it for the moment. Is that statement ready for the press yet?'

'It's being delivered now.'

'Fine.' Chris stood up. 'Meeting adjourned, gentlemen. And, Frank, I have to go down to Wall Street and straighten some people out on what's been happening. I want to know who leaked the information when I get back. O.K?'

'Do my best.'

Chris gave him a long, warning look. 'Consider yourself fired if you don't.'

Discus security guards tried to form a human chain to keep back the reporters as Chris' car swept out from the rear entrance of the building. Several of the reporters broke through and clustered around the car, bringing it to a halt.

'Mr Mallory, Mr Mallory.' A ginger-haired girl tried to push a microphone through the partially opened window. 'Have you any statement to make about Tundra Corp?'

Chris shook his head.

'Mr Mallory. Tundra Corp have categorically confirmed rejection of your bid. What's your next move?'

'We are currently evaluating the position with regard to Tundra.'

The girl took that to mean the battle for Tundra was still on, and pushed the microphone further into the car. 'Meryl Stewart Beaumont is quoted as saying that you are entirely unfit to run a corporation like Tundra. What is your response, Mr Mallory?'

By this time the security guards had managed bodily to remove the clutch of reporters from the front of the car and it hastily sped away. Chris sat back in the seat. If Meryl Stewart Beaumont thought a little cheer-leading on behalf of Tundra changed things, she was mightily mistaken.

PART 4

David Barclay paced up and down his office. He stopped by the desk and looked down at the report, cursed softly, and continued pacing. He came back to his desk and picked up the telephone.

'Josie, I asked you to get me Miss Beaumont five minutes ago. What the hell is going on?'

'Sorry, Mr Barclay, I'm still trying to reach her. I've left a message at Wajiki International and at her apartment.'

'O.K., O.K.' He slammed the telephone down. It rang immediately. He picked it up again. 'Yes.'

'I have Miss Beaumont on line two for you, Mr Barclay.'

'Hello, Meryl?'

'Yes David. Can you speak up a little? The line is rather faint.'

'I have some serious news for you. I have just received the report on the explosion at the refinery. It *was* sabotage. The police have found traces of nitro-glycerine in the wreckage.'

There was absolute silence from the other end of the telephone.

'Hello, Meryl, are you still there?'

'Yes, yes. David, I can't believe it. Who would do such a thing?'

'I hate to say this, but your father wasn't exactly short of enemies.'

'Who is? Do you have any idea who it might be?'

'Could be a disaffected employee.'

'You mean someone with a grudge against my father?'

David's hand tightened around the telephone. Jesus Christ, he should have thought of it himself. It could just be that stupid bastard Rufus Mackenzie. He was crazy enough to try something like that. 'Ah – it's possible, Meryl. Don't worry too much about it. The police are investigating.'

'It's very difficult not to worry, David.'

'I know, I know. I wouldn't have called except I guessed you would want to be kept informed.'

'Indeed.'

'When can we expect you back in Canada?'

'Very soon, David. I am just working out the details here on a project that I think you will find very exciting.'

'What is it?'

'I can't discuss it now, David; I should have been in a meeting five minutes ago. I will explain when I see you.'

'Meryl, I –'

'Sorry, David, I have to go.'

David stared at the mute telephone then slammed it down. What the hell was she up to now? He checked his watch. It was time to see if he could track down Rufus Mackenzie. Blowing up the cat cracker was precisely the crazy kind of act Rufus would be capable of. Beaumont was now out of Rufus' reach for ever. The next best thing was to blow up half the refinery. David thumped a clenched fist into the palm of his hand. He had to get to Rufus before the police thought of questioning him.

Gerry Schmidt stuck a small cheroot in his mouth and lit it, while he waited for his call to England. He had some good news for the blonde bombshell. God help the men if she ever found out what they had christened her. He leaned back in his chair and propped his feet up on the desk. She had done more for morale in the last twenty-four hours than an oil strike in the Beaufort Sea. Even the crackerjacks had abandoned their usual topic of conversation in favour of the merits of rights issues and vigorous expansion plans. Not that any of them knew what the hell they were talking about, except what they had read in the newspaper.

The telephone rang. He took the cheroot out of his

mouth. 'Miss Beaumont? Gerry Schmidt here.' He
stretched out an arm and picked up a folder on the side of
his desk.

'Gerry, nice to hear from you. How are you?'

'Oh, I'm fine, thanks. You?'

'Same here.'

'Glad to hear it. Look, I've been looking at that patent
specification you sent. I think I have good news for you. I
had the boffins do some tests on the bonding application
and I think I've come up with something. In the specification it gives silicon carbide as the bonding material, which
works quite well. You remember our last conversation? I
said there had been problems in the past because the
ceramic material proved to be too brittle. Seeing the silicon
carbide behave satisfactorily under test set us thinking. We
conducted more tests, this time using silicon nitride as the
bonding material, and that is looking pretty good. We set
up a model decanter centrifuge and it's still running non-
stop without any problems.'

'That sounds very impressive. Do you still have more
tests to do?'

'A few more. Take about a week or so.'

'O.K., Gerry, thanks for the information. Let me know
what the final results are.'

'Will do.'

Mrs Mayes smiled cheerily at David Barclay when he
arrived at Rufus' lodgings. A dishevelled, tired looking
woman, she rented the room below Rufus'.

'Do you know if Mr Mackenzie is in his room, Mrs
Mayes?'

'Er – I think so.' She wrestled to keep a firm grip on a
sack of rubbish. 'Haven't heard him come down the stairs.'

'Thanks.' David bounded up the flight of stairs to Rufus'
room.

The door was unlocked. David opened it and stepped
inside. Rufus lay in a heap of soiled blankets on the bed.

David went up to him and roughly shook his shoulder. Rufus groaned and opened his eyes blearily, propping himself up on one arm. 'Oh, it's you, Mr Barclay.'

'Got it in one.' David pulled a tube of Alka Seltzer from his pocket and went to the washbasin in the corner of the room. He dropped the tablets into a toothmug and filled it with water. 'Here, drink this down.'

Coming back to the bed, he handed the mug to Rufus, who groaned loudly as he sat up. 'Jesus, could you do something about the hammer drills in my head?'

David didn't answer. He went and filled a kettle and began making a pot of coffee.

After two mugs of hot coffee Rufus looked as if he was once more capable of noticing his surroundings.

'O.K., time to get up.'

Rufus stared about him. David grabbed him by the shoulders and hauled him off the bed. 'I said get up.' He half dragged Rufus to the table and sat him down on a chair. 'O.K. then, what've you been up to?'

Rufus stared at him in bemusement. 'Nothing, Mr Barclay. I ain't been up to nothing.'

David shook him roughly. 'The explosion at the cat cracker. When the police come round here, you're going to be in real trouble.'

'Police?'

'Police, Rufus. And if they find traces of nitro-glycerine on your hands, you are going to be in even more trouble. Serious trouble.'

'Don't know what you're on about, Mr Barclay.'

David stared into his face, uncertain whether or not he was telling the truth. 'You're a lying bastard.' He shook Rufus furiously, like a rat. Rufus put up his hands to protect himself, but David brushed them away.

'You're a stupid bastard, Rufus. The way to get back at Beaumont is to find the specification, not to blow up half the goddam refinery and risk the lives of honest working men.' David let go of him and he slumped back in the chair.

Pushing his hands into his pockets, David stared down at Rufus. 'I've worked my ass off to help you, I don't know why I fucking bother.'

The older man wiped his nose on his sleeve and mumbled something.

'What?'

Rufus buried his head in his hands. 'I didn't mean for anyone to get hurt.'

David shut his eyes and let his breath out very slowly. He had been right. Rufus *had* caused the explosion. 'Rufus, you could spend a long, long time in jail for what you have done. Probably the rest of your natural days.'

Rufus jerked his head up. 'Please, Mr Barclay, don't tell the police. Please don't do that. It would finish me off. I know it would.' He raised a hand to clutch at David's sleeve. 'Don't do it, Mr Barclay, please. I've no quarrel with the guys at the refinery. Good bunch of workers. The very best, yessir. The very best. Never intended anyone should get hurt. You've got to believe that, Mr Barclay.'

David went to the bed and picked up the mug from the floor. He switched the kettle on again and made more coffee. As a disaffected ex-employee, Rufus would be a prime target for the police. He was known to have a grudge against Beaumont. If Rufus went to jail, he would never find the specification. He spooned a heap of instant coffee into the mug and filled it with hot water, before taking the mug back to the table and putting it in front of Rufus. 'Drink that.'

Rufus wrapped his hands around the mug and took a sip. David pulled out the other chair away from the table and sat down. 'Why, Rufus?'

Rufus took another sip of coffee. 'Wanted to get back at him. He cheated me.'

'Beaumont is dead. He's out of reach. Why did you blow up the cat cracker?'

'Don't really know now, Mr Barclay. Honest, I don't.'

Rufus took another mouthful of coffee. 'Suppose because Beaumont's dead.'

David stared at him. 'What the hell are you talking about?'

'He's dead. You said yourself. Never going to get my money now, am I?'

'Listen to me, Rufus. You *are* going to get your money. I am going to see that you get paid. But I am not going to do it if you keep blowing up the fucking refinery every time you get drunk. Do you understand that?'

'You're not going to tell on me, are you? Jail would kill me.' Rufus looked pleadingly at David. 'I meant no harm to –'

David raised his hand. 'O.K., O.K. I believe you, and no I won't tell the police.'

'You're a real pal, Mr Barclay. The only friend I've got.'

'Sure, sure.'

Rufus looked at David slyly. 'What about the police?'

'Don't worry about them. I'll deal with it.'

Rufus drank the remains of the coffee. You got no problem, Rufus, no problem. If Barclay says he'll fix something, he fixes it.

'What the hell are you grinning at?' David looked at Rufus angrily. Rufus scratched at his armpit, frantically trying to think of an answer.

'I said what the hell are you grinning at?'

'Nothing, really, Mr Barclay. Thought just came into my head that old Beaumont went to his grave never knowing you gave me money. His money. Kind of –' Rufus gestured with his hand. 'Kind of how you say?'

'Ironic.'

'That's it. Ironic.'

Rufus' gaze followed David's hand as he slipped an envelope out of his inside pocket and placed it on the table. He quickly reached out to take it, but David held on to it. 'Have you remembered where the specification is?'

Rufus withdrew his hand sulkily. 'At the Patent Office, isn't it?'

David spoke slowly. 'The other specification, Rufus. The one Beaumont stole from you, without paying you one dollar for it.'

Rufus clasped his hands around his coffee mug. 'Can't remember.' He looked up at David belligerently. 'Why do you keep going on so much about it? What do you want it for, anyway?'

'I don't want it, Rufus. *You* want it. If you know where the specification is,' he raised his arm and gestured at the room, 'it can take you out of all this.'

Rufus stared about him, as if not particularly interested where he was.

David tried again. 'If you got the specification you'd be worth a mint. It would bring Bella back, Rufus.'

Rufus sniffed. 'She wouldn't have me back.'

'She would if you had money. If you could afford to give her a decent life.'

Rufus stared down into the depths of his mug again.

David stood up. 'O.K., O.K., if you don't want to get the better of Beaumont, dead or alive, that's up to you.'

The older man straightened up at the mention of the name. 'He cheated on me, Mr Barclay. I trusted him and he cheated on me.'

David sat down again. 'I know, Rufus. It's why I'm here. To see you get what is rightfully yours.'

'You're a good man, Mr Barclay.'

'But I can't help you, Rufus, unless you remember where the specification is.'

'Must be in the files somewhere.'

David rubbed the side of his jaw. 'It isn't. I've checked everywhere at the office and at the plant. It isn't on the company files. You must remember where you last saw it. It's your only chance.'

Rufus rubbed at his brow. 'I'll try to think. Not now. Give me a couple of hours.'

David stood up again. 'I'll be back tomorrow, Rufus, and this time get your head together. Do you understand me?' He jerked a thumb at the empty whisky bottle on the floor. 'Leave that alone.'

Rufus nodded.

David hurried downstairs and paused outside Mrs Mayes' door, which opened before he had a chance to knock. Mrs Mayes poked her head around the door. 'Thought it might be you, Mr Barclay. Mr Mackenzie in was he?'

'Yes, thanks.' David pulled out a roll of money from his hip pocket.

'See he gets a couple of hot meals down, Mrs Mayes. That liquid diet of his is going to kill him one of these days.' He handed her the money, knowing full well that half of it would go to buy her own favourite liquid.

'I was only saying to the girl in the deli last week, one day they'll find him dead, you know.' She tucked the money down the front of her blouse as she spoke.

'You could be right, Mrs Mayes, but see he gets some hot food down him, will you?'

'Don't worry, Mr Barclay, I'm going out in a few minutes. I'll bring him something back and stand over him to make sure he eats it.'

David smiled. 'Thanks, Mrs Mayes.'

Mrs Mayes watched him walk down the stairs until he was out of sight. She fingered the money in her blouse. He was certainly a looker. If she had been thirty years younger she would have asked him in for a bit of what he fancied . . .

Retaliation by Discus Petroleum to the rejection of their bid was fast and below the belt. An increased offer of $50 for every Tundra share was deliberately made after the markets had closed with Tundra's shares standing at around $46. Every single shareholder of Tundra had been contacted on behalf of Discus, with the exception of Meryl. She was contacted when it was just too late to leak the information to the stockmarkets; preventing any speculative rise in Tundra's share price. With Tundra's share price standing at

$46, the renewed bid of $50 by Discus was looking very attractive: too attractive for speculative shareholders to dismiss.

Meryl's hasty meeting with Graham Vose quickly wiped out the euphoria of the previous day. Vose rested his hands behind his head. They had been discussing Discus' renewed offer for two hours without coming up with any satisfactory answers. Meryl got up from her chair and went to stand by the window. 'There is one way.'

'What's that?'

'Recapitalization. We could arrange a package of incentives to the shareholders. More stock, perhaps with an extra special dividend. We would have to borrow the money. Such a move would increase Tundra's indebtedness to such an extent that the company would be worthless to Mallory.'

Vose removed his hands from his head. 'I would consider that an extremely drastic measure.'

She gave a dry laugh. 'So would I.'

He rested his hands on the desk and clasped them together. 'You couldn't recapitalize *and* launch a rights issue.'

Meryl didn't answer.

'I'm afraid, Miss Beaumont, I couldn't go along with the idea of recapitalization. It's far too risky, and would set back Tundra's projected profitability by an unacceptable time scale.'

Meryl stared out of the window at the building opposite. 'Deserting the sinking ship?'

'I have done my best for you, Miss Beaumont, because I am sympathetic to your aims, to the aims of Tundra; but Anglo-Allied Life could not countenance what you have suggested. If you went ahead, it would have to be without our support for the idea.'

Meryl pressed her lips together. 'Very well, Mr Vose, there is no more to be said.' She walked back to the desk and packed her briefcase. She glanced briefly in the direction of Vose. 'Thank you for your time.'

Vose got up to see her out, but she had already swept to the door and opened it.

Haruki Kushida had booked a table at Simpsons, a restaurant famed for the quality of its beef. He and Meryl chatted about anything except the reason for the meeting. They discussed the merits of roast beef and sukiyaki; Haruki confessing to having a fondness for British roast beef and Yorkshire puddings.

Meryl was almost running out of conversational small talk when the matter of the Osaka consortium was broached by Haruki. With Vose backing out, she had had little alternative but to contact Haruki and request a meeting to discuss the Osaka offer. Haruki stared down at his coffee cup. 'In the light of the renewed offer by Discus Petroleum, I am glad that we have the opportunity to discuss the offer from my clients. I appreciate that the threat of a future takeover worries you. I can, of course, vouch for the good faith of my clients when they say that would not be their intention.'

Meryl pursed her lips, wondering how to express as politely as possible that good faith, however well-intentioned, was insufficient.

Haruki placed his hands together and rested them on the table in front of him. 'But, of course, in some situations, such an understanding is not enough.'

Meryl looked at him with relief. He had said it for her.

'If we accept that this is one of those situations, I would like you to consider a proposition of my own,' he continued blandly.

'Certainly, Mr Kushida.'

'Good, I shall speak plainly in the English manner and trust that this is what you would wish of me.'

'I would very much appreciate it, Mr Kushida.'

'I have looked at the situation very carefully, both from the consortium's viewpoint and from yours. Perhaps you would consider the splitting up of the Tundra organisation into relevant parts, and the setting up of a new company within the organisation encompassing the upstream business and research and development of the Greywolf field. The name is irrelevant for the moment, but say something like Tundra International, Tundra Exploration. A proportion of the shares in the new company could be purchased by the consortium. Put simply, the consortium would achieve their stake in Tundra's future exploration in the Athabasca tar sands and Tundra would retain most of its independence. The sale of such shares would of course raise substantial and much needed capital for Tundra. A most harmonious answer to the problem, I believe. What do you think, Meryl?'

Meryl looked down at her hands. That was the most harmonious suggestion she had heard all day. The idea definitely had potential. 'May I ask what gave you the idea, Mr Kushida?'

He smiled. 'You. I went very carefully through the statements that have been made by Tundra. You did at one stage say that you did not rule out mutual research and development with another company.'

She nodded.

'I believe, Meryl, that such a proposal would be keeping within the spirit of your father's wishes to keep Tundra an independent company.'

'I agree. I think it would.'

He smiled. 'Then we are a step further to solving the dilemma.'

'That will depend on whether or not the consortium will agree.'

'If you will forgive me, I took the step of ascertaining the consortium's reaction to the idea before I mentioned it to you. They agree in principle. Naturally, details need to be agreed upon. The price at which the shares in the new company would be offered is obviously crucial to both sides. One would have to take into account that the new company's prospects would not at first sight look particularly attractive to a buyer. Its major asset is an as yet expensive and partially developed method of extracting oil.'

'Indeed.'

'You will obviously wish to consult with your other shareholders, but in the meantime, is it possible for you to make your own thoughts known?'

'I like the idea very much, Mr Kushida. Very much.'

'Good. This will allow us to consider the form negotiations should take. As there is only a week before the acceptance date of the new Discus offer, I assume you will wish to appoint someone immediately, to act on your behalf in these matters?'

Meryl made a quick decision. There was no one else she knew of Kushida's calibre. With the wrong person representing her, negotiations with the Japanese could only end in disaster. 'I had hoped that you would find it possible to take on the role of honest broker and act for me, too. As an employee of Wajiki, I have come to respect and admire you, Mr Kushida.'

Haruki's face creased into a genuine smile. 'I am most honoured that you think so. I am equally honoured to find myself in a position to act on your behalf.'

'I think that will be best. I fear I shall sound rude when I say that differences in English and Japanese cultures can make discussions prone to misunderstanding on both sides, but I hope you will forgive me for saying that.'

'Ah, now I believe the Americans would say that is an understatement.'

Meryl laughed. 'I believe they would.' She clasped her hands together and stared at them. Now was as good a time as any. She picked up her bag and opened it, and withdrew a white envelope. 'Mr Kushida, there is something I have to give you. I have considered the matter very carefully and I think it is only fair to Wajiki and myself if I tender my resignation. I hope you will understand.'

He took the envelope from her. 'I understand perfectly, Meryl. You are not a person who gives anything less than one hundred per cent. Your work for Wajiki International is held in great esteem. You are going to be very much missed.'

She smiled. 'Thank you very much, Mr Kushida.'

'Do you wish me to consider a name for your successor?'

Meryl thought for a moment. She owed Ian Fellowes one for that report on Christopher Mallory. 'Ian Fellowes. He is my deputy. He has stood in for me while I have been away. I wouldn't want to recommend anyone else.'

He nodded. 'I shall bear your recommendation very much in mind.'

Meryl wrapped the telephone flex around her fingers. She had told the switchboard operator at Tundra that she would hold until Gerry Schmidt was found. That was seven minutes ago. She heard a sharp noise followed by a muffled expletive. 'Hello, hello.'

'Gerry Schmidt here, Miss Beaumont.' He sounded out of breath.

'Gerry, how are the tests going on this new specification?'

'Very impressive. We calculate that using silicon nitride will lower running and maintenance costs by something like seventy-five per cent.'

'What does that mean when compared to the price of conventional crude?'

He gave a low whistle. 'That's a tough one to answer.'

'Try. It is important.'

She heard him suck air through his teeth. She crossed her fingers tightly. Please, Gerry. Please.

'I would say that if conventional crude was say, $30 a barrel, we would be competitive. Just.'

Meryl uncrossed her fingers. 'Have you finished all the tests?'

'Should take a couple of more days.'

'O.K., Gerry; can I rely on you to keep a very strict confidence?'

'Your father could, no reason why you shouldn't.'

'You know about the renewed offer by Discus?'

'I would have to be deaf, dumb and blind, not to.'

'It is possible that we may have Japanese funding to develop extraction and treatment of tar sands to produce synthetic crude. The backing would enable us to shake off the Discus bid. Nothing has been decided yet with the Japanese, but will you finish the tests as soon as possible? It could prove very important in negotiations.'

'Will do.'

'And, Gerry, could you get hold of Rufus Mackenzie? I think we should make a patents pending application straight away, as a matter of top priority. Obviously, we will need his say so.'

'Not necessarily, Miss Beaumont. We wouldn't be filing his specification using silicon carbide, would we? We would be filing a specification based on our work on silicon nitride. There's a difference there if you can spot it.' He reached across the desk for a packet of cheroots and his lighter.

'So what are you trying to say? We have the right to file a specification without recourse to Rufus Mackenzie?'

Gerry paused to light up a cheroot. 'That is what I am trying to say. We have modified the improved design sufficiently to legitimately claim that the process is ours.'

'That's a bit tough on Rufus Mackenzie, isn't it?'

'So it's a tough world. Look, Miss Beaumont, the last time I saw Rufus Mackenzie he was lying semi-conscious outside the refinery gates, suffering from alcohol poisoning. I had to get one of the security guards to call an ambulance. If you want to give this thing top priority, forget about Rufus Mackenzie. He would have to redraft the specification to take into account the work we have done on silicon nitride. He simply couldn't do it. He's shot to pieces, believe me. If you feel bad about it, give him a bonus payment.'

'I'll think about that one. I suppose if he's as bad as you say, he would simply drink himself to death.'

'Probably would.'

'Gerry, have you mentioned the tests you have been doing to anyone, by any chance?'

He gave a low laugh. 'I figured that wasn't what you wanted.'

Meryl raised her eyebrows. 'What gave you that idea?'

'I have a wife and five daughters. I'm pretty good at understanding women.'

'Then you must be a most remarkable man, Gerry.'

He laughed again.

'But I don't buy it. You'll have to do better than that.'

'O.K. I have worked for your father too long not to know how the Beaumont mind works. There had to be a good reason why you went over the head of our acting president and came to me direct. I figured the reason had to be a good one.'

'As you know so much about women, Gerry, you will know that we are blessed with intuition, and my intuition tells me that I have only heard half the story.'

'I'll come clean. Barclay and I do not get on.'

'And . . .'

'And in the recent past we have lost out to Discus Petroleum so many times it just isn't true.'

'How so?'

'Drilling rights in the Beaufort Sea. Outbid on the NWT Pipelines deal. Either Chris Mallory has second sight, or . . .'

'. . . or he has insider information.'

'You got it. Look, your father was not in the best of health. You know that. It isn't too difficult to start thinking someone is taking advantage.'

'O.K., Gerry, I read you.'

'Miss Beaumont?'

'Yes?'

'I – ah, said something a little earlier which may have caused offence. It wasn't intended. Like I said, I have a wife and five daughters. A man either learns to understand or he goes crazy. I guess we really are the weaker sex.'

Meryl laughed. 'That sounds like special pleading.'

'Probably.'

'Let me know the results of your final tests and get some-one on that patent application straight away.'

'Will do. Will you still be in England?'

'Yes, I have one or two things to tie up, but if I have a change of plan, I'll let you know. Bye.'

'Bye to you.' Gerry put the telephone down and cursed softly as ash from his cheroot fell on to his lap. He brushed the ash away. The blonde bombshell had been very busy indeed. Japanese funding. He stubbed out the cheroot. Not surprising when you considered who she worked for.

Haruki Kushida raised his hand and examined the tips of his fingernails. He had asked JJ to meet him in his office to impart the news that the senior vice-president of their mother company, Wajiki of Japan, had been approached by the Osaka consortium and had personally instructed Haruki to take over the negotiations with Tundra. He now regretted the haste of that invitation. Unaware that JJ knew nothing about Meryl's resignation, he had spoken in a way which must now be considered tactless.

JJ brushed an imaginary piece of fluff from his knee. If Meryl was trying to tell him something, she was going the right way about it. He appeared to be the last to know that she had resigned, and he didn't like to be made a fool of. Most certainly not in front of Haruki Kushida. He brushed at his trouser leg again. 'I shall of course be more than happy to assist you in any way I can.'

Haruki nodded politely. 'I think, JJ, under the circum-stances, it is better if I do not call upon your assistance, unless of course Miss Stewart so requests.'

'Yes, of course. I understand perfectly.' JJ spoke rather stiffly.

'Miss Stewart is no longer my employee. She is now my client.'

'I do understand, Haruki.' JJ recrossed one leg over the

other in irritation. He understood perfectly. If he was not *au fait* with Meryl's resignation, he was not going to be allowed to be privy to the negotiations on behalf of Tundra.

Haruki got up from his chair. 'Well, JJ, thank you for coming to see me. I am pleased that we have reached mutual understanding of the situation.'

JJ nodded and walked out of the office. Haruki stared after him. Meryl had taken on the burdens of her ancestors. It was inevitable that in doing so, many things would change. He took a cigarette out and lit it. One must strive to face change with equanimity. JJ had not yet learned that lesson.

JJ returned to his office and told his secretary not to put any calls through. He was a man little given to outward signs of temper, but he slammed the door of his office so hard his secretary literally jumped in her seat. He dragged the chair away from his desk and sat down. He had been pushed aside. No discussion allowed. No logical explanation given. He had about as much mutual fucking understanding with Kushida as the commissionaire on the door downstairs.

Meryl made herself a quick cup of instant coffee and took it into the sitting room. She sat down, looking at the rough notes she had made. There had to be a public response from Tundra to the renewed offer. She would have to confer with David. It would look odd if she didn't. If Gerry Schmidt was correct in his suspicions – and, apart from the overt male arrogance, she felt she could trust him – David was still an unknown quantity. She picked up her pen and went over the question mark she had made by David's name again.

The telephone rang. She fervently hoped that it would be Edwin Reece: she was going to have to rely on him even more.

'Hello, Edwin?'

'Yes, Meryl, I rang as soon as I received your message.'

'Edwin, listen, I don't have much option but to enter into

negotiations with the Osaka consortium. The other alternative is recapitalization. I spoke to Graham Vosc earlier, and he wouldn't buy that idea so he has returned to his favourite position of sitting on the fence. I need time to hammer something out with the Japanese, but I don't want David to know anything about it.'

'Meryl, you can't keep him permanently in the dark about what's going on.'

'I have to. For the moment I have to. Gerry Schmidt thinks David has been giving information to Discus for a lot longer than we imagined. He says Discus has outbid Tundra on deals in the past, as if Christopher Mallory has had second sight.'

Edwin drew his breath in. 'It is a possibility, but one that would be difficult to prove.'

'I'm not for the moment interested in proving it, Edwin. I just want to make sure it doesn't happen again. I am going to contact David as soon as I have finished speaking to you. To keep him busy, I shall tell him to draw up plans for recapitalization. That should keep him occupied for a few days. And, Edwin, I think to quash any suspicions David may have, you should be seen to be trying to get me the best personal loan available. Use everything I have as collateral, if you have to.'

'Meryl, is it necessary to go to such lengths?'

'Yes, for the simple reason that I may just need such a loan to inject into Tundra, if I can't reach an agreement with the Osaka consortium.'

'I suppose it would kill two birds with one stone, so to speak. Mallory will expect some action from us. Apparent attempts at recapitalization would give him cause to re-think his strategy.'

'Quite so, Edwin.'

'Very well, Meryl, I will do as you say. One further thought, though. I think you should return to Canada as soon as possible. It will look suspicious if you are seen to remain in London for no good reason, and I think it will help to calm fears here, if you return. Our stockbrokers have reported some brisk selling of Tundra shares this morning.'

'Selling is inevitable, I suppose, but I agree it would look better if I kept a high profile back home. I could manage a couple of days. There is not much I can do in England, until Mr Kushida comes back with facts and figures from the Osaka consortium.'

'Good. See you soon then, Meryl.'

Christopher Mallory looked out of the window at what he could see of the New York skyline through the misty rain. The statements from Tundra about Discus' improved offer were emphatic. Tundra would remain an independent trading company with a strong and healthy future. He pushed his hands into his pockets. The statement had contained the usual crap. Tundra's directors were meeting to consider further options open to them and to prepare a formal statement of intent to its stockholders. He whistled softly through his teeth. Meryl Stewart Beaumont had only one option left. Recapitalization. An option that would make her British stockholders cut and run.

There was a light tap on the door of the office and a young girl entered. 'Good morning, Chris. One tuna and mayonnaise. One beef and pickle.' She placed a lunch box on the desk.

'Thanks.'

Ordinarily, Chris would have engaged her in a couple of minutes' conversation; more as a reflex action than anything else. She was quite attractive. This morning, he stayed looking out of the window. He had another lady on his mind: Meryl Stewart. He would show her just how 'unfit' he was to run Tundra Corp.

Frank collided with the young girl as he rushed into the office just as she was leaving. He set her aside with a brief smile. 'Excuse me.' He shut the door firmly behind her. 'Chris, I think we may have a problem. There's a rumour spreading fast on Wall Street that your favourite lady of the month has got herself a Japanese white knight.'

Chris cursed under his breath. Rumour instantly became fact on Wall Street. 'Know the source?'

Frank gestured with open arms. 'Come on, Chris, when do we ever know who starts what rumour.'

'O.K.' Chris walked slowly back to his desk. 'Get me a list of every client Wajiki of Japan has back home.'

Frank placed a sheet of paper on the desk. 'You've got it.'

Chris picked up the list of names. 'Thanks, Frank. Remind me to get you to read my mind sometime.'

Frank grinned.

Two share option traders had reached the same conclusion over a cup of coffee, just before the start of the day's trading. They couldn't understand why they hadn't thought of it before. A photograph of Meryl Stewart in one of the newspapers had triggered the idea. The lady had friends in Japanese high places. She worked for an offshoot of one of Japan's leading merchant banks, whose assets quadrupled those of any of the leading American banks. Neither of the traders could remember afterwards who had made the connection first, but Meryl Stewart had a white knight tucked away somewhere. It was so blindingly obvious it was just a question of time when he would appear. Within ten minutes of trading on the New York Stock Exchange, Discus' share price started to fall. No one had ever taken on the Japanese and won. Not even Christopher Mallory.

Chris took one of the sandwiches out of the box and took it with him back to the window. Staring out of the window again, he bit reflectively into the sandwich. Tundra would remain independent. Such rigorously pursued independence would not, of course, rule out joint ventures with other companies in the field of research and development. Mallory turned and tossed the sandwich into the waste bin. Meryl Stewart Beaumont had managed to leave the back door ajar. Christ, Mallory, you don't need someone to read your mind; you need someone to give you a new brain. He strode to the desk and picked up the telephone.

Meryl placed two candlesticks either side of the bowl of flowers on the table. When JJ arrived home she would have to break the news to him that she had resigned from Wajiki and was returning to Canada for a short while. A gourmet dinner from the local restaurant would help to soften the blow. She checked her watch. Just after six. The happy hour. Time to try and relax with a glass of wine. She had a long, long way to go before she would see a happy hour for Tundra. Just for the moment she was still managing to keep in step with Discus Petroleum. David had welcomed her telephone call and heartily agreed that a plan to recapitalize was the only answer to the improved offer. She poured a glass of wine. Perhaps she was being too suspicious, but she had the feeling he had been just a little too enthusiastic.

The front door of the apartment opened and closed with more noise than usual. Meryl popped her head around the sitting room door. 'JJ, you're back earlier than I had expected. What was the seminar at the DTI like? Useful?'

'O.K.' He dumped his briefcase by the side of the hall table.

'Come and have a drink, darling, I've got lots to tell you, Edwin thinks –'

'Meryl I have got something to say to you first. Come into the sitting room and sit down.'

Meryl glanced at him wondering what could be wrong. JJ very rarely spoke in such a clipped manner. She sat down on the sofa and looked up at him.

'Meryl, I can appreciate that our relationship may not be as important to you now as it once was, but I do expect you to have the courtesy to tell me what you are doing at Wajiki International, instead of my having to be informed by Haruki Kushida.'

She looked at him for a moment, unable to follow what he was saying. 'Oh, my resignation. JJ, I'm sorry. There simply wasn't time to tell you; you left so early this morning. I honestly hadn't got my head together then. I'm sorry. I just decided later that it was the only sensible thing to do.'

'Really. You just decided. I am not stupid, Meryl. You must have thought about it before now.'

'In a way, I suppose, it did cross my mind. I've had so many things to think about, I didn't give it much priority until I had to.'

JJ turned on his heel and went to the sideboard, and mixed himself a whisky and soda.

'I had, Meryl, a most humiliating meeting with Haruki Kushida. I was first informed of your resignation then I was obliquely informed by Haruki that as you were now his client, I would not be asked, as I would have normally expected, to assist in negotiations on your behalf without your permission.' He swallowed a large mouthful of whisky and set the glass down again. 'What the hell do you think you are doing?'

'I'm sorry; what do you mean?'

'I mean, Meryl, that I will not be treated like a bloody office boy by Haruki Kushida, just because of you. You could have, at the very least, consulted me first. Instead you go rushing off to Haruki.'

Meryl got up from the sofa. 'Please, JJ, let me explain. I *did* want to discuss things with you. Very much so. But you were at the DTI seminar all day. Please try to understand, JJ, things are moving so fast at Tundra I have to think on my feet. I don't have time to wait.'

JJ finished the remains of the whisky and refilled the glass.

'I don't understand why you are so angry. Why should Haruki Kushida refuse to allow you to handle the negotiations?'

He spun round to face her. 'Because, you stupid little bitch, the orientals operate on trust. *Trust.*' He took in a deep breath. 'God Almighty, don't you understand how Kushida's mind works? If you didn't tell me that you were resigning, what other things have you not told me and why? It is the bloody *'why'* that was obviously bothering him.'

Meryl went to him and put her arms around his middle. 'JJ, I'm terribly sorry. I didn't think. I'll explain to Kushida what has happened. That it's all my fault. Don't worry.'

He removed her arms from around his waist. 'Don't bother. It's too late.' He looked at his watch. 'I'd better get showered and changed. I'm going to be late.'

'Where are you going?'

'Dinner engagement.'

'But, JJ, I wanted to tell you before. I have to go back to Canada tonight.'

'Really?'

'Please, do try to understand. I must go back. It's only for a couple of days.'

'Do whatever you want to do, Meryl; you seem to be making a habit of it of late.' He walked towards the door, removing his jacket and tie as he went.

She hurried after him. 'Please, darling, don't go out. I've ordered your favourite meal from that restaurant you like. We need to talk before I go.'

'I'm sorry. I am having dinner with a client, and I can't cancel it. The way things are going, I shall be lucky to have any clients left at all.'

'JJ, please: I need to talk to you. I really do.'

'Well, talk to me while I change.'

The stewardess led Meryl to her seat in the first class cabin. Meryl sat down and placed her briefcase on the seat next to her. The stewardess handed her a menu. 'We shall be taking off soon and dinner will be served shortly afterwards.'

'Thank you.'

She leaned back and shut her eyes: she could understand why JJ was angry, but she could have sorted things out with Haruki Kushida, if JJ would have let her. While he was shaving, a sudden thought had prompted her to sneak a look at his Filofax. There was no dinner engagement with a

Crackerjack

client. It couldn't have been an oversight; JJ always kept
a note of every engagement. She opened her eyes at the
instruction to all passengers to fasten their seat belts. Drawing the ends of her seat belt together, she snapped it shut.
They had done more than quarrel. A barrier had arisen
between them. It had started when she said she would go
and see her father. Then she thought she had imagined it.
Now, she was certain she hadn't.

PART 5

Meryl sat in the back of the limousine. Her eyes unconsciously followed the neat line of hair beneath the chauffeur's cap. He had been waiting at the airport for her when she arrived. She had half expected Edwin Reece to be there as well, but Scott was alone.

'We'll be arriving in just a couple of minutes, Miss Beaumont. Sorry about the delay. Traffic's really heavy today.'

'That's O.K., Scott.'

He dipped his head slightly in acknowledgement.

Meryl turned and look out of the window. A long and sleepless overnight flight had given her ample time to mull over her quarrel with JJ. Someone had once jokingly referred to JJ as her mentor: the man she couldn't live without. It had been meant to be offensive. She sighed. Perhaps it was true, and perhaps JJ was getting bored with her. There might even be someone else on the scene. There would always be older, more sophisticated women who would give their eye teeth to sew a name tag into his jacket. She bit her lip pensively. The brash kid from Edmonton was losing her attractions. If she was honest, she would admit that his love-making had become perfunctory. Ultimately satisfying, but lacking the ginger and snap it used to have.

Scott stopped the car in front of the house and leapt out smartly to open the rear door. 'Here we are, Miss Beaumont.'

'Thanks.' She looked him full in the face as she stepped out. He was quite attractive when he smiled.

Marsh the butler and Mrs Kemp both stood on the steps waiting to greet Meryl.

'Miss Beaumont, welcome home.' Mrs Kemp beamed happily. Now she had someone to plan a week's menu for.

'Thank you, Mrs Kemp. Glad to be back.' Meryl had stepped into the hall before she had realised what she had said. She glanced up at the wide, curving staircase. A week ago, this would have been the last place she would have thought of as home. She turned to Mrs Kemp.

'Any messages?'

'Oh yes, Miss Beaumont. I'll go and fetch them.' Mrs Kemp went into the library and returned with Charles Beaumont's diary.

Meryl rubbed her brow. That was something else. While she had been away people had unconsciously lapsed into calling her Miss Beaumont. Not that it mattered any more. Mrs Kemp put on her spectacles. 'Now then, Mr Reece will drop by on his way home from the office. Mr Barclay left a message to say he would be away for the day. He's had to go to Ottawa to attend Mrs Bianca Barclay's funeral.' Mrs Kemp looked over her glasses and lowered her voice. 'His mother, Miss Beaumont. Very sad. She'd been ill for a long time. If you ask me it's a blessing.'

'Oh dear, I am sorry. How sad for David.'

Mrs Kemp removed her spectacles. 'Now, Miss Beaumont, you look as though you need a cup of tea to revive your spirits.'

'Thank you.' Meryl walked slowly to the study. It would take much more than that to revive her spirits.

Edwin sat in a chair opposite Meryl and looked as if he had been sandbagged. Meryl remained silent, thinking it better to let him digest the information about the contents of the deed box at Dixon & Dixon in his own good time. It had obviously come as a shock to him to realize that he hadn't known her father as well as he thought he had done. He hadn't known anything about the assets her father had kept in England.

Edwin raised his head to look at her. 'I was your father's attorney for fifteen years. I believed our friendship was based on trust, on honesty.'

'Don't take it too much to heart, Edwin. I don't believe it was personal in any way. Pops never trusted anybody, not even his own flesh and blood.'

'My feelings are not important, Meryl. What is important is that the estate accounts have been filed containing what we now know to be serious omissions.'

'No problem putting it right, surely?'

He tightened his mouth in irritation. 'I have put in many hours of work to ensure that your father's estate was kept completely in order to avoid unnecessary delays and precisely this kind of complication.'

Meryl pursed her lips. It was a bit rough on poor old Edwin. A lawyer's competence rested in some measure on full disclosure by the client.

'I suppose your father never forgot the days when he was poor.' Edwin spoke slowly as if still in the process of formulating his thoughts. 'I remember he once told me he went to school without any socks inside his boots, his mother was so short of money. He must have kept the assets secret as insurance against bad times: like a rainy day account. Although what he imagined could ever reduce him to such poverty again, I cannot think.' He picked up his glass of rye and took a sip. 'Yes, I think that must be it.' He nodded to himself. 'It must be.'

'Like a squirrel hoarding nuts for winter.'

Edwin gave a faint smile. 'Well, I will get in touch with Dixon & Dixon tomorrow. As they have acted for your father in the past, no doubt they will be prepared to act on behalf of the estate.'

'I'm sorry, Edwin, this has caused problems for you.'

'Not your fault. Besides, it is what I am here for. Now, Meryl, what are your plans for tonight?'

'Oh, I really don't know.'

'I don't want you to sit mulling over Tundra's problems

all night. Would you like me to stay and keep you company? That is if you can put up with the company of a boring old man.'

'You're not boring, Edwin, and you are certainly not old. I shall be delighted if you will stay. We can have dinner together.' She got up from the chair. 'If you will excuse me for just a minute, I'll go and tell Mrs Kemp there will be two for dinner and try to persuade her not to roast an ox for the main course.'

He laughed. 'You will never change her.'

'I've got to, Edwin. I simply do not have my father's appetite.'

The commotion outside somewhere in the garden woke Meryl with a start. She sat up in bed and fumbled for the bedside lamp. Someone was shouting at the top of his voice. She switched on the light and looked at the alarm clock. It was just after two in the morning. She rubbed at her eyes. She had been dreaming about David, but couldn't remember exactly what about. She leapt out of bed and ran to the window. Lights downstairs had already been turned on and clearly illuminated the figure weaving about unsteadily in front of the fountain, just as Marsh and a handyman ran from opposite directions to overpower him. She rushed to the door and hurried downstairs.

Rufus Mackenzie was still shouting although he was firmly pinned to the ground. 'You bastard! I know where it is. I'll get you, Beaumont!'

Between them Marsh and the handyman hauled Rufus to his feet. Meryl stood by the door clutching the front of her bathrobe to her chest. She stared at the drunken figure of Rufus in bewilderment.

'I've called the police, Miss Beaumont. They'll be here very soon.' Mrs Kemp patted Meryl's arm in reassurance.

'Who is he?'

'I've no idea, Miss Beaumont. I can't think how he managed to get into the grounds.'

When the police arrived Rufus was unceremoniously bundled into the back of the car, still struggling and shouting obscenities at those around him. A little later a second police car arrived and a plain-clothes policeman carefully took down statements from Marsh and the handyman. The grounds were carefully checked, but it was something of a mystery how Rufus had managed to get in. The massive lock on the front gates and the one on the side gate hadn't been tampered with. The only way in would be to scale the eight feet high walls – a considerable feat for a drunken man.

The following morning Meryl received a telephone call from the police station to say that the previous night's intruder had been a man called Rufus Mackenzie. He was well known to the police, being regularly picked up for drunkenness and causing an affray. After breakfast Meryl decided to go along to the police station and see Rufus Mackenzie for herself.

It was difficult to imagine that the scruffy drunk half propped up on a bunk in the cell had once been a brilliant research engineer. The sergeant pulled at Rufus' shoulder. 'Come on, on your feet.'

At first, Rufus refused to speak to anyone until the sergeant threatened him with permanent detention in an alcoholics' clinic. He peered at Meryl. 'Who are you?'

'I am Meryl Stewart Beaumont.'

Rufus wiped his nose on the cuff of his sleeve.

'I'm Charles Beaumont's daughter.'

He didn't reply.

Meryl sighed inwardly. She ought to be feeling very angry, but she couldn't. He was a complete physical wreck. Something in his life must have happened to reduce him to this state.

'What were you trying to do?'

Rufus looked at her out of the corner of his eye. 'Wanted to see Beaumont.'

'My father is dead, Mr Mackenzie.'

He stared up at her, his eyes wavering, as if struggling to focus on her face.

'I said my father is dead.'

Rufus pretended to shut his eyes and peered at Meryl through his eyelashes. She wasn't as angry as she was pretending to be.

'Sorry, Miss, I didn't know. Didn't mean to upset you, Miss.'

'What did you want?'

Rufus remained silent. Meryl gave a sigh of exasperation. The sergeant touched her arm. 'You're not going to get much out of him, Miss Beaumont. He's not properly sobered up yet.'

'I didn't do it.' Rufus struggled to get to his feet.

The sergeant pushed him down on the bunk again. 'Save your explanations for the judge.'

Rufus flailed his arms in the air as he fell back on the bunk. Meryl intervened. 'Mr Mackenzie, listen to me. If you will tell me what you were doing last night causing a disturbance at my home, if you tell me the absolute truth, I won't press charges.'

The sergeant stared at Meryl in disbelief. 'Miss Beaumont!'

She raised her hand. 'Please. Let me deal with this.' She turned to Rufus and used her most authoritative voice. 'What were you doing?'

Rufus jumped. He narrowed his eyes and looked at her. She was no pushover. He licked his lips. 'Came to collect a debt. Your father owes me.'

Rufus staggered slightly as the cold morning air hit him. Meryl grasped his arm and walked him down the steps of the police station. 'I don't know why I'm doing this, except that I feel more pity than anger for you.' She glanced up and down the street and noticed a coffee bar on the corner. She tugged at his arm. 'Come on, let's get some hot coffee inside you.'

Rufus followed her without protest, like a subdued child. Meryl waited until he had downed a bowl of soup and two thick slices of bread, and was enjoying a cup of coffee and a cigarette from the pack she had bought him. 'Now, Mr Mackenzie, I want an explanation.'

'Rufus. Everyone calls me Rufus.'

'O.K. Shoot, Rufus.'

He pushed his coffee cup to one side. 'You're very like your father.'

'So everyone keeps telling me. Get on with it.'

He hunched his shoulders and rested his elbows on the table. 'I wasn't always like this, you know.'

Meryl nodded.

'I worked my ass off for that father of yours, back in the sixties when you were a kid.' He stabbed a finger at his chest. 'They were my ideas that put Tundra on the map, not his. You won't remember, you were too young, but back in the seventies when the Arabs started playing games, everybody was falling over themselves to find other supplies of oil.'

He stubbed out his cigarette and immediately lit up another one. 'It was my invention, you know.'

'What invention?'

'My invention to improve the design of decanter centrifuges.'

'I know. We still hold the patent specification for it. But what's the problem? You were paid for it.'

'I didn't get a cent for the other one. I improved the process. Did all the tests. Improved extraction by 50%. I handed the idea over to Tundra.' He looked up at her. 'Whatever anyone says about me, I was loyal to your father. I could have made millions out of the idea, if I'd wanted, but I gave the patent rights to Tundra, to your father.'

'And?'

'Nothing. Bloody nothing. Said now that the oil price had dropped, the process was too expensive to operate. He cheated me. Your father made the one single brilliant thing I had done in my life worthless. Completely worthless. I couldn't even sell it to another company, as he had the rights to patent it.'

'Would you like some more coffee?'

'Could do with a drink.'

'Don't you even *think* of taking more alcohol. Look at your hands. They're shaking.'

He shrugged. 'Have to be coffee then, won't it?'

Meryl turned round in her chair and signalled to the waitress to bring more coffee. Gerry Schmidt was right. Rufus was in no fit state to be re-employed. She turned back again and watched him, rubbing at the ashtray with the butt of a cigarette. She felt guilty. Whether he gave the rights to the second, improved specification to Tundra or not, the company owed him something, if only on purely moral grounds. She picked up her coffee cup. 'And what brought you to this state? Don't tell me my father is responsible for that as well.'

'He fired me. Couldn't get another job. Then the drink took a hold of me. Wife left me. Wouldn't even let me see my daughter.'

Meryl raised an eyebrow. She wasn't in the least surprised to learn that. 'So, you expect compensation, Rufus?'

He didn't answer.

'O.K., Rufus. Tundra has a reputation for looking after its workers, and although I know you have brought a lot of your present condition on your own shoulders, I will see what can be done for you.'

He raised his head. 'What do you mean?'

'I mean, we will probably try to arrange for a lump sum to be paid to you for your previous research work. Although, on second thoughts, perhaps a monthly pension might be more suitable, then we can't be held responsible for your drinking yourself to death.'

'When will I get it?'

He pulled out the lining of his jacket pocket. 'I'm skint. Miss Beaumont. Not a cent.'

'I believe you, but I bet the proprietor of the local liquor store is a wealthy man.' She pushed her chair back and stood up. 'Wait here a minute.' She went to the counter and asked if the manager would let her cash a cheque.

The manager came out from the back and spoke to Meryl himself. The name of Beaumont was good enough for him. He gave her fifty dollars from the cash register and a further fifty dollars from his back pocket. She went back to where Rufus sat hunched over his cup of coffee. 'Here's some money to tide you over, but don't spend it all on drink.'

Rufus picked up the wad of notes and flicked through them with his thumb then hastily stuffed them in the inside pocket of his jacket.

'I meant what I said, Rufus. No drinking. It's about time you got your act together. I'm not surprised your wife left you. You are a disgrace. When was the last time you had a bath?'

He folded his arms tightly across his chest, as if guarding the money safely stashed away in his pocket.

'Come to the office tomorrow morning and I will get someone to sort out some kind of pension for you.' She picked up her bag and slung it over her shoulder. 'Bring your birth certificate with you, as well. I don't know how long we keep records of ex-employees.'

He nodded.

'Don't forget. Tundra first thing tomorrow morning. Bring your birth certificate. And don't drink. Right?'

'Right.'

Rufus waited until Meryl had left then cast a furtive eye around the coffee bar. Assured that no one was watching, he pulled the money out of his pocket and counted it again.

Bella Mackenzie put the saucepan to drain on the rack and quickly dried her hands at the sound of the telephone ringing. When she realized the caller was Rufus she went to slam the telephone down.

'Bella, Bella, I've got money for you. Don't hang up.'

She pushed a lock of hair behind her ear. 'I told you never to call me.'

'Listen, I've got money for you. It's not much, but there's

more where that came from. Tundra are going to give me a lump sum and a pension.'

A look of disbelief flashed across Bella's face. 'Why should they do that?'

'For my research for them. I'm going to be paid properly.'

'Who told you that?'

'Miss Beaumont.'

'Oh yeah, saw her picture in the paper a couple of days ago. What's she bothering with you for?'

Rufus chewed at his lip. 'Er, I saw her at the refinery. She knew all about my work for Tundra. Told her I'd been very ill. She said I should have a proper pension.'

'Are you drunk, Rufus?'

'Not touched a drop, Bella, I swear it.'

'I suppose you didn't tell her *why* you had been ill.'

'Listen, Bella, I'm going to send you some money. It's not much, but I want to see you and Liz right. When I get my pension through, I'll send you half each month. I promise. Bella, do you know where my birth certificate is? I've got to take it up to the office first thing tomorrow morning.'

'What have you got to do that for?'

'Don't know. Miss Beaumont said something about their records. Do you know where it is?'

Bella thought for a moment. 'We used to keep important papers in the deed box in the bank. I suppose it could be there.'

'Oh, Bella, you're always so efficient. Thanks.'

'Rufus, listen. Don't go touching anything in the box that doesn't belong to you. I've got insurance policies in that box. So don't touch anything that isn't yours.'

'I won't, Bella, I won't.'

Rufus put the telephone down and wiped his mouth with the back of his hand.

The assistant manager of the bank looked suspiciously at Rufus, but didn't say anything. He led Rufus to a small ante room and told him to wait. Someone would bring the deed box presently. Rufus sat down on a chair and stared about him. He had had to call Bella back and ask what the name of the bank was, it was so long since he'd used it. He rubbed his hands together. He was going to stay off the drink for good this time. Get his act together. He stood up as the door opened and a young man entered and placed the deed box on the table, then left without speaking one word.

Rufus turned the key, unlocked the cheap metal box and rummaged through the bundle of papers. He plucked out an illuminated certificate. A tear came to his eye. Those were the days when a degree in engineering meant something. You were somebody. He pushed it back in the box and searched for his birth certificate. He gave a gasp of astonishment when he saw the photocopy patent specification. He dragged it out and flicked through it. Oh, my God. He laughed out loud. This was it. He stared at it dumbfounded. He, or Bella most likely, must have got a copy of it and put it into the deed box for safekeeping. This was the missing specification. He shut his eyes. God bless you, Bella. I'll see you right, I truly will. Rufus carefully folded the specification and put it into his pocket, then shut the lid of the box and locked it. Fuck the birth certificate. He was going to make his fortune. Tundra knew what they could do with their pension.

David greeted Meryl's arrival at the office with relief more than enthusiasm. Her return increased the risk of the missing specification being discovered before he could get his hands on it.

'Meryl, I'm glad to have you back. We are climbing up the walls at the moment. What's all this about a Japanese white knight? There are rumours flying around all over the place.'

'So I understand, but don't ask me.'

'Beats me how these rumours start in the first place.'

'Wall Street couldn't survive without them.'

'Discus' share price has dropped again.'

'Good. That gives Christopher Mallory something to

think about and gives us a little more breathing space. At least for the time being.'

David crossed to the desk and picked up a folder. 'Here are some preliminary figures for the recapitalization of the company, Meryl. It will, of course, create serious indebtedness, but that is something we will just have to live with for the moment.'

Meryl took the folder and slipped it into her briefcase. 'Good work, David. I'll take these away and go through them properly.'

'When do you want to discuss things?'

'I suppose as soon as I can. We haven't got much time, have we? The new offer expires in a few days.'

He checked his watch. 'I've got a couple of meetings to attend this afternoon. Look, why don't we have a working dinner together? Away from the office, we'll be able to get through much more.'

She looked at him in surprise. 'Why not? Come and have dinner with me at home, then we won't be disturbed. Sevenish, O.K.?'

'Fine. Look forward to it.'

'By the way, talking of home reminds me. I had a visit in the early hours of this morning from one of our erstwhile employees, by the name of Rufus Mackenzie.'

David swallowed. His mouth had suddenly gone very dry. 'Rufus Mackenzie?'

'Mmm. Drunk as a lord. Shouting and falling about all over the place. We got the police to cart him away.'

David pushed his hands into his pockets and clenched his fists. 'What did he want?'

'I didn't find out until this morning. The police telephoned to say who he was and I thought I should go to the police station and see what it was all about. I don't take kindly to ex-employees waking me up in the middle of the night with their grievances. Apparently he feels my father cheated him. He was going on about the patent we hold for one of his designs.'

David stared at her. He felt as if he had suddenly been turned into stone. 'What did he say?'

'Nothing that made very much sense. I suppose I should have been very angry, but I felt rather sorry for him, actually. Anyway, I said we would try and do something to help him out of his difficulties. Perhaps a monthly pension. He seemed happy at that. Actually, could you get someone to work something out for him, David? You and I have more important problems than Rufus Mackenzie to worry about.'

'Indeed. I'll put someone on it right away. I'm sorry you have been troubled.'

'Not to worry.' She picked up her briefcase. 'Right, David, see you sevenish.'

'Yes.' He stood where he was until she left the office then went to the drinks cabinet and poured himself a stiff drink. The stupid bastard. What in God's name did he think he was doing?

Mrs Mayes cocked her ear. She thought she heard someone on the landing. She went and opened the door and spotted Rufus leaning against the wall. She stared suspiciously at the parcels clasped to his chest. 'What've you been up to then?'

'Mind your own business, you old cow.'

'Hey, mind who you're talking to. Remember who looks after you.'

'All right, all right.' Rufus fumbled in his trouser pocket and pulled out a couple of dollars. 'Here, have this. Buy yourself something.'

'You've not been stealing have you?'

'No.'

'You've been up to something. What is it?'

He leaned forward and spoke in a whisper. 'I'm coming into money.'

She hooted with laughter.

'It's true I tell you.' He pushed the money into her hand. 'And there's more where that came from. My ship's coming home. My ship is definitely coming home.'

Mrs Mayes folded the dollar bills and slipped them into the pocket of her skirt. 'Er – Rufus, I was just going to put some soup on to heat. Would you like some?' She held the door open wider. 'There's enough for two. Bit of bread and cheese after, if you fancy it.'

He hitched the parcels higher up on his chest. 'Yeah, O.K. Give me a couple of minutes.'

Mrs Mayes stared in astonishment at Rufus when he reappeared at her door. He had shaved and put on a navy blue, but not matching, jacket and trousers and a pristine white shirt he had bought earlier from an Army and Navy surplus store.

'Come in, Rufus, come in.' She wrinkled her nose as he walked past her. He still smelt like a polecat.

He stood in the middle of the room as if awaiting inspection. 'I'm staying off the drink for good.'

'About time, Rufus. It will kill you eventually.'

'I'm going to get my act together.'

She shot him a sideways glance. Someone must have given him a good talking to.

The Osaka consortium were pleased at the news Teriyaki Iwano had brought them. He had assured them that, as the Americans would say, they had made Meryl Stewart Beaumont an offer she couldn't refuse.

Teriyaki smoothed the front of his tie. 'I think gentlemen, that C\$10 per share is about right for the shares in the new company to be formed by Tundra. However, news has leaked out, or it could be simply minds thinking alike, that Tundra has a so-called white knight. My latest information is that this has caused a drop in the price of Discus shares and a slight rise in Tundra's. If this state of affairs continues, it is possible that shares in the new company may require to be re-evaluated.' He smiled. 'I should imagine Miss Stewart Beaumont would agree with me.'

The men seated around the table broke out into laughter.

'I think perhaps we should consider the possibility of

having to agree a price for the new shares at say C$15.'

His words were met with complete silence. 'Negotiations can then, of course, be conducted within a framework of C$10 and C$15.' Teriyaki looked down at his tie again. 'Miss Stewart Beaumont would, I think, experience difficulty negotiating outside that framework.'

The men around the table nodded. Teriyaki lit up a cigarette and waited. There was just one outstanding matter to be discussed and agreed upon. The leading member of the consortium and close friend of Teriyaki, Tatsuo Furukawa, glanced across at Teriyaki.

'Tatsuo, perhaps we should now discuss the question of Miss Stewart Beaumont.'

Tatsuo looked relieved. The consortium, to a man, were as concerned about holding a meeting with a foreign businesswoman as they were about the negotiations themselves. There was the difficult question of etiquette to be considered.

They listened intently as Teriyaki explained that although he had only met her once, during a visit she made to Wajiki in Tokyo, he had been very favourably impressed. Haruki Kushida spoke very highly of her as an employee. Although Teriyaki was quick to point out circumstances had changed considerably; she was now a client. She spoke fluent Japanese and could be relied upon to understand the protocol of the negotiations. All in all, she was an extremely charming young lady with, he understood from Haruki Kushida, something of a passion for Japanese food.

Tatsuo glanced at his companions and they nodded. The protocol of the meeting was quickly agreed. The negotiations would take place at Wajiki's head office in Tokyo; a place that Miss Stewart Beaumont was familiar with and, as a mark of respect to a Western businesswoman, the language of the negotiations would be English. Teriyaki glanced at his watch. It was almost noon. Exactly time for lunch.

* * *

Rufus pulled the bottle of whisky out from under the bed. He looked at it for a moment then pushed it back under. He was going to keep his word. No more drink. He was going to get his act together. He got to his feet and decided to make some coffee. Perhaps it would take the craving for a drink away.

David rapped on Rufus' door. After a couple of seconds Rufus opened it.

'Oh, Mr Barclay, come in.'

David took in the new outfit and clean shirt, but didn't comment. Instead he went on to the attack. 'What you did last night was very stupid. Very stupid.'

'What do you mean, Mr Barclay?'

'Come on, I know all about it. Miss Beaumont told me. You must have been out of your mind to go round there and make a scene.'

'Must have had a drop too much, Mr Barclay.'

David leaned against the door and folded his arms. 'Why, Rufus? Why did you do it?'

'Forget now. Think I remembered where the specification was. Last time I saw it was in Beaumont's study. He put it away in his safe.'

David shook his head slowly. 'I get it. So you thought you would go round there, break into the house, force your way into the study and crack open the safe. Is that it?'

Rufus grinned. 'But I've got the specification.'

David stared at him. He slowly unfolded his arms. 'Have you been at the drink again?'

'No, sir. Not a drop.'

'Where is it?'

Rufus pulled the photocopy of the specification from his jacket pocket and handed it to David. His grin broadened as he watched David quickly flick through the pages.

David felt sick with relief. He carefully smoothed the curled corner of the first page. 'Where was it?'

'In a deed box Bella and I keep at the bank. Went to look for my birth certificate. Found it lying at the bottom.'

David looked at him quickly. 'What does Bella say about it?'

'Doesn't know. Going to keep it as a surprise. She wouldn't believe me even if I did tell her.'

'No, she wouldn't, would she.'

'She'll believe me soon enough.'

'Sure she will.' David slipped the specification into the pocket of his overcoat. 'I'll get this filed first thing tomorrow morning.'

'What then?'

David ran his hand down the back of his head. 'I think I know someone who would be very willing to pay you a lot of money to use your design. I think I know just the person.'

'Bella won't believe this when I tell her.'

'Don't jump the gun, Rufus. It will take a while to get a proper agreement. You want things done right this time, don't you?'

Rufus nodded.

'Well.' David rubbed his hands together. 'How about a little drink to celebrate your good fortune.'

'I'm off the drink, Mr Barclay. I'm getting my act together.'

David smiled. 'Sure you are, Rufus, but one drink won't hurt you. You deserve to celebrate. Come on, we'll just have one glass each.'

Rufus cast a glance in the direction of the whisky bottle under the bed. Just one drink to celebrate.

Gerry Schmidt was less than amused to get a call from Meryl just as he sat down to his evening meal. His wife rolled her eyes and put his dinner plate into the oven to keep warm. Gerry propped one elbow up on the kitchen wall. 'Yes, Miss Beaumont, the tests are completed and are satisfactory.' He glared at the wall. 'What do you mean is the application filed? Miss Beaumont, the preparation of a specification is not like writing a love letter. We have sent a draft to the patent agents and they are going through it.' He clamped his hand to the back of his neck. 'I should think a week, two weeks. Look, Miss Beaumont, there is no point in filing an inaccurate specification. It will simply be thrown out by the Patent Office. O.K., O.K., I'll chase the agents. You have to realize that this specification is not the only one they have to deal with, you know. Right, Miss Beaumont, I'll certainly tell them if they don't get it filed by the end of the week, it will be the last specification they ever handle for us. I will most certainly do that. Thank you, Miss Beaumont and goodnight to you.'

Gerry slammed the telephone down. Crossing to the refrigerator, he wrenched the door open, took out a bottle of beer and opened it. His wife looked at him as she removed his plate from the oven. 'Trouble?'

He took a swig of beer. 'Whatever gave you that idea?' He took the bottle to the table and sat down again.

'She's rather beautiful, isn't she? I saw a picture of her in a magazine.'

'Yes, and she is also a superbitch. And I do not want to discuss Miss Beaumont while I am eating my dinner. Please.'

During their working dinner, Meryl was exposed to the less formal side of David Barclay. The relaxed, sociable and very charming David. Discussion of Tundra's problems gave way to discovering links in their past that put them both on a slightly more intimate level. They had both attended Toronto University, but not at the same time. He was three years her junior.

'I think we should finish this, don't you?' David picked up the decanter and refilled their glasses. 'What made you decide to become a lawyer?'

'My father. I had a choice of two careers. To be a very successful lawyer, or to be a world famous brain surgeon.'

He laughed. 'Come on. Seriously, what made you decide?'

'I am being serious. I could either become a lawyer or a surgeon.

'Pops used to say, "Marylin, when was the last time you met an unemployed lawyer? When was the last time you saw a surgeon drawing security?" I never had an answer to that one. I chose law, mainly because I can't stand the sight of blood.'

He laughed again. 'I'm not sure I believe a word you are telling me.'

'It's absolutely true. You surely know what my father was like. My turn now. What made you chose business management and economics?'

David picked up his wine glass and took a mouthful to give himself time to think of an equally lighthearted explanation. 'We-ell, funnily enough I had vaguely thought of something like law, but when I visited the campus, you know the get-to-know-the-place day they have, I saw this ravishing blonde. She looked somehow lost and I went up to her.'

'Of course.'

He grinned. 'And, I discovered she was doing business management so I got myself listed on the course.'

'Now that story I can very well believe.'

He gave a semi-embarrassed grimace. 'I see people have been talking about me again.'

She chuckled in amusement.

'Have they?'

'Have they what?'

'Have they been talking about me at Tundra?'

Meryl looked at him quizzically. A note of seriousness had crept into his voice. 'No. I don't think they would dare. Everyone is terrified of you at Tundra.'

'Except you.'

Meryl smiled. 'Except me.'

They went back into the sitting room for coffee and some of Mrs Kemp's special rum-flavoured truffles. While Meryl busied herself pouring coffee, David glanced around the room. It had been a long time ago, but he still remembered. He had come to the house with some urgent papers for

Charles Beaumont and had been told to wait in the hall. Meryl had come into the room dressed in riding clothes. She had looked at him as if he was some strong-smelling substance adhering to the sole of her boot and demanded to know where her father was.

David felt a wave of anger sweep through his body at the remembered scene. He glanced downwards and noticed a strand of blonde hair on his sleeve. He plucked at it and dropped it to the floor. He had the specification. He would now have her.

An hour later, Marsh appeared to enquire if Meryl required anything further. He had been sent to the sitting room by Mrs Kemp. It was almost midnight and by Mrs Kemp's thinking it was time that Mr Barclay left. Meryl looked at David, 'Would you like a nightcap before you go?'

David hesitated for a moment. It was difficult to suggest something else that he would like in front of the butler. 'Actually, I suppose I'd better be going.'

Meryl smiled politely. Before David could say anything further Marsh went to the front door. 'I will fetch your coat for you, sir.'

David got up from the chair. Not tonight, but definitely some other night. And soon.

Meryl held out her hand. 'Goodnight, David.'

David deliberately turned his back on Marsh, who was standing ready to open the door. His lingering gaze quite openly displayed his sexual desire. Meryl was faintly relieved that Marsh was still dutifully in attendance. David ignored her outstretched hand and lightly kissed her cheek. Her eyes widened, but she quickly pulled herself together. 'See you tomorrow, David. Goodnight.' She nodded to Marsh and he opened the door. Meryl stood in the doorway and waited until David had reached his car. Before David left he gave a brief wave without actually turning round to do so.

* * *

David parked his car in a secluded cul-de-sac about half a mile away from the apartment block where Rufus lived. He got out and looked around him. No one was in sight. He walked back quickly to the road leading to the cul-de-sac and when he reached it took care to stay out of the light of the street lamps.

The sheet pinned across the window of Rufus' room as a makeshift curtain showed a sliver of light shining within. David looked up at the window then quickly ran to the fire escape. He flattened himself against the wall for a moment at the sound of footsteps in the alley, waited until it was quiet, then sped up the stairs. At Rufus' window he paused and looked back down the alley to make sure no one could see him. He could hear Mrs Mayes' television blaring away in the room below. Shading his eyes, he peered into the window.

Rufus sat slumped at the table, the empty whisky bottle at his side. David smiled to himself. He had known Rufus couldn't stop at just one drink. He rapped on the window. Rufus raised his head and looked around him. David risked standing in the full light and banged on the window. Rufus got to his feet and stumbled across the room: he raised the sheet to one side and looked out. It took him a few seconds to realise who it was standing outside the window. He bent down and raised the heavy old fashioned sash window a few inches.

'Mr Barclay? Is that you?'

David raised a finger to his lips. 'Keep quiet. Someone might see me.'

Rufus leaned against the window to stop himself swaying. 'What's wrong, Mr Barclay? What are you doing out there?'

'Listen to me, Rufus. When I got back to Tundra House the Japanese were already there.'

Rufus stared at him. 'Japanese? What Japanese?'

'I told you. The Japanese are taking over the company.'

Rufus rubbed his hand across his mouth. He didn't remember anything about the Japanese.

'They want the specification you found. They are going to steal it from you. For God's sake, listen to me, Rufus. That's why Miss Beaumont promised you a pension. It's a trick to get you to give up the specification. She's going to sell it to the Japanese. There is no pension. She's going to cheat you like her father cheated you.'

Rufus rubbed at his eyes. He didn't know anything about the Japanese except his uncle had been captured by them. When he was brought back home, he was put into a special hospital. He never uttered a word from that day until the day he died. They said what he had suffered had turned his mind. Rufus swayed slightly and clutched at the window frame to steady himself. Japanese. The Japanese were coming. He poked his head out of the window. 'What are we going to do, Mr Barclay?'

'We are going to get you to a safe place. You and the specification.'

Rufus rubbed at the side of his face. 'Where are we going?'

'My place. Now.' David raised the window higher. 'Come on, it's your only chance. You'll be safe at my place.' He grabbed at Rufus' arm and pulled him through the window.

'Hang on, hang on. Need my jacket.' Rufus looked over his shoulder trying to remember where he had left his jacket.

'You haven't got time. Come on.'

The older man allowed himself to be pulled through the window. He put one foot on the window still, but nearly toppled backwards. David grabbed both his shoulders and steadied him.

David pushed Rufus back into the shadow of the wall. 'Ssh. I thought I heard someone.' He waited for a couple of seconds then pushed Rufus in front of him. 'It's O.K. now. Go on.'

Rufus was confused by David turning him one way then another. His head began to spin. He reached out for the handrail to steady himself. David lunged at him and grabbed him by the collar of his shirt and the seat of his trousers. With one massive burst of strength he heaved Rufus over the side of the fire escape. Rufus uttered only a muffled cry as he fell fifty feet to the ground. David pressed himself back into the shadows straining to hear if a window was being opened, any sign of someone investigating the low thud Rufus' body made as it hit the ground. He let his breath out slowly in the continuing silence then ran as softly as a cat down the stairs. Rufus lay half on his side, his head angled oddly to his body. David stopped to check that he was dead before running off down the alley.

When David returned to his car, he was breathing heavily. He got inside and quickly started up the engine. When he reached the top of the cul-de-sac he glanced around, but the street was deserted. Turning left, he quickly accelerated away.

He was just disposing of trash, like he disposed of his step-father. Tony Barclay had been too easy. An asthmatic with a weak heart, just the sight of a cat would bring on an attack. He had died crawling on his hands and knees pleading for his inhaler. David glanced at the speedometer. He was driving too fast. He slowed down. Trash. He was just disposing of trash.

The gates of the cemetery were locked. David parked the car a few yards away from the gate. He leaned back in the seat and shut his eyes. Slowly his breathing quietened. 'I'll come and see you tomorrow, Momma. I'll bring you some of those pink carnations you like.'

His visits to his mother's grave were secret, not because he felt ashamed of her, but because they meant so much to him. Only his mother could stop the voices filling his head, driving him mad. Visiting her soothed his disturbed senses like nothing else could. As he grew up he had come to recognize the strange restlessness that preceded the voices in his head. Deprived by age of the soothing comfort of his mother's embrace, he had been driven to frequent and anonymous sexual solace. Now that had become too much of a risk. He opened his eyes and switched on the engine. 'I'll see you tomorrow, Momma. I promise.'

* * *

Mrs Kemp popped her head around the study door. 'Would you like some more coffee, Miss Beaumont, and Scott says the car is ready when you are?'

'Thank you and thank you.'

Mrs Kemp laughed. 'It's nice to hear you sounding so cheerful.' She came in, picked up the coffee tray and bustled out again.

Meryl tapped her pen on the file in front of her. There had been cheering news and not so cheering news. Graham Vose had called her up. His methods of communicating were almost as obscure as those of the Japanese. However, it was evident that following the rumour of a white knight coming to Tundra's rescue, together with the fluctuations in the share prices of both Tundra and Discus, Vose had rekindled his interest in Meryl's intentions. He had listened with a great deal of interest to the idea that Tundra should be split into separate groups: the division dealing with exploration and research to put its shares up for sale to the Osaka consortium at an agreed price, thereby raising sufficient cash to eliminate either the question of a rights issue, or recapitalization.

The other news Meryl received was less cheering. Haruki Kushida had telephoned with a proposition that the consortium would be prepared to negotiate buying shares in the new company at C$10. She had turned the suggestion down flat. Haruki was unperturbed and suggested that perhaps a meeting in Tokyo with the consortium might produce more favourable terms.

Meryl stretched her neck back and then forward. She had one card to play with the Osaka consortium. Patent rights to the new design for decanter centrifuges that would make extraction of oil from tar sands much more competitive. Patent rights which Tundra had not yet obtained officially. She drummed her fingers on the desk. Without some kind of patent protection, she was not in a position to give the consortium the kind of detailed information they would require about the design.

The telephone rang. She picked it up expecting Edwin Reece to be on the line. Much to her surprise she found herself being greeted by JJ.

'Meryl, good morning. I hope I'm not ringing at an inconvenient time?'

'No, no.' She waited for him to speak again.

'My secretary left a message on my desk for me. Haruki is out of the office at the moment and I understand you wanted either him or me to call you back.' He gave a small embarrassed laugh. 'I'm afraid I have to cope with a temporary secretary at the moment, so I don't know how accurate the message is.'

'Not entirely accurate, I'm afraid.'

'Oh dear.'

She waited for him to take the initiative, but he lapsed into silence. 'Actually, it was Haruki I wanted to speak to. I was simply returning his call.'

'Ah, I see.' JJ paused. 'I hope things are working out. Tundra's share price rose again in London this morning. That is good news, isn't it? Makes the Discus offer look a little less attractive. Well, Meryl, and how are you?'

Meryl pursed her lips. She thought the last time they had talked he had expressed a certain lack of interest in Tundra's affairs. 'I'm fine, JJ. How are you?'

'Well, as always. I noticed your daffodils in the window box are coming out. Quite spring-like weather here this morning in London.'

She suppressed a smile. If you can't think of anything else to talk about, you can always rely on the weather. 'Well, thanks for the weather report, JJ.'

He laughed. 'Look, I'd better go. I have a meeting shortly. When shall we be seeing you in England again?'

'I'm not sure. It is possible that we may be seeing me fairly soon.'

He laughed again. 'Well, I'll say bye-bye for now.'

Meryl put the telephone down and leaned back in her chair. And bye-bye to you too, as Gerry Schmidt would say.

She must be dreaming. She thought she had left England on the worst possible terms with JJ. Now he was ringing up as if there was absolutely nothing wrong. She twirled gently from side to side in her father's chair. JJ had sounded uncomfortable. She wasn't quite sure she believed the story about the secretary and the message. Turning to face the desk again, she checked her watch. Edwin, Edwin, will you please call me.

As if on cue, the telephone rang again. Meryl snatched it up. 'Ah, Edwin, I want you to do something for me. Gerry Schmidt has sent this new specification off to the patent agents and is talking about a week before it can be filed. I must have it filed right away. Gerry's a good man in his own field, but I need someone to get on top of this situation.'

'I'll try and find someone for you.'

'Edwin! I was talking about you. Take over from Gerry on this one, will you? Put a rocket up the patent agent's you-know-what if necessary, but that specification *must* be filed straight away. I have just been acquainted with the price the Osaka consortium are prepared to pay for shares in the new company. They are expecting us to sell for the price of a jellybean. I think we can get them to increase the offer, if I can show them evidence that we can, if necessary, produce synthetic crude as competitively as conventional crude at a certain level, but I can't risk divulging technical know-how which isn't patent protected. You understand me?'

'I understand you perfectly. Don't worry. I'll get on to it.'

'The other thing, Edwin: Haruki Kushida has dreamed up yet another harmonious suggestion.'

He laughed.

'Seriously. He suggests that I should meet the consortium in Tokyo. A personal meeting might produce some better results for us. Also Graham Vose has suddenly reappeared out of the woodwork, so I thought I would return to London, see Vose and discuss things, then travel on to Tokyo with Haruki. Now, can you put David on hold for me again?'

Edwin groaned.

'Don't panic. Graham Vose can demand to have personal discussions about the recapitalization plan. O.K.?'

'I'll do my best. I hope you realize, Meryl, that David is convinced I am plotting a conspiracy against him.'

She grinned. 'Well, you are, aren't you? Look, don't worry, he left here last night a very happy man. I approved the details of his recapitalization plans.'

'What was he doing at home with you?' Edwin spoke quite sharply.

'Having a working dinner.'

'I see.'

'Actually, it was quite enjoyable.'

'I must say, Meryl, I am rather surprised. I don't think your father would have approved, under the circumstances. Besides, don't you think it a little unwise to entertain David Barclay alone? People gossip, you know, Meryl.'

She raised her eyes to the ceiling. 'Edwin, it was a *working* dinner. We were not alone. Mrs Kemp and Marsh were there. And I know my father, he would have very much approved. I don't want there to be any risk of David leaking information to Christopher Mallory about the Osaka deal, until I am ready to make it public, until it is in Tundra's interests. If I have to have a working dinner with David to keep him happy, I shall do so. Edwin, I am a big girl now. I must be allowed to know what I am doing.'

'I know that, Meryl, and I respect how hard you are striving to save the company, but David does have a certain reputation with women.'

'Edwin, I had worked that out for myself, thank you.' She clamped a hand to her brow. 'Look, I know you care about what happens to me, and I do appreciate it, but there is really nothing to worry about. I have no intention of being seduced by David Barclay. Happy?'

'I know you think I am old-fashioned about these things, Meryl.'

'No, I don't. I never take your advice lightly, you know that.'

'Thank you.'

Meryl puffed her cheeks out. Edwin sounded slightly more mollified.

'I'll get on to this patent agent, then put David on hold for you.'

'Thanks, Edwin.'

The plain-clothes detective walked across the room and stood in front of the photograph of Franklin Reeve Beaumont. Tundra Corp was an institution in Edmonton. If it crashed, there would be serious unemployment and that meant more crime to deal with. He turned round as the door opened and stared at Meryl. She was more beautiful than the newspaper pictures had given her credit for.

'Good morning; it's Sergeant James isn't it?'

'Yes, Miss Beaumont.'

'How can I help you?' She gestured to him to sit down.

'I am investigating the death of a man called Rufus Mackenzie. He was a one-time employee of Tundra, I believe.'

Meryl stared at him. 'Rufus, dead? I only saw him the day before yesterday. What happened?'

'He was found lying at the bottom of the fire escape at the apartment block where he lived.' He flipped open his notebook. 'And the day before yesterday was the last time you saw him?'

'Yes. He had created a disturbance outside my home the previous evening. He was completely drunk. I went to see him at the police station the next morning.'

'Yes, we do have a note of that, Miss Beaumont.'

Sergeant James turned in his chair as the door opened and David walked in.

'Oh, David, this is Sergeant James. Rufus Mackenzie is dead. He was found lying at the bottom of the fire escape where he lived.'

'Really?' David looked at the sergeant with an expression of total surprise. 'My secretary said you wanted to see me. Is it something to do with this?'

'Yes, sir. It is. We understand from a Mrs Mayes who lived in a room below the deceased that you paid frequent visits to Mr Mackenzie.'

Meryl turned to stare at David. David ran his fingers through his hair. 'Before you go on, Sergeant James, there is something I have to explain. Not just to you, but also for Miss Beaumont's benefit. However, it is confidential, and I would be grateful if it could be treated as being off the record.'

Sergeant James didn't reply. David pushed his hands into his pockets. 'I visited Rufus Mackenzie every month to give him money on the instructions of Charles Beaumont. Although Charles had fired him and, I may say, for very good reason – Rufus almost killed one of the crackerjacks in a drunken brawl – he felt concerned when it was obvious that Rufus had fallen on hard times and was in fact a very sick man. He had before his alcoholism been a brilliant engineer. He had done valuable work for Tundra. Obviously, it was out of the question that Tundra should be seen to show favour to a man who had been fired. You would have a queue a mile along outside the refinery gates, so he asked me to get the money to Rufus every month to help him out. It was nothing to do with Tundra. It was straight out of Charles' own pocket. Cash. No questions asked. Not as far as Rufus was concerned.'

Sergeant James looked down at his hands. 'Yes. When was the last time you saw Mr Mackenzie?'

'Yesterday afternoon. Lateish. I didn't stay very long. He had been drinking. I usually stay for as little time as possible when he is in that condition. The slightest remark can set him off into a violent rage. I gave him his money and left.'

'I see.' Sergeant James wrote quickly in his notebook.

'Perhaps I should also explain, if Miss Beaumont has not mentioned it already, that she instructed me to arrange a proper pension from Tundra to be paid to Rufus, in recognition of his past services. I had wanted to make sure Rufus clearly understood that the payments from me would stop when his pension became available. I didn't have the chance. He was too befuddled by drink to understand anything.'

'Why didn't you acquaint Miss Beaumont with this arrangement of her father's?'

David shrugged his shoulders. 'Partly because it was a private matter between myself and Charles. It seemed unnecessary to burden Miss Beaumont with something that is really quite a trivial matter. Partly because we have been under considerable pressure here at Tundra during the last week. Quite frankly, Sergeant James, I considered the payments made to Rufus Mackenzie the least of our problems.'

Sergeant James nodded. 'Well, sir, I think that explains everything.' David looked down at the floor. There was something wrong. He had overlooked something. The glass. He had forgotten the glass. 'Oh, there is just one more thing. I don't know if it is important or not. I did have a drink with Rufus. You probably think it a stupid thing to do, but he insisted and – well – anything for a quiet life.'

Sergeant James nodded again. 'I understand, sir.' He glanced at Meryl. 'That will be all, Miss Beaumont. It is necessary that we check everything out under these circumstances.'

She smiled. 'Yes, of course. Tell me, what do you think happened to Rufus?'

'Hard to say.' He flipped his notebook shut and returned it to his pocket. 'Off the record, it looks like accidental death. He was still suffering from an attack of bronchitis. The night he was arrested and taken to the cells, he complained of breathing difficulties. We had to have him checked out by a doctor. On the night of his death, we estimate he must have drunk the equivalent of a bottle of whisky. He might have needed fresh air. The window of his room was still open when we examined it. Maybe he climbed out on to the fire escape. In his drunken state, perhaps he stumbled or lost his balance. We will probably never know exactly what caused his fall.'

David pushed his hands into his pockets. 'Perhaps I should have stayed with him longer and tried to persuade him to leave the bottle alone.'

Sergeant James shrugged. 'I don't think it would have done much good, sir. He would have died anyway given another month or so. Medical reports say he was suffering from chronic cirrhosis of the liver. It was just a question of time really.'

David nodded. 'As you say, just a question of time.'

Sergeant James went to the door. 'Miss Beaumont, Mr Barclay, I'll see myself out.'

David took in a deep breath. That had been too easy. Meryl waited until the Sergeant had shut the door behind him then turned to David. 'Why didn't you tell me about the payments?'

He sighed. 'I am sorry, Meryl. It wasn't deliberate. It just wasn't important. You said yourself we have other problems. We have a company to save. Rufus Mackenzie just wasn't important. Perhaps I was wrong in thinking that; if so, I am sorry.'

'I don't suppose it matters now, he is dead. Poor fellow.'

David looked at his watch. 'It's almost lunchtime. Would you like a drink? I could certainly do with one. I was beginning to think at one stage Sergeant James was going to arrest me on suspicion of murder or something.'

She laughed. 'You, of all people, under suspicion. Don't be silly, David. You know what the police are like. Some like doing their job more than others.'

'True.' He clapped his hands together. 'Right what can I get you?'

'A glass of sherry, please. By the way, David, getting back to business, I had a call from Graham Vose this morning. For some reason he has decided to crawl out of the woodwork.'

David laughed.

'He is insisting on personal discussions about our recapitalization plans. I should really go back to London for a couple of days. Will that be a problem?'

'Not at all. Good idea.' He smiled to himself as he turned his back and opened the drinks cabinet. It is an excellent idea, Meryl.

Meryl listened to her own voice informing her that neither she nor JJ Reynolds were able to take a call and instructing her to leave a message. She put the telephone down, but kept her fingers on the handset. It had just been a silly quarrel. JJ wouldn't have called her, if it had been anything more. She lifted the telephone again. She would patch things up with him when she returned to London. It was stupid to go on like this. She dialled the number once more and left a message saying she would be returning tomorrow morning.

An assistant gravedigger pushed a wheelbarrow along the path. He cast a casual glance at the man squatting down in front of the grave. The man's mouth moved as if he was talking to himself. The gravedigger walked on unsurprised. People did strange things in graveyards.

David leaned forward and adjusted the stem of a pink carnation. 'The police came round today asking about Rufus. You know, Momma, you couldn't convice them it wasn't an accident even if you tried. Just like it always was. They like to think they know everything, don't they, Momma? I've got the specification in a safe place and she's taking herself off to London again. Be patient for a little while longer, Momma.'

Meryl took a taxi to the flat she shared with JJ, but when she arrived the place was empty. She went to the answering machine and played it back. Several other messages had been left after hers. She called Wajiki International, but was told JJ was away in Glasgow. He was expected back next morning.

Meryl took her travel bag into the bedroom and dumped it on the floor. If she could sleep for a couple of hours it might clear her head. Even if the Discus deadline was looming ever closer, she couldn't cope with talking to either Vose or Haruki Kushida at the moment. It would have to wait until tomorrow morning. She drew the bedspread back then stopped as a whiff of stale, musky perfume wafted up. She tore at the sheets in anger. If you must sleep with someone in my bed, JJ, at least have the courtesy to change the bloody sheets. Five minutes later the bed had been stripped and remade, the sheets dumped on the bathroom floor. Meryl pressed her hands to her eyes. Her head was throbbing.

JJ shook Meryl's shoulder. 'Meryl, Meryl.'

She opened her eyes and looked up. For a moment she had believed herself to be back in Edmonton.

'Meryl, what are you doing here? I didn't expect you back so soon.' Now fully awake, she sat up and swung her legs off the bed.

'Obviously not.'

'What do you mean?'

She stood up. 'I think you have something to tell me, JJ.'

He gave a small laugh. 'I do?'

'You do.'

He stared at her in silence.

'I am going to take a shower and whilst I do, would you do something about the sheets in the bathroom.'

'Sheets?'

'Yes, JJ. The sheets.'

Meryl sat in a chair by the television. JJ stood looking out of the window. 'What do you want me to say, Meryl?'

She clasped her hands together tightly. 'I don't want you to say anything. I just want to know what is going on. We agreed that we would always be honest with each other.'

He continued staring out of the window, only turning his

head slightly when he eventually spoke. 'I would like to know what is going on, as well. Things have changed. *You* have changed, Meryl.'

'What do you mean?'

'Ever since you went to Canada, your father's business has become your sole, undivided interest. Your job here; our relationship, are no longer of any importance.'

'That is just not true.'

'It is, Meryl. Lie to me if you must, but don't lie to yourself.'

She jumped furiously up from the chair. 'Lying. I am lying! What the hell have you been doing?'

'I haven't lied, Meryl. I was going to tell you. It seemed better if I waited until I could see you again, to tell you.'

She dug her fingernails into the palms of her hands. 'Tell me what?'

'That, as you have guessed, yes, I have been sleeping with someone.'

She bit her lip.

'For God's sake, Meryl, what do you expect me to do? Wait around on the off chance that occasionally you might be able to spare me some time? Is that what you expect of me?' He turned back to the window again. 'I have never tried to hold you back in your ambitions, Meryl, and I don't intend to now. I accept, naturally with reluctance, that you now have an interest in which I cannot play a part.'

'It isn't true. Just because I have to manage my father's affairs, doesn't mean things have changed.'

JJ shook his head. 'But they have, Meryl. You are now a multi-millionairess. You don't call that change?'

'I am still the same person I was before.'

'You're not, Meryl, that's the point I'm trying to make. You are not the same person, you couldn't possibly be.' He turned away from the window again and faced her. 'I have been waiting for you to tell me, but it looks as if I am going to be left to say it. You talk about honesty between us,

Meryl; then admit the relationship is over. We have had very good times, but it is over.'

Tears sprang to Meryl's eyes. She swallowed. 'I just can't believe you are saying this.'

'Someone has to. Forget about me. I am no longer of any importance, of any use, to you.'

'You are.'

'I am not, Meryl. When was the last time you asked me for my opinion, my advice? All I ever hear about is Edwin Reece. "Edwin says that." "Edwin thinks I should do this." You don't need me any more.' He stared down at his shoes. 'Go back to Canada, Meryl. Where you belong. Run your company as it should be run. You are perfectly capable of it.'

She fought back the tears in her throat.

'I am not being unkind, Meryl, but I need a relationship with a woman who has more to offer me than the occasional long distance telephone call.'

'So that's it, is it? You get bored, so you sleep with someone else. Now it's all my fault. Well, let me tell you something, JJ. I may not have always been everything that you have expected me to be, but I have never cheated on you, I have never broken our agreement. We said – we agreed – if our feelings for each other changed, we would tell each other. Each of us would be the first to know. Whatever happened between us, we would always give each other that. We promised each other.' She swallowed back the tears that were threatening to choke her. 'And you call yourself a gentleman.'

'I don't. That is what other people call me.'

'Then they're wrong. You're just another goddam crummy bastard.'

JJ didn't see the bowl of flowers she flung at him. He just looked down at the broken vase on the floor. He didn't say anything, but quietly brushed the drops of water and petals from his jacket. Meryl covered her face with her hands. Tears fell hard. She heard him walk past her. The front door opened and closed.

*   *   *

When Meryl arrived at her mother's apartment it was shortly after midnight. She helped her mother make up the bed in the guest room and didn't confess the real reason why she had come until they were sitting in front of the electric fire in the sitting room, drinking cups of cocoa.

Mary glanced at her. 'What is the matter, darling?'

Still hurt and confused that JJ had wiped out their relationship as easily as wiping chalk from a blackboard, Meryl burst into a flood of tears. She fished out her handkerchief from her dressing gown and blew her nose. 'He just decided at some predetermined moment that everything had changed. *I* had changed. That's it. Finish.' She wiped the end of her nose. 'I don't even get to be consulted.'

Mary reached across and patted her shoulders. 'Darling, I wish I knew what to say. I am hopeless at giving advice about men. Are you in love with him?'

Meryl shook her head.

'Then you'll get over him.'

Meryl looked across at her mother. 'Were you always in love with Pops?'

'Despite everything. Silly, aren't I?'

'No, not silly.' Meryl pushed the handkerchief back into the pocket of her dressing gown. 'I'm the silly one. I don't even know why I'm crying.' She wrapped her arms around her knees and hugged them to her. 'I suppose because I was happy, I assumed he was happy.'

Mary picked up her mug of cocoa and held it in both hands. Charles had been like that: he had automatically assumed if he was happy, she would be too – something that couldn't have been further from the truth. She wiped a drip of cocoa from the side of the mug. 'Men stop wanting women when they change. I think it must frighten them.'

Meryl looked across at her mother in surprise. It was rare for her to be so profound.

'It's true, darling. The price women pay for security is never to be able to change.'

'Unless of course the man wants it.'

'Only unless.'

'Is that my trouble with JJ?'

Mary nodded and took a sip of cocoa. Meryl suddenly felt ravenously hungry. 'How about a toasted cheese sandwich?'

'Oh, not for me, darling. It would keep me awake all night.'

Meryl got to her feet. 'Mom, you go on off to bed. Don't stay up. I'm fine now.'

'Are you sure?'

'Sure, sure.' She planted a kiss on the side of her mother's cheek.

Meryl wiped a crumb of bread from the side of her mouth and took her plate and mug to the sink. She rinsed them under the tap and left them to drain. Returning to the sitting room, she turned off the light then curled up on the sofa with just the glow from the electric fire casting a comforting light. When she woke up it was daylight. She got up and switched the electric fire off and opened the curtains. She must make her mother accept some money from her. She must have run up an enormous electricity bill, leaving the fire on all night.

The drive back to London gave Meryl time to put her thoughts in some semblance of order. JJ had ended things. So be it. Although she ought to have seen it coming, she shouldn't have pretended nothing was wrong, shouldn't have ignored the emotional distance he had been carefully putting between them. By the time she reached the outskirts of London she had convinced herself that she was glad it was over. The last week or so JJ had made her feel like a little girl sensing adult disapproval, but not quite knowing what she had done that was so wrong.

Somehow she managed to get through the meeting with Haruki Kushida and the lunch with Graham Vose, although she thought at times the food would stick in her throat. Vose gave his backing to an agreement with the Osaka consortium, but wanted to see a figure of C$30 for the new shares.

Haruki welcomed the opportunity to travel with Meryl to Tokyo. It would give them time to hammer out her negotiating stance. She had been given the use of his office to make a call to Edwin asking for news about the specification. The information was encouraging. The specification and application for patents pending had been filed. Edwin knew someone in the Patent Office. They had been to law school together. The man had promised to see the application was processed without any delay. Edwin hoped to have the patents pending document in twenty-four hours. They would just make the Discus deadline, if the negotiations in Tokyo were finalised.

Meryl returned to the apartment, feeling more dead than alive. The basket of freesias left on the table in the sitting room almost undid Meryl's resolve. She picked up the envelope and opened it. 'Thank you for everything. I wish you well and I hope we can remain friends, JJ.' She crumpled the note up and dropped it in the waste basket along with the flowers.

Meryl briefly glanced around the room. There was nothing she wanted to take with her. Nothing at all. She went into the bedroom and packed up her remaining clothes. She left a note on the dressing table asking JJ to send them on to Canada when convenient.

While the taxi driver took her travel bag downstairs, Meryl took a last look around. There was everything she wanted to take with her. Love. Warmth. Understanding. She picked up her briefcase and checked the contents. Beaumonts don't cry. Even when they hurt themselves. She slung her bag over her shoulder. Pops said that when she fell off the pony he was trying to teach her to ride when she was five – and she wasn't going to start now.

PART 6

The mirror-glass windows of the buildings reflected images of each other, adding to the claustrophobic atmosphere of Tokyo. Meryl had visited Japan on two previous occasions, but was still struck with the sense of having been swept into an alien eco-system. The chauffeured car stopped outside the Imperial Hotel and Meryl and Haruki were welcomed as honoured guests. Haruki begged her permission to leave her at the hotel for a couple of hours and visit the office. Meryl acquiesced gratefully. As Haruki had intended, it gave her some time to wind down and collect her thoughts for the task ahead.

A maid in her suite politely suggested a soak in a hot tub and a massage. Both were very good for the jet-lagged body. The hot tub turned out to be the size of a swimming pool, filled with steaming hot water and exclusively for Meryl's use for as long as she wished. The guardian of the hot tub looked a little disappointed when Meryl explained about her delicate skin and requested a cooler tub, but she smiled and bowed and took her into another room. This room had a spa tub and Meryl slid into it, allowing herself to be buffeted by the strong currents of water swirling around her.

The masseuse helped Meryl to remove her bathrobe, at the same time managing to pass her a towel with which to cover herself. Meryl got on to the table and lay on her stomach. She smelt something fragrant being wafted in the air, and shouted when thumbs were pressed hard just below her neck. The masseuse agreed that was where the tension was. In the neck and shoulders.

Meryl arrived at Wajiki of Japan feeling in much better shape. There was something to be said for a hot tub and a massage after a long flight. Haruki stepped to one side to allow her go ahead of him into the reception hall. Computers controlled and monitored everything in the building from the air conditioning to the whereabouts of each individual employee. Meryl was handed a 'smart' card by a smiling receptionist who requested her to insert it into the terminal, and who took great pains to point out that Meryl must keep it on her person at all times. The size of an ordinary credit card, it contained information about Meryl and gave her access to each department she wished to visit. It could even pay for her lunch, or purchases at the courtesy shop. Each time it was used computers recorded her exact position in the building. Haruki Kushida told her it was an inbuilt safety system. In case of fire or an earthquake all of the staff in the building could be quickly located and accounted for. A comforting thought, but Meryl could not quite shake off the Big Brother feeling. A light flashed on the monitor and, as she keyed in a code, a map rather like a street map was displayed on the screen. Her destination was the conference room that had been specially set aside for the meeting between herself and the Osaka consortium.

The first meeting with the Osaka consortium, chaired by Haruki Kushida, progressed extremely well. Meryl quickly guessed that Tatsuo Furukawa was the leading voice of the consortium. She made a conscious effort to consider herself as part of a committee required to reach a consensus of opinion, rather than as an individual who had come to barter. Her confidence had increased when, during a coffee break, Haruki had quietly praised her controlled and skilful performance. The consortium were very impressed with her.

Meryl hurried back to the conference room in full knowledge that the second meeting was not going to be quite so easy. She was now beginning to worry seriously that she had not heard anything from Edwin about the patents pending application. She was going to need it very shortly, if she was going to be able to cope with some hard bargaining. It had been agreed that Tundra was to be divided up, the new company to be called Tundra Enterprises. The sticking point was the price to be set on the shares in the new company. Meryl had suggested C$30. The consortium was now suggesting C$12. It was an improvement, but she only had Vose's agreement to go down to C$25 if she had to, but no further.

Haruki rose to his feet when Meryl entered the conference room. She glanced around, relieved to see that the others hadn't returned yet.

'Meryl, I think we should use this quiet moment to find a solution to the impasse.'

'Yes, I agree.' Meryl took a deep breath. She had already decided to play her last card with or without confirmation that Tundra had been granted a patents pending. 'But first I would like to seek your advice.'

'Of course.'

'Tundra, as you know, holds a patent specification for the treatment of oil extracted from tar sands. We have looked very closely at the whole operation, particularly with regard to decanter centrifuges, and we are in the process of filing a second patent on a significant improvement to the process. It is estimated that this advanced process will increase the extraction rate of synthetic crude by 75%. This means, of course, that given a certain level, it makes the extraction of synthetic crude competitive with conventional crude. My problem is that although a patents pending application has been entered, the formal documents have not yet come through and, technically speaking, we have no cover and therefore are not in a position to allow sight of the specification.'

Haruki frowned slightly. 'I wish you had told me this earlier.'

'My colleague in Canada promised to let me know as soon as the papers had gone through. I had hoped to have heard something this morning and obviously if I had, there wouldn't now be this problem. I appreciate the consortium cannot consider a share price of C$30 without this information, but –'

Haruki nodded. 'I understand your position. Shall we agree to mention this to the consortium? It will give them an opportunity to reconsider their position and hopefully you will have good news from Canada.'

Before Meryl could reply a young man knocked on the door and entered.

'Excuse me for the interruption, but there is a telephone call for Miss Stewart Beaumont from Edmonton Canada. A Mr Edwin Reece.'

Meryl puffed her cheeks out in relief. 'Haruki, I think this might be what I was waiting for.'

'Let us hope so. Perhaps you would care to take the call on the telephone over there.'

Edwin Reece, never a man to rush things, enquired after Meryl's health, but she interrupted him impatiently. 'Edwin, are the papers through?'

'Yes, yes. No problem.'

'Can you fax them to me here at Wajiki immediately? It is extremely important.'

'Will do. By the way David Barclay is breathing smoke through his nostrils. Wants to know what the blankety blank is going on?'

Meryl grimaced. 'Keep him on the back burner for me, Edwin.'

'That isn't going to be easy. He's chewing over his conspiracy theory again. He says he tried to reach you in London, but was told you had gone away. I think you should speak to him.'

She groaned. 'Edwin, I am in the middle of some tough negotiating. I simply can't talk to him. Stall him for a little while longer. Lock him up in the men's washroom if you have to.'

'Very well.'

'And, Edwin, don't forget to fax those papers immediately.'

'I won't, Meryl. Bye bye.'

'Bye.' Meryl put the telephone down and stood in silence for a moment, waiting for the ripples of relief in her stomach to settle.

The second meeting with the consortium was adjourned after ten minutes when a facsimile copy of the specification arrived. It was agreed that the meeting should be reconvened the next morning. The consortium required time to have the specification examined by experts. Meryl anticipating, correctly, that Haruki would welcome the opportunity to bring himself up to date with his own affairs, announced that she was taking herself on a shopping and sightseeing trip. Haruki's relief was carefully concealed, but he insisted in that case they should dine together that evening and promised a visit to a *ryotei* famed for its *sukiyaki*.

Edwin Reece sighed and looked at his watch. The rush to get the patents pending application granted had left his other work scarcely touched. He dragged the bundle of papers in front of him and untied the faded pink tape. Dixon & Dixon of London had not been as helpful, one lawyer to another, as he had expected. He withdrew a dogeared envelope and shook the stock certificates out, automatically checking to see that the envelope had emptied itself. At the bottom was a very crumpled piece of paper. He removed it and straightened it out. He gave a wry smile as he read the hand written note.

The writing was ragged as if written by an unsteady hand. 'I, Rufus William Mackenzie hereby transfer all rights of usage of the process described in this specification to Charles Beaumont his heirs and successors in consideration of the sum of $1,000 dollars. In receipt of this sum I hereby confirm that the contents of this specification are a true and accurate version of my further research work and results on decanter centrifuges. Dated this 19th day of May 1986.'

Edwin sat back in his chair. The schemes of mice and men. The specification had belonged to Tundra all along. Rufus had been paid for it, despite his claims. He got up from his desk, suddenly feeling very weary. He moved across and stared out of the window, although it was now dark and he could only see his own reflection. Secrets. Sometimes they were valueless in the light of the trouble they could cause. He pressed a forefinger and thumb either side of his nose and shut his eyes. God knows what the cost would be of keeping yet more things secret. David Barclay was an attractive man and Meryl was an attractive woman. They were also half-brother and half-sister. He walked back to his desk. Time would tell whether Charles' secret would have to be revealed to them both.

There was a palpable air of carefully suppressed excitement in the conference room at Wajiki. Expert opinion shared Tundra's assessment of the new specification. In the light of that the consortium were prepared to agree a share price of C$25 for Tundra Enterprises. Meryl knew the Japanese would expect her to give way a little in response, but she was content for the time being to play it tough. She informed the consortium that the new development would create international interest in the new company. That interest should be properly reflected in the share price.

The meeting took a short break for coffee. Meryl quietly sat to one side, having already decided that when the meeting recommenced she would offer to split the difference, but no more. She would accept a price of C$27.50. Occupied by her own thoughts she didn't notice that the consortium were taking longer than usual over their coffee. When they finally returned to the conference table they formally agreed a price of C$30. Meryl leaned back in her chair, not quite believing that she had pulled it off without having to make any serious concessions. It took a moment for her to react to everyone rising to their feet and offering to shake her hand.

There remained one further problem for the consortium to resolve. What form the celebrations should take, following the signing of the agreement. Ordinarily, they would have taken a private room in a restaurant then gone on to a nightclub in the Ginza district, and happily whiled away the remainder of the night. Unfortunately, that would not be at all suitable for their female guest. When they consulted Haruki on this delicate matter, he resolved the problem instantly. A tea ceremony. He was quite certain Meryl would enjoy it. There then followed a lengthy discussion as to which teahouse she should be taken to. They finally agreed upon the Rikugien Garden. It was a pity that it was not the season of the plum and cherry blossoms, but it was the most attractive garden in Tokyo.

Meryl retired to a small office to make lengthy telephone calls to London and Edmonton. The consortium had agreed that the agreement reached with Tundra should be announced to the press without delay. She looked through the agreement between Tundra and the Osaka consortium for the last time before slipping it into her briefcase. With twenty-four hours to spare, she had won the fight to keep Tundra independent and out of the clutches of Discus Petroleum, though much of her success she owed to the negotiating skills of Haruki Kushida, who had carefully smoothed out each step of the way to agreement.

Meryl had taken the precaution of wearing a skirt with a very wide, full hem. She dropped down into a kneeling position with as much grace as she could manage and smoothed the sides of her skirt. The room in which the tea ceremony was to be conducted was stark by Western standards. Apart from a painted scroll on one of the walls there was just a simple flower arrangement in the formal *rikka* style: the three flowers carefully arranged in height to symbolize man, heaven and earth. She turned to Haruki Kushida, who sat on her left.

'What beautiful flowers. Their symmetry is quite perfect.'

He smiled with great pleasure. She then looked at the painted scroll then turned to Tatsuo Furukawa, sitting on her right. 'How beautiful that scroll is. It must have been painted by an artist truly in sympathy with his work.'

Tatsuo inclined his head, showing great pleasure in her remarks.

Meryl leaned back a little on her heels and wriggled one ankle to avoid the onset of cramp. Fortunately, on one of her previous visits she had been taken to a tea ceremony and was fairly confident she could get through this one without causing serious offence, or unintentionally insulting her hosts. Having paid lavish compliments about the beauty of the room, she could relax until the *manju* cakes were served. These too would require further compliments.

When the little cakes were served, Haruki went to great pains to show her how to use the little wooden stick to cut the cake up and to eat it.

The actual making of the tea itself seemed to take for ever, or so Meryl began to feel, as pins and needles slowly began to travel up her legs, however much she tried to discreetly wriggle her feet. The implements of tea-making were numerous. A small brazier, tea kettle, tea caddy, a jug for the hot water, bowls, a tea scoop, a whisk. Meryl smiled and nodded at each act performed by the tea master. He produced a small whisk and began swishing it back and forth until the liquid produced a fine froth.

As honoured guest, Meryl was served first. She accepted the bowl with her right hand and balanced it in the palm of her left; remembering to turn the decorated side outwards. She bowed to the tea master and then to Haruki and Tatsuo. 'Please excuse me for drinking this delicious tea before you.'

They bowed even lower in recognition of the honour she did them in speaking in Japanese. She took a sip of the rather bitter tasting mixture and smiled at everyone. She wiped the rim of the bowl then turned it around. 'How beautiful. This is the finest decoration I have ever seen.'

Once again her words produced more bows and more smiles. Meryl breathed a sigh of relief when attention was turned away from her and Haruki and Tatsuo were served with bowls of tea. She winced slightly as each of them slurped their appreciation of the excellence of the tea.

When Meryl thought both her legs were completely numb, the tea master signalled that the ceremony was over by removing the caddy and tiny scoop from in front of him and passing it to an assistant. She gritted her teeth: this was the most difficult part of all. Standing up. She rose to her feet then realised that gentle hands were supporting her elbows. Haruki and Tatsuo had risen to their feet seconds before she did and were at her side. It would have been unthinkable to have allowed their honoured guest to toppled forward when she stood up.

The business sections of national newspapers in Canada, the U.K., and the U.S.A. carried reports of the eleventh hour intervention by the Osaka consortium in the Tundra/Discus takeover battle. Some arrived at the same association of ideas and carried cartoons depicting a giant samurai clad in feudal armour glowering down at a quivering and much miniaturised Chris Mallory. The information given to the press was embroidered upon and the rumour that Tundra had developed a revolutionary process to extract non-conventional crude from tar sands, making it twenty per cent cheaper than conventional crude, quickly became accepted fact. On the London and Toronto Stock Exchanges, Tundra's share price rose dramatically, but investors jumping off the Tundra/Discus merry-go-round sent the Discus share price plummeting on the New York Stock Exchange.

Chris Mallory sat at his desk with a telephone clamped to either ear, shouting alternately into each. He slammed

one telephone down and snarled down the other. 'I repeat,
I have no knowledge of a counterbid for Discus Petroleum
by Tundra. If you repeat that rumour, I will sue you.' He
hung up abruptly, pushed his chair back and went to stand
at the window. He pushed his hands into his pockets. 'O.K.
Frank, release a statement that as of this moment in time
Discus Petroleum formally withdraws its offer for Tundra
Corp.'

'Wise decision, Chris. We couldn't afford getting
involved in a bruising fight with the Japanese.'

'Frank, please do not tell me things I already know.'
Chris ran his fingers through his hair. 'I must be going crazy
or something. I knew it. In the back of my mind, I knew it.
She was always too confident. Never once was Tundra
stampeded into making a mistake. She kept me hanging in
there until she was ready to move. Jesus, I really should
listen more often to myself.' He glanced round at Frank.
'Get that statement out right away. We've got to stop this
freefall we've got ourselves into. Hopefully, Discus and
Tundra will be stale news by lunchtime. We should get some
confidence back before the markets close.'

'No problem there, Chris. We have people lined up to
congratulate you on the wisdom of your decision. We've
got one of the stockholders ready to express his respect for
your judgement as president of Discus Petroleum.'

'Thanks a lot, Frank, that makes me feel very good.'
Chris picked up the telephone again and spoke to his secretary. 'Arrange for flowers and a magnum of champagne to
be sent to Miss Meryl Stewart Beaumont, will you?'

'Yes, Chris. Any message?'

'Sure there is. Send her my congratulations and tell her
I'll be back.'

Edwin sat opposite David's desk. He couldn't remember
the last time he had felt such a warm glow of pleasure.
David stood with his back to him, staring out of the window. Edwin had never liked him or his upstart ways and his

arrogance. His assumption that he could twist Charles around his little finger. That he owned Tundra even before Charles had been pronounced dead.

Edwin placed his hands together and rubbed them. If only Charles could see what his daughter had pulled off, almost single handed. If only he could witness the expression on David's face. Who knows? Perhaps he could.

David sat and stared fixedly at Edwin when he broke the news, not ungently, that Meryl had won the fight against Discus. David would, of course, understand only too well that the negotiations with the Japanese had to be kept so secret that he himself could not know about them. He wasn't to take it personally. Meryl had even had to keep it a secret from her live-in companion of long standing, in London. David made it plain that he couldn't care less about her lover and made it equally plain that he felt he had been treated very shabbily as president of the company, although he stopped short of resigning because of it.

David turned away from the window. 'If you will excuse me,' He strode out of the office. He went to the men's washroom and nodded briefly to a man already standing in front of one of the urinals. He fumbled at the zip of his trousers, his hands shaking with rage. She had cheated him. Like her father had cheated him. Like Rufus Mackenzie had cheated him. The bastard had already sold the specification to Beaumont. He hurriedly zipped up his trousers again.

Edwin Reece had taken great pleasure in informing him that Rufus had assigned the unfiled specification to Charles Beaumont and his heirs and successors. Therefore, it formed part of his estate and legally belonged to Meryl. David went to a basin and turned on the tap, splashing cold water on his face. He felt sick. He grabbed a handful of paper towels and rubbed at his face. He needed to think. He gripped the sodden towels in his hands. The voices were returning. He shut his eyes, willing them to go away.

* * *

David turned round sharply at the sudden sound then realised it was a couple of birds fighting in the bushes. He turned to face his mother's grave again. 'Don't worry, Momma. No one is going to cheat on us. No one, Momma, I promise.' A tear rolled down his cheek. 'Trust me. That's all I ever need you to do.' He pulled a handkerchief out of his pocket and blew his nose. He pushed the handkerchief back in his pocket and got to his feet. 'I love you. I always will.' He walked slowly along the path to the gates of the cemetery. If there was any justice, real justice, everything would be his. *Everything*.

Gerry Schmidt chewed at his cheroot. 'Jesus Christ, put your backs into it, will you. I want those core samples in the laboratory by tonight, not next week.' He turned on his heel and stomped back to the jeep, pulling his personal radio from his belt. 'Site 1 to Base. That you, Ronnie?'

'Yes, Mr Schmidt.'

'Stand by to receive the third section of core samples. How are things?'

'Looking pretty good. What's it like with you?'

'O.K. Ronnie, could you do me a favour?'

'Sure.'

'Call my wife, tell her I haven't a hope in hell of getting back from Athabasca by tonight. We should finish the test drilling by tomorrow morning. Tell her I'll be home in time for lunch.'

'O.K. Mr Schmidt.'

Gerry clipped his radio back on to the belt of his trousers. He walked back to the test site. 'I thought I told you guys to put your backs into it. Goddam, the place is going to be swarming with fucking Japanese before we know it. We are supposed to be good at our job. We are supposed to look efficient. *E-f-f-i-c-i-e-n-t*. Remember that word, or doesn't it form part of your vocabulary?'

* * *

As the limousine approached, the security officer at the gates of the refinery raised the barrier. When Meryl and David alighted from the car, they were greeted by the manager of the plant and taken into the administration block. They went through the ritual of donning overalls, hard hats and sturdy protective boots.

'Those boots comfortable, Miss Beaumont?'

'No, but I'll manage.' Meryl jammed her hat firmly down to her ears.

'Right. Ready to go.'

They walked slowly across the yard to the control room, at a pace that allowed Meryl to keep up. From there they would witness the No. 1 cat cracker going back on stream. Whilst carrying out repairs after the explosion, the cracker-jacks had also discovered hairline cracks, almost invisible to the human eye, in the feedstock pipes, in two of the nearby distillation chambers, necessitating a full videoscan of the complete system and its replacement.

The manager guided Meryl into position in front of the huge control panel. 'Would you like to press the button, Miss Beaumont.'

'Yes please.'

'It's that one there.'

'O.K. Now?'

'Whenever you like.'

Meryl pressed the red button in front of her and waited. Lights flashed on the control monitor and bounced of their own accord along a grid system of coloured lines. She turned to David. 'I don't know why pressing a little button gives one such a feeling of power, but it does.'

He laughed. 'You should try sitting in my chair sometime.'

She clapped her hands together. 'Well, is that it?'

'That's it.' David took her arm. 'Would you like some coffee to celebrate? Alcohol is out, I'm afraid.'

'Good idea.' Meryl turned to shake hands with the manager then followed David out of the control room.

When they returned to the administration block, Josie

had relayed a message from Tundra House for David. It was from Gerry Schmidt. His laboratory team had completed the first of the tests on the oil extracted from the Greywolf Field. After treatment in the newly built experimental decanter centrifuge, the end product was an oil of 40° API gravity. David slipped the note into his pocket. Nice timing, Josie. Just the lead in I need.

'You've got something else to celebrate, Meryl. Gerry Schmidt has finished the first tests. They've got oil samples of 40°.'

'Does that mean the proportion of light products will be higher?'

'It does indeed.'

'Well done, everyone. That will put a smile on the faces of our Japanese friends. I suppose we should start making arrangements to ferry them out to Athabasca. They seem very keen on a visit.'

David passed her a plastic beaker of coffee. 'Have you ever been out to Athabasca?'

'No, never.'

'Would you like me to fly you out there on Sunday? We could have a picnic by the lake.'

She stared at him in surprise. 'I didn't know you could fly a plane.'

'Sure. My one and only hobby. Can't afford any more. Keeping a plane is ruinously expensive.'

'You mean you've got your own plane? Wow.'

David raised a hand in protest. 'Don't get the wrong idea. It's not a jet-set carrier. Quite old actually, but a hell of a lot of fun.'

'Believe you.'

'Want to come then?'

'Love to.'

Mary Beaumont held on to Simon Fairfax's hand while she waited to be put through to Meryl. She squeezed it and smiled at him. 'Darling, hello? Is that you, Meryl?'

'Hi, mom.'

'Meryl, Simon and I had to ring although we are sure you are very busy. Congratulations, darling, on your success. I hope you have taught that horrid man Christopher Mallory a lesson.'

Meryl burst out laughing. 'I doubt that very much, Mom.'

Mary paused and looked at Simon. He nodded encouragingly. 'Meryl, darling, we've got some news of our own. Simon has asked me to marry him.'

Simon leaned down to speak into the handset. 'For the umpteenth time.'

Meryl laughed again. 'I heard that, Simon.'

Mary shooed Simon's head away. 'Listen, darling, I have accepted. What do you think?'

'I think, Mom, it is the most sensible thing you have done in a long, long time. It's wonderful news and I am very, very happy for you both.'

Mary put her hand over the mouthpiece. 'She says she is very happy for us.'

Simon took hold of her hand. 'Did you expect otherwise?'

'Mom, Mom. Are you still there?'

'Yes, darling, still here.'

'When's the wedding and what do you want the chief bridesmaid to wear?'

'Oh, Meryl, give us time to think. We haven't even set a date yet.'

'Make it soon. Mom, I'm sorry but I have to go now. I will call you back later. When I do, I want to know the date of the wedding. No excuses, I mean it.'

'All right, darling. Speak to you later.'

Mary put the telephone down and turned to Simon. 'She says we have to set the date of the wedding, before she calls back.'

Simon took her arm and led her to the sofa. 'Then let's do as we are told.'

The float-equipped light aircraft swung away from the line

of the Athabasca River. David took one hand off the controls and passed a pair of binoculars to Meryl. 'We're just approaching Wood Buffalo National Park to your left. I'll reduce height a little and if you look through these you may see some bison.'

Meryl took the binoculars and peered out of the side window at the thickly forested land below. After a couple of minutes she rested them in her lap. 'I can't see anything except trees.'

'They should be down there somewhere.'

She looked through the binoculars again. 'Why are we turning?'

'Making the approach to the lake.'

Meryl put the binoculars down again. 'Where are we going to have our picnic?'

David shrugged. 'Don't know. Somewhere.'

She gave a little laugh. 'You are the worst possible guide anyone could have.'

'And the worst possible thing a passenger can do is to annoy the pilot.'

'Sorry, sorry.'

As the plane landed on the water and skimmed to the north end of the lake, David eased the throttle and gently turned the plane towards the shoreline then switched off the engine. Meryl looked about her, savouring the sudden quiet. 'This is so attractive. Right away from the madding crowd.' She took a canister out of her bag and gave herself a final spray of mosquito repellant.

'Not too quiet for you?'

'No, it's lovely.' She unclipped her harness and opened the passenger door. She dropped one foot on the float, slipped, and landed with both feet in the water.

David climbed out and helped her on to the shore. 'If you had waited ten seconds I would have gallantly offered to carry you.'

Meryl looked down at her wet feet and grimaced. 'He tells me now.'

They chose a picnic spot not far away from the plane and unpacked their lunch of cold chicken and coleslaw. Meryl heard a bird cry. She shielded her eyes with her hand and looked up, not noticing that David had produced a previously opened bottle of wine. He shot her a quick glance, but she was still staring upwards. Swinging the bottle gently from side to side, he made sure that what remained undissolved of the barbiturate powder was well mixed into the wine. He removed the cork and poured out a glass.

'Look, David, up there. Is that a crane?'

David raised his head. 'Probably. Here, have some wine?'

She glanced down. 'Wine? This is a surprise.'

'Well, you said you had developed something of a taste for wine in England. Thought you might like to try this. It's French, a good Bordeaux.'

Meryl took the glass and sipped at the wine. It tasted rather bitter.

'Like it?'

She smiled politely. 'It's really very nice. Thank you. Aren't you going to have some?'

'The pilot isn't allowed to drink.'

'Just one glass?'

'Maybe later.'

A light wind ruffled the surface of the lake. Meryl shaded her eyes. 'Strange isn't it? Here we are sitting, and beneath us is an awful lot of oil.'

'No talking shop. It isn't allowed here.' David refilled her wine glass. 'What would you like to do after lunch?'

'What would you like to do?'

He thought for a moment. 'Take a stroll in the woods.'

Meryl burst out laughing. 'And provide a good meal for the mosquitoes. No thank you.' She stifled a sudden yawn. She felt strangely drowsy. David filled her glass again.

'David, stop. Are you trying to get me drunk?'

'Just relaxed. You are,' he flicked her chin, 'very desirable when you are relaxed.'

She glanced around her looking for something to distract

his attention. 'Oh, what's that over there?' She pointed to nothing a few feet behind him.

David turned round and Meryl quickly tipped most of the contents of the wine away. She didn't want to offend him, but the wine wasn't particularly nice. It left a nasty bitter taste at the back of her mouth. She couldn't stop herself from giving a loud yawn.

He turned back and laughed. 'You're just not used to the outdoor life.'

'I am.'

'Come on, when was the last time you breathed in air as fresh as this?'

She put her hand to her mouth and stifled another yawn. 'This is ridiculous. Sorry.'

He ruffled her hair. 'Take a siesta. I need to check the oil in the engine. I'll just be a few minutes.'

Meryl stretched out and propped herself up on one elbow. She watched David walk back to the plane until the urge to close her eyes became irresistible. When David returned, the barbiturate had fully taken effect and she was fast asleep. He quickly packed up the picnic and slung the bag over his shoulder, then scooped Meryl up in his arms and carried her to the plane. As the plane took off under full throttle he glanced across at her, but she gave no sign that the noise of the engine had penetrated her sleep.

Meryl dreamed that she was flying with David. Holding on tightly to his hand as they drifted over the trees. She could hear his voice calling to her not to be frightened. If she was frightened she would fall to the ground. Meryl's eyelids moved as she became conscious of her surroundings and realised she wasn't dreaming. She was somehow back in the plane with David. Still drowsy and confused, the sound of David talking slowly filtered through to her brain.

'Do you remember that day in the garden? Do you? The day you were playing with your new puppy? I do.'

Meryl's eyelids fluttered as she struggled to hear what David was saying.

That day had also been David's birthday. His mother had taken him to the Beaumont house and made him promise to be very quiet while she did her work. When she was finished they would go into town and she would buy him a birthday present. She made him stand outside the kitchen door to wait for her. He wasn't to move. He wasn't to wander about the gardens. He musn't disturb Miss Marylin. She was in one of her moods because her daddy had gone away. The slightest thing would set off one of her tantrums.

Meryl tried to swallow. Her tongue felt like a piece of felt. She tried to keep her mind on what David was saying. 'Oh yes, people like me weren't allowed to exist in your world, were we? Little Miss Marylin Importance in her big garden playing with her expensive pedigree puppy. No one must upset Miss Marylin Importance otherwise she would have a tantrum.'

She tried to open her eyes, but the effort was too great. Honey. Yes. She remembered now. That was the name of her puppy. Honey. A frown creased her brow. Why was he talking about Honey?

David continued talking out loud to himself. It had been a hot day. A very hot day. He had become bored standing outside the kitchen door and went to the fence and climbed up to see what was on the other side. He had seen his mother carefully carrying a tray into the garden. She put it down on a wrought iron table and called to Meryl to come and have a nicely iced orange drink. He called to his mother. He was thirsty too. She shouted to him to get down and go and wait by the door like a good boy. She would bring him out a glass of water.

Meryl moved her head slowly and managed to open her eyes briefly.

David was shouting. 'Nicely iced orange drinks were only made for Miss Marylin Importance, weren't they? I had to drink fucking water.'

She opened her eyes fully, moved her hands in her lap and realised she wasn't wearing a safety harness.

'Do you remember what you did?' His voice thickened with anger. 'Do you?'

Meryl tried to lift her head up, but it was weighed down by some invisible pressure. Although she could hear David's angry voice very clearly, her thoughts drifted and settled on snatches of conversation with Edwin Reece. She managed to look sideways at David. Edwin was right. She and David had met before. He was the boy with the spots on his face, clinging to the other side of the fence. A piece of fence snapped of and he disappeared with a scream. Miss Cane had rushed through the gate and begun shouting at him.

David turned his head and realised that Meryl was awake. 'You shouldn't have done that.'

Frightened by the expression of rage on his face she struggled to sit up. She swallowed and tried to speak.

He grabbed at her shoulder. 'You shouldn't have done that.'

'What have I done?' Her voice was thick and slurred.

'You know what you did. You know!' He shook her violently, forcing her head to roll from side to side.

Fear dispelled the foggy sleep from her mind. What had she done to make him so violent? She froze at the remembered image. She had followed Miss Cane to see what had happened. He was lying on the ground clutching at his ankle, crying loudly. She had laughed at him. Crybaby. Crybaby. She licked her lips. She had laughed at him.

David turned round in his seat and spoke in a flat monotone. 'The twenty-eight days are almost up. This is one deadline you are not going to keep.' He stretched across her and opened the passenger door. 'Must get these hinges replaced. This door swings open too easily. It's very dangerous.' He grabbed Meryl and pushed her hand towards the open door.

She tried to turn her head. 'What do you mean?'

'I mean that we have to say goodbye now.'

For a moment Meryl couldn't believe what he was doing

or saying. She looked down at the forest hundreds of feet below and screamed. His sheer physical strength propelled her further towards the open door.

'Goodbye, Miss Marylin Importance. You will not survive your father. And I will inherit everything you ever thought you owned.'

Meryl screamed again, but the rushing air snatched the breath from her lungs. She managed to hook her foot beneath the seat and half turn her body. Flinging her arms out she clawed desperately at his face, but was almost numbed by a stinging blow to the side of her head. Her fingertips found his mouth and she dug her nails into his lower lip. David gripped her wrist and twisted it until she thought it would break. With her free hand she tore at his face until he was forced to take his other hand off the controls.

The plane dropped its nose and began to lose height rapidly. David raised his fist to his shoulder then punched Meryl full in the face. Blood spurted from her nose. A second punch on her chin rendered her unconscious. David leaned over as far as he could and struggled to push her limp figure out of the door. He was flung back against his side of the plane as it started to go into a spin. He grabbed the controls and wrestled with them. Shouting as much to himself as to the plane, he managed to correct the spin and level the plane out. It was too late. The plane was already at tree-top height. One of the floats caught on a branch and was ripped away. Frantically David tried to steer the plane towards a small clearing. The last movement he made was to switch the engine off before the plane bounced sharply over the tree tops and crashed into the clearing.

When Meryl regained consciousness the sun was beginning to set. She tried to move then realised that she was on her side and almost upside down. She moved again, then screamed at the sudden pain shooting up her left arm. Freeing her right hand from underneath the tree branch that jutted through the window of the plane, she supported her broken arm. Slowly she managed to turn round and sit up. David was still strapped in his seat, his head lolling awkwardly to one side. She stared at him, not remembering for a moment what he had tried to do. Turning, she looked at the remaining fragments of what had once been the passenger door and shivered. He had tried to push her out. He had tried to kill her.

Meryl nursed her left arm close to her body and wriggled and pushed her way out of the doorway. She tumbled to the ground and lay there for several moments. The pain in her arm made her feel sick. She raised her head and looked upwards at the sky, not knowing where they had landed, only knowing that it was remote and she would never be found. She raised herself to her knees. Blood trickled down the side of her face. Meryl got to her feet and leaned against the side of the plane, looking back inside the cabin. David was still unconscious. She shivered. It might not be for long. She shut her eyes. There was no point in crying for help. No one would hear her. She opened her eyes.

ELT. When the helicopter pilot had flown her from Tundra House to the hotel, she had asked about all the controls. One had been an emergency location transmitter. All aircraft had to have one by law. Ordinary aircraft had the ELT fitted in the tail of the plane. It was triggered off automatically if there was a crash. People often thought it safer to go and find help, but the best chance of survival was to stay with the aircraft until its position was located by the rescue people.

Meryl looked again at David. His eyes were still shut. She hauled herself back inside the plane, pulling the scarf from around her neck. She struggled to bind his hands together, tugging at one end of the scarf with her teeth and using her good arm to pull the other end through and tighten the knot. She looked around her. There was nothing more she could do, except find a safe place. She couldn't stay in the aircraft with him. She crawled out of the plane and stumbled off.

About half a mile away she found a small grassy hollow protected by a large stone on one side. She sat down to catch her breath. The pain in her arm was growing worse with every move she made. Meryl got to her knees and peered over the top of the stone. She couldn't go on any further. She had to stay here. She sat back again and rested against the stone. If David woke up and came to find her, perhaps he wouldn't see her. She closed her eyes. She should have looked for a torch. There was bound to have been one in the plane. He would be able to find her with the light of a torch.

Meryl opened her eyes. It was dark. She struggled up into a sitting position, almost crying out as pain surged through her arm. She peered over the top of the stone. There were no lights. No sounds. She leaned back against the stone again. A sudden snuffling sound made her freeze in terror. Bears. She had only seen bears in pictures or on television. She swallowed. Don't move. Bears can't see very well. She strained her ears. The snuffling sounded closer. She swallowed again. She should have tried to climb up a tree. Grizzly bears couldn't climb trees, or was it brown bears? Oh God, please don't let it be either. She sat hardly daring to breathe. What felt like minutes went by, but there was nothing but silence. No movement. Slowly she relaxed her body against the stone.

Sometime during the night she woke up with a cry. A howling had woken her up. She stared around her in terror. Wolves. It must be wolves. She listened carefully, but there was only silence once more. She told herself off for being so stupid. Wolves only howled if there were other wolves to call to. She must have imagined the noise. Meryl shivered violently in the bitterly cold night air. She had to keep warm. She rubbed at her feet then at the hand of her injured arm, but the pain was too intense. She unbuttoned the front of her blouse and raised her injured arm and slipped her hand inside. The support gave some relief to the searing pain.

The next time Meryl woke up it was daylight and the

sound she heard was the sound of a helicopter up above. She scrambled to her feet and waved frantically. A loud-speaker told her to stay where she was. She would be rescued soon. She screamed at the top of her voice. 'He tried to kill me. He tried to kill me.' The helicopter banked steeply and flew on a few yards to a clearing in the forest. She stumbled after it.

An air rescue officer caught Meryl as she fell into his arms. He picked her up and took her to the helicopter.

'He tried to kill me. He tried to kill me.' She cried and cried, but no one seem to take much notice of what she was saying. She was lifted into the helicopter and someone began gently examining her broken arm.

'Just relax now. Everything's going to be all right. Just relax.'

Mrs Kemp bustled up to the bed. She patted Meryl's hand. 'Good girl, you've eaten your soup.'

Meryl didn't answer. Mrs Kemp glanced anxiously at the portable television at the foot of the bed. The poor girl did nothing else but stare at it. The only time Meryl spoke was when Mrs Kemp asked her if she would like it turned off. Mrs Kemp sighed to herself and removed the tray from Meryl's lap. 'Would you like me to sit with you for a little while?'

Meryl shook her head.

'I'll come back later on then.'

Meryl stared intently at the television screen as the early evening news commenced.

The anchorman led off with the current news of the day. The near fatal flying accident that had nearly cost the lives of the president of Tundra Corp, David Barclay and its major stockholder, Meryl Stewart Beaumont. Meryl leaned forward. No. No. It wasn't an accident. He tried to kill me. She sank back against the pillows and shut her eyes. The newscaster repeated what he had said on an earlier broad-cast. David Barclay had broken his spine in the accident. It was probable that he would be paralysed for the rest of his life. Meryl Stewart Beaumont had been more fortunate, escaping with a broken arm and severe cuts and bruises. Meryl moved her head from side to side on the pillow in anguish.

Edwin had listened patiently to her story, so patiently that she feared he didn't believe her. He had held her in his arms while he explained that the story could never be told. She was safe. They had that to be thankful for. But the story must never be told, it would do irreparable damage to Tundra. The publicity would never end either for herself or for the company. She had to be brave. Very brave.

Meryl had sobbed into his chest until there were no more tears to shed. Edwin promised to stay with her always. She was safe. David Barclay could do her no more harm. He would spend the rest of his life trapped, confined to a bed. He was completely paralysed from the neck down. That would be his terrible punishment. Edwin had stroked her hair until the dry, hoarse sobs subsided.

Edwin came out of the sitting room as Mrs Kemp came down the stairs. 'How is she, Mrs Kemp?'

'Just the same. She's had some soup. I suppose that's an encouraging sign.'

'Shall I go up and see her?'

'Yes, Mr Reece.'

Edwin carefully opened the bedroom door and walked quietly to Meryl's bed. 'Meryl, it's Edwin.' He sat down on the edge of the bed and took hold of her hand.

At first she gave no sign that he was there, but she slowly turned her head to look at him. 'It did happen, didn't it? What I said did happen, didn't it?'

He nodded. She looked at the television screen again. 'I can't keep it a secret on my own, Edwin.'

He raised a hand to her head and stroked her hair. 'I will help you.'

Mary and Simon walked hand in hand out of the church.

They stood for a moment on the steps, faces raised, as if admiring the bright sunshine. One of Simon's friends rushed forward to take a photograph.

'Kiss the bride, please.'

The handful of guests laughed at the clichéd instruction. Simon bent his head and kissed Mary.

'And again, please.'

Simon obliged enthusiastically until Mary raised a hand to his shoulder in gentle protest.

Meryl secretly removed a bag of rice from her bag and crept behind Mary and Simon while they were kissing. The guests began laughing again. Simon turned round just as Meryl raised her uninjured arm and flung a handful of rice straight into his face. He coughed and spluttered. The amateur photographer clicked his camera just in time to capture the scene.

The wedding reception was held in a hotel on the sea front in Bournemouth. After the cake was cut and the speeches made, everyone relaxed and got on with the serious business of enjoying themselves. Simon carefully circled the room until he reached Meryl's side. He put his arm around her shoulders. 'Feeling all right?'

'Yes, I'm fine, Simon, really.'

'I didn't have a chance to say this before, but thank you for coming. You have been through a terrible trauma, but thank you for coming. It means so much to Mary and me to have you here.'

She smiled. 'It means a lot to me too. Wild horses couldn't have kept me away.'

He looked down at the floor. 'I know you have to return to Canada for the memorial service. When do you have to leave?'

'Not for a few hours, yet. Besides, I'm not leaving until I have seen the bride and groom off on their honeymoon.'

He checked his watch. 'I think we should be making a move.' He glanced across the room and made an unsuccessful attempt to catch Mary's eye.

'I think you had better go and rescue her, Simon. Once Mrs Jollife starts talking . . .'

He lowered his voice. 'I know, I know.'

Meryl tugged at his sleeve. 'Simon, before you go, where are you taking Mom on honeymoon? I am dying to know.'

'Well, as we are leaving soon and if you promise not to breathe a word, I'll tell you.'

'Promise.'

'Bali.'

'Simon, how terribly romantic!'

He flushed slightly. 'Well, not so much romantic, but I think Mary will like it. Well, I'd better go and get her organised.'

Mary turned before stepping into the car and threw her bouquet of flowers into the air in Meryl's direction. Meryl stepped back slightly, leaving someone else to rush forward and catch it. She suppressed a smile. It was Mrs Jollife, Mary's next door neighbour.

There were cries of, 'You're next.'

Mrs Jollife blushed happily. She hoped it would be true. Meryl moved forward to give her mother a final embrace. 'Be happy, Mom.'

'I will, darling.'

Meryl turned to Simon. 'Simon.'

He gave her a hug and a kiss on the cheek. 'Thank you for everything.' He turned back to Mary and helped her into the car.

Meryl waved as the car moved off, laughing at the same time at her mother, trying to blow kisses through the window without knocking her hat off.

The memorial service for Charles Beaumont, delayed for two weeks following the plane crash, was attended by some-time friends, sometime enemies and the plainly curious. Television men including crews from Japan and the U.K. were jammed together outside the church. They surged forward as a limousine pulled up and Christopher Mallory stepped out. He walked slowly up the path, ignoring the cameras. One hardbitten reporter joined him at his side. 'Have you any comment to make on the failure of Discus Petroleum to gain control of Tundra Corp?'

'Excuse me, I am here on a strictly private and personal visit to honour a truly great man.'

One of the ushers hurried forward and quietly escorted the reporter back to his place.

Ten minutes later a second limousine drew up, and this time the patience of the camera crews was rewarded. Meryl got out and walked up the path with Edwin Reece at her side. Zoom lenses searched her face seeking out signs of bruises under the thick make-up and dark glasses. They lingered over the not quite healed cut on the side of her lower lip then panned down to the arm still in plaster.

Meryl entered the church and stood for a moment. Every pew was packed. People were even standing at the back of the church. Edwin Reece touched her elbow. 'Are you all right?'

She nodded. As she walked down the aisle people turned to smile, offer their hands; some got to their feet. Near the front she noticed Haruki Kushida and the members of the Osaka consortium. On the opposite side sat JJ Reynolds. A man loomed in front of her and took both her hands. 'Miss Stewart Beaumont, I'm Chris Mallory. I hope my being here will not offend you, but I wanted to come to pay my respects to a truly great man. I admired your father very much.'

She looked up at him. The warmth of his gaze was genuine. He squeezed her fingers. 'I admire you, too.'

Chris Mallory was replaced by the figure of JJ Reynolds. He kissed Meryl's cheek and took hold of her arm and guided her to her seat. He sat her down and held on to her hand. 'My poor darling, I can't believe what has happened. I came as soon as I heard.'

Meryl removed her hand from his, irritated by the hushed tone of his voice, as if he was talking to an invalid. She glanced over her shoulder and saw Edwin trying to squeeze into the pew behind her.

'JJ, thank you for coming, but could you change places with Edwin Reece? I want him to sit next to me.'

JJ looked down at the hand she had rejected. 'Yes, of course.' He got up and switched places with Edwin.

David Barclay had been transferred to a longstay hospital. He lay motionless, but by rolling his eyes to the right as far as he could, he could just see the male nurse and the television monitor on the corner of the desk. They never left him alone. Sometimes he would cry out. The words would tumble from his mouth as confused as the images in his mind. Sometimes, he would drift off to sleep and wake in terror at the sight of Tony Barclay standing by his bed with a raised fist.

He swivelled his eyes and stared up at the ceiling, listening to footsteps approaching the bed. The short sleeve of his nightgown was pushed up. He felt the prick of a hypodermic needle as it entered his arm. Words of protest formed in his mind, but they weren't uttered. A tear formed and rolled down his cheek. I only ever did it for you, Momma. No one else, Momma.

Meryl stepped into the office and walked slowly to her father's chair. She swept from her mind the thought that it had also been the chair David had sat in. She pulled the chair away from the desk and sat down. She rested her hands on the desk and looked at the man in the photograph on the opposite wall. Franklin Reeve Beaumont had been a real man, like Pops had been.

Seeing JJ at the house after the memorial service had been like seeing him for the first time, but not quite. She had a new awareness of him. It had come to her in a flash. The difference between Christopher Mallory and JJ couldn't have been more apparent. Chris had been sympathetic, true. He talked, rather touchingly, about his elder brother who had been killed in an automobile accident over twenty years ago. He took hold of her elbow and told her that whatever people might say, time doesn't heal, but it does ease. She should thank God she was still alive and get right out there and show the world what she was made of.

JJ had tried to smother her with concern, subtly reinforcing her vulnerability, drawing her back to him. Cosseted. She needed to be cosseted. She had been through a terrible experience, but she wasn't alone. He was here. They would forget the past. He had talked to her as if some unspoken act of misbehaviour was known to him, but was being graciously overlooked. Meryl leaned back in her chair. There had been a time when she would have puzzled over it until she had worked out what it was that had displeased him. She hunched her shoulders. Pleasing JJ had been rewarded by affection in carefully measured doses. Never enough to satisfy. Just enough to prolong the addiction. Her father had been less sophisticated. He had given affection indiscriminately. In return he had expected, demanded, all of her love, refusing to share it with anyone, least of all her mother.

The telephone rang. She picked it up and took a call from Christopher Mallory.

'Meryl, I hope I am not calling at an inconvenient time, but I did want to talk to you.'

'No, it's not inconvenient.'

'Good. How are you?'

'O.K., and you?'

'Fine, just fine. I just wanted to say that I enjoyed the opportunity of meeting you last week. I took it as a great honour to be asked back to the house after the service. I wasn't exactly an invited guest.'

'As you had travelled from New York to be here, it was the least that I could do.'

'I appreciate it.' He paused for a moment. 'I wondered, Meryl, if perhaps we could have a meeting sometime. There are a couple of things I would like to discuss with you, over dinner say?'

'What things?'

'Well, I hope you will agree it is stupid for you and I to be at each other's throats, businesswise. I figured there are a couple of projects that we could get together on that would be to our mutual advantage.'

'Would you like to get straight to the point, Chris?'

He laughed. 'O.K. I hear on the grapevine that your process for extracting non-conventional crude is proving very successful. I wondered if you would consider the possibility of negotiating a licence to Discus to use it.'

'I would be prepared to consider it.'

'Good, I can come back to Edmonton at the end of the week. Would that be O.K. for you?'

'Yes, I think so.'

'Great, I'll be in touch. And, Meryl, I look forward very much to meeting you again. What little time we had for conversation last week, I enjoyed very much.'

'Thank you.'

'See you soon.'

Meryl put the telephone down and smiled to herself. Chris Mallory was working very hard on both fronts.

She walked across to the photograph of her grandfather. Beneath the photograph stood a newly cast bronze head of her father. She gazed at the sculpted magisterial expression. Pops hadn't been all bad. He had simply been what he had to be. She clasped her hands together. Three generations of Beaumonts. One day someone would hang her photograph on the wall. Someone else would sit in her chair. Perhaps a fourth generation Beaumont. Perhaps he or she might say the same of her.

B.J.ROCKLIFF

PAYDIRT

**'A SPIRITED AND FASCINATING HEROINE . . .
A MINEFIELD OF DEADLY PERILS . . .
FAST-MOVING, INTELLIGENT AND TOPICAL'**
LOOK NOW

**Jani Ashworth – one of the new breed of
City high flyers – is poised to pull off the
business coup that will secure her a coveted
promotion and give her company sole
mining rights to a rare mineral deposit in the
heart of the Andes.**

**But then a geologist on a routine assignment
is murdered in a back street of La Paz.
Arriving to investigate, Jani finds the
presence of such a senior European
executive has not gone unnoticed; either by
the authorities – themselves a byword for
corruption – or by Heinz Kesseler, a
German businessman who seems to have
taken her interests a little too closely to
heart. But Jani is very well aware that in the
game of international finance the dangers of
the boardroom are as lethal as any in the
South American wilderness – and that
friend can be every bit as deadly as foe . . .**

FICTION/THRILLER   0 7472 3010 2   £2.99

THE TRADE OF ANGELS

DEREK
P A R K E R

'Readable, shapely, with a pleasantly evil
denouement . . .' *She*

As the last person to see little Jonny
Brackenbury alive, illustrator John Opie is an
obvious suspect when the boy disappears. And
when a strange Greek dies practically in his
arms, Opie realises he's mixed up in a very
nasty business indeed.

Following his only clues – half a train ticket to
Cornwall, a pornographic magazine and the
muttered word 'Tiberius' on the dying man's
lips – Opie sets out to clear his name. His first
port of call is the fishing village of Polperro, his
birthplace, where there is an unexpected
Greek connection – and a brush with violence.

The trail leads to the ruggedly beautiful
southern coast of Greece, but the deceptively
idyllic setting cloaks a sinister vice ring of
depraved and evil men whose deadly trade
leads to innocence abused and an
international network of corruption,
torture . . . and murder.

FICTION/THRILLER   0 7472 3245 8   £2.99

A selection of bestsellers from Headline

FICTION

THE MASK	Dean R Koontz	£3.50 ☐
ROWAN'S MILL	Elizabeth Walker	£3.99 ☐
MONEY FOR NOTHING	John Harman	£3.99 ☐
RICOCHET	Ovid Demaris	£3.50 ☐
SHE GOES TO WAR	Edith Pargeter	£3.50 ☐
CLOSE-UP ON DEATH	Maureen O'Brien	£2.99 ☐

NON-FICTION

GOOD HOUSEKEEPING EATING FOR A HEALTHY HEART	Coronary Prevention Group	£3.99 ☐
THE ALIEN'S DICTIONARY	David Hallamshire	£2.99 ☐

SCIENCE FICTION AND FANTASY

THE FIRE SWORD	Adrienne Martine-Barnes	£3.99 ☐
SHADOWS OF THE WHITE SUN	Raymond Harris	£2.99 ☐
AN EXCESS OF ENCHANTMENTS	Craig Shaw Gardner	£2.99 ☐
MOON DREAMS	Brad Strickland	£3.50 ☐

All Headline books are available at your local bookshop or newsagent, or can be ordered direct from the publisher. Just tick the titles you want and fill in the form below. Prices and availability subject to change without notice.

Headline Book Publishing PLC, Cash Sales Department, PO Box 11, Falmouth, Cornwall, TR10 9EN, England.

Please enclose a cheque or postal order to the value of the cover price and allow the following for postage and packing:
UK: 60p for the first book, 25p for the second book and 15p for each additional book ordered up to a maximum charge of £1.90
BFPO: 60p for the first book, 25p for the second book and 15p per copy for the next seven books, thereafter 9p per book
OVERSEAS & EIRE: £1.25 for the first book, 75p for the second book and 28p for each subsequent book.

Name ....

Address ....

....

....